Jane Dunbar Chaplin

Gems of the Bog

A Tale of the Irish Peasantry

Jane Dunbar Chaplin

Gems of the Bog
A Tale of the Irish Peasantry

ISBN/EAN: 9783337125882

Printed in Europe, USA, Canada, Australia, Japan

Cover: Foto ©Andreas Hilbeck / pixelio.de

More available books at **www.hansebooks.com**

PADDY'S OPINION OF HIS MISTRESS. p. 16.

GEMS OF THE BOG;

A TALE OF THE IRISH PEASANTRY.

BY

MRS. JANE D. CHAPLIN.

PUBLISHED BY THE

AMERICAN TRACT SOCIETY,

117 WASHINGTON STREET, BOSTON,

HURD AND HOUGHTON, 13 ASTOR PLACE, N Y.

The Riverside Press, Cambridge, Mass.

The principal characters and scenes in the following pages are drawn, very nearly, from real life. The story was first published as a serial in the "Watchman and Reflector."

J. D. C.

CONTENTS.

GEMS OF THE BOG.

CHAPTER I.

THE FIRST FAMILIES OF KILLYROOKE.

THE picturesque little hamlet of Killyrooke consisted of one long row of straw-thatched cottages, each having its garden patch stocked with potatoes and cabbages, and graced by a pig-pen. In most of the dwellings a hole in the wall sufficed for a window, while the floor was only the hard-beaten earth. Art had never entered Killyrooke; but nature, so lavish of her bounties to all beautiful Ireland, had not forgotten this remote and quiet nook. The green lawns, the fields of flax and barley, the high old hedges, the bluest and brightest of waters, the blackest and richest of bogs had

charms unutterable for the hearts of her simple
children. As the Switzer mourns for his
mountains, and the Icelander for his snows,
so they, when exiled, mourn for their native
bogs.

The society of Killyrooke, humble as it was,
boasted of its distinctions as much as did that
of neighboring towns. The farmer — so called
— sat upon the pinnacle of the little social
fabric. He leased a bit of land, and owned a
donkey, two or three cows, and pigs whose
name was legion. The next grade were the
laborers, many of them meriting that name
only in harvest, living as they did in idleness
and want most of the year ; while the lowliest
of all were the professional beggars, who lived
on the bounty of the gentry and larger farmers
in the surrounding region, and who made their
headquarters in Killyrooke, finding shelter in
dilapidated huts and cow-houses, or with the
tender-hearted peasants.

At one end of the long street lay in quiet
beauty the little " Lough," a heritage of mercy
to the people. Beside its bright waters the

ruddy daughters of the hamlet met once a week to wash their garments and to gossip over affairs of common interest. All day these nymphs stood knee deep in the water, splashing it about, either in work or play, while their plaintive Irish airs, chanted in time with their rubbing, and their merry wild laughter, woke the echoes from the neighboring hills. The washing done, they spread their clothes on the bright turf around the " Lough," and then sat down to wait for sunset, which always brought brothers, friends and lovers, as well as the older people, who came from curiosity to see and hear all that interested the girls and boys. What " Change " is to the city merchant, what the tavern and the store are to the remote villager, what the " sewing-society " is to ladies among us, the Lough was, at the time of which we write, to the dwellers in Killyrooke. Here the old men bargained for donkeys and discussed the probable price of potatoes; here the young " boys " planned long tramps to fairs and horse-races, and ex

changed soft words with the ruddy-cheeked
girls resting on the green banks. And in
the background the mothers whispered their
secrets of joy or woe in each other's ears, and
the grandmothers — always the nursery-maids
among the the lowly Irish — swung themselves
to and fro, wailing the babies to slumber, and
varying their motion and their music by an
occasional blow or epithet aimed at the older
urchins, who thwarted their efforts by tickling
the toes of the drowsy infants.

We have said there was an aristocracy in
this humble Killyrooke. It comprised the
rival houses of Sheehan and O'Gorman, and
arose mainly from the fact that their ancestors
had more land and better cottages than their
neighbors, and that their dwellings alone had
each a glass window to admit the light and to
exclude the rain. But alas for human greatness! There must be always some drawback
to its perfect enjoyment. These families had
for generations been bitter rivals as well as
equals, and the distinction enjoyed by both

above their neighbors could not atone for the
heart-burnings and envy on the one hand, and
the wounded feelings on the other.

But at the time when our story begins, the
equality was broken, and the rivalry was
waning. Sloth had taken captive the represen-
tative of the O'Gormans; while that "which
biteth like a serpent and stingeth like an
adder" had bound in its not less ruinous coil
the wife, Biddy. Thus nine young scions of
the house were left without care or restraint,
save the brawlings exchanged between themselves, and the beatings bestowed on the
younger eight by the first-born of the family,
Nan, a bright girl of seventeen.

Nan O'Gorman was very fair, having in
some way monopolized all the beauty in the
family. Once in a while the dying energy of
her race would suddenly flash up in her breast,
and for days she would scrub and sweep the
cottage, wash the children's faces, switch the
pigs from the door-way, and begin to spin yarn
for the winter's stockings. Then the embers
would die out, and Nan was off to a race or

a show, returning in such company and at such
a time as pleased herself.   Meanwhile the little
ones got a meal, or a crust, or went supperless
to bed, according to the quantity of whiskey
their mother had been able to procure.   Is it
any wonder, then, that the clay chimney had
fallen, and that the envied glass window had
been boarded up for want of panes?

While the O'Gormans were thus falling to
decay, the Sheehans, who lived across the way,
still prospered in worldly things, and kept up
their honor and their name.   Prudence and in-
dustry, long the guardians of their humble
dwelling, still spread their wings above it;
plenty blessed the cottage and the land, and
none in want were ever sent empty from the
door.

There was not, and never had been, one point
on which these two families could meet in sympathy.   "We are no farther apart now," said
John Sheehan, the farmer of Daisy Farm,
"than we iver war. The O'Gormans have been
Papists since the time when there war darkness
on the face o' the deep, as mentioned in Scrip-

tur', and the Sheehans have been Protestants since the day in which God said, ' Let there be light.' "

But neither of these men, we are sorry to say, was a consistent defender of his own faith ; for while Pat O'Gorman would roll up his sleeves and fight in defence of. the " mother church " and all her mummeries, he lived in utter disregard of the decalogue she commanded him to obey. And John Sheehan, with the Assembly's Catechism on his tongue, and a hatred of all Popery in his heart, was only a self-righteous Pharisee, walking in the light of the fire his own hands had kindled. He gloried in his " larning," in his Protestantism, in his Scotch descent, in the piety of his parents, in the respect paid him in the little Presbyterian church of the next town, and in every thing he had and did. He lacked humility, and was in great danger of striking a rock, as he sailed on with his eyes shut to the dangers around him. He was blind while boasting of his clear sight; dead in sin while he fancied himself a living and active member, to whom

the "body of Christ" was under great obliga-
tion. "It's a fine thing to be a Christian," he
said, "but a finer thing to be a rispectible
Christian."

But,for all this self-deception, John Sheehan
led a very different life from his neighbor. The
dormouse-like existence of O'Gorman we have
mentioned already. John Sheehan, like his
ancestors, was noted for his mercy to the poor
and his strict attention to his own business. It was his proudest boast — and John
was a proud man — that his ancestors were all
of his own way of thinking, and that the great-
great-grandfather back of them all, Hugh Mc-
Millan, was a Scotch Covenanter; and that
while a drop of that holy blood was left in his
veins he would hate sin and cleave to temper-
ance and virtue; and that no beggar or outcast
should be sent hungry from his door; he would
feed and shelter Protestants for their own
sakes, and Catholics for the love of God, who
made and bears with them.

Daisy Farm was well-tilled, and divided by
wide ditches and hedges of long growth, and

John's harvests were always the richest in the region. His cattle were well fed and housed, and treated almost like members of his family. Not seldom did he address a restless cow in soft tones, saying, " Gently, dear, gently." He was the soul of good nature, so that the O'Gormans had found it much harder keeping up enmity with him, than with his stern, resolute old father before him. It was very hard to hate the man who called their dirty children " dearies," and who fed them with ginger-bread.

As John kept up the reputation of the farm, so did his wife that of the dairy and poultry-yard. His aged mother was still regarded as head of the family, and treated with a defer-ence amounting to veneration. Her husband, while he lived, had always called her " Honey," so her dairy-maid and the farm-servant fell in-to the way of calling her " Misthress Honey," and to John she had always been " Mammy Honey." And when John brought a young mistress to the cottage, the good woman found herself called " Mammy Honey," by way of distinction from the new Mistress Sheehan, by all Killyrooke. Never was a sweet name more justly applied. Her gentleness, love of peace and true generosity had long made her a wonder — almost an object of awe — among her neighbors. To her was due the peace which had cheered the last hours of the old rivals — her husband and the father of Pat O'Gorman, — and her soft word had often turned away from John and his wife the wrath of the present occupants of the ruined cot.

Mammy Honey was not merely a good-tempered woman; she possessed a strong mind and a noble heart. The stern blood of the old McMillans flowed through her veins, and the faith which had enabled them to sing psalms of triumph in the face of their foes still burned in her heart and lighted up her eyes. Had she lived in the days of the Covenanters, rather than have yielded her conscience to a tyrannical king she would have added her blood to that which then moistened the Scottish moors.

For fifty years, since she came a bride to

Killyrooke, Mammy Honey had walked blame-
less among her neighbors, yielding her inter-
ests, her feelings, every thing but her conscience, for peace's sake. While no bitter
words ever escaped her lips against the pre-
vailing religion, she set her face with Puritanic
firmness against all which she believed to be
heresy, so that while serving and watching, as
had always been her wont, by the sick-bed of
her neighbors, she had never suffered her eyes
to look upon, nor her ears to hear, the forms
and mummeries which she regarded as the
idolatry forbidden in the Word of Truth.

While the thriftless women about her envied her neat cottage, her fruitful garden, and
her whole glass window, they loved her, and,
aside from the rival O'Gormans, there was
scarcely one in the hamlet who would have
listened silently while her name was lightly
spoken; a few were even sensitive, for her sake,
when the church of her love was reviled.

When, arrayed in her brown Sunday gown,
and cloak of duffle gray, with her broad frilled
cap bound to her head by a black ribbon, and

leaning on John's strong arm, Mammy Honey walked erect and firm to the little Presbyterian church at Cloynmally, she looked like a duchess in disguise rather than like the humble peasant she was.

One Sunday morning as she set off thus, her farm-servant, Paddy Mannon — of whom more anon — exclaimed to a trail of companions who passed on their way to mass, while he, easy soul, sat astride the stile gazing at them, "Look at her, b'ys, this gold morning! Heaven smile on her beauty! Sure, thin, she was made for a throne, but sint in mistake to a farm; and will ye dare to say that because she turns her back on the church, and 'his riverence,' and the saints, and the picturs, and the beads, that she'll not enter heaven? 'Dade I'll fight the first one as dares say it; and I'll bet my new brogues with any of ye that there's not as fine-looking a woman in heaven now as herself is — the bet to be paid when we gits there and proves it." And Paddy winked at his comrades, to impress them with his shrewdness, while they laughed and called back, "How comes it, Paddy, that ye 'bides in the true church yerself, while ye believe that Protestants will enter heaven as well as ourselves?"

"How is it, indade?" replied Paddy. "It's because I was born in it, and can't throw it off like my coat, and I wouldn't if I could, be so mane. I'm not plazed with the freckles on my face, but do ye think I'm going to skin myself to get clear o' them? I don't like these dull little eyes o' my own, but do ye think I'll pull them out o' my head for that same? Indade, no! I stands on my honor, I does, in this matter o' religion; and though themselves has fed, and clothed, and rared me from a starved workhouse-child, I'll not throw up my religion to plaze them. I'm great on conscience, and I'm not the b'y to sell my principles for a home, my birthright for a bowl o' porridge, as one mean-sperited lad in the Scriptur' did; not I."

Paddy was a man made up of contradictions. He was faithful to the Sheehans but he was so careless of the poor wages he earned that

he either gave or threw them away as soon as
he got them. He had a wife and child, and
would go almost wild with joy when they came
to see him, but if months elapsed without a
visit, he never sought them out, nor felt any
anxiety for their welfare. He made all manner of sport of "his riverence and the church,"
but almost fell on his knees at sight of the
priest, and shook with fear when rebuked by
him for unfaithfulness. He was as light-
hearted as the colt he was rearing, and felt no
more care for the future. It was joy enough
for him to live, and " sarve Misthress Honey."

CHAPTER II.

A NEW MISTRESS.

JOHN Sheehan had lived many years after his father's death with no companion but his mother and Paddy Mannon. Being of a very social nature, he sometimes complained that the cottage was "a dale too silent and lone" for him; and yet he had reached thirty without a thought of marrying. When one suggested that he needed a wife, he would ask, with filial jealousy, "Do ye see any thing goin' wrong about the cottage or farm, that a wife could mend? And where would I ever find a woman that would bide bein' subject to Mammy Honey? And *that* every body about me shall be, while Heaven spares her — the darling."

He had scarcely uttered these words to a neighbor who was bantering him one day, when he drove off to sell five "lovely young pigs"

to Farmer Doane, a prosperous man in the next
county. Arrived there, he received a welcome
both as merchant and as guest, and after
pocketing his silver, took his place at the long
deal table, on which smoked the sweet bacon,
potatoes and cabbage raised on the farm. Here
his eye fell on Peggy O'Canty, a young orphan
who assisted the good wife in the dairy, and
whom the worthy couple always addressed as
" Peggy, jewel." He stole one sly glance at
her as she poured out the buttermilk at table,
and another when he left the kitchen to accompany Doane to the cow-house; and then
he mustered courage to ask her name and
history.

In a marvellously short time John had pigs
to sell again, to the great amazement of Mammy Honey, who looked upon it very much like
selling her relations; and in this second visit
to Doane's he fairly lost his heart, and came
home laying plans to brighten up the cottage,
and buy a new donkey-cart and a suit of
" younger-lookin' clothes."

When he got Paddy Mannon off to his bed

in the loft that night, John opened his mind to
his mother, dwelling on Peggy's charms of
face, and manner, and heart, as if he had
known her for years, while the truth was he
had never yet spoken to her! "And now,
Mammy Honey," he said, "here's the way
open for me to have company, and for ye to
have help in the cottage and the dairy; what
would you say to my bringing her here?"

"I'd think well o' it, John," replied the old
woman, "if I knew she war a humble, God-
fearing child, for it's such a one ye need, and
not a flighty thing that would be running off to
fairs and races and leading ye farther off from
God — which same is unneedful. Ye must ride
over to Doane's some day and ask him is the
girl a Protestant and a Christian, and does she
mind her duty humbly, as if she felt the
Masther's eye on her. And more, John, dear,
ask is she tinder and loving; for I could niver
give ye up without getting back love as my
payment; for ye are all I have left in the world,
now! O, lad, it's a great thing for a mother
to give her only son to another woman, and

one she niver saw! But as I have not been a selfish mother, no more will I be now! May ten thousand blessings rest on ye both, darling, and may I live to see ye happy together."

John soon " got leave of his mother" — he was a man of six feet two, weighing two hundred pounds! — " to ask a line of character from the minister of Cloynmally to Peggy's master, begging his leave to marry her." Hitherto Peggy had never heard of his intentions, and was quite amazed when her master explained matters to her in presence of the suitor. After John had left the house, she expressed great surprise to her mistress why such a fine, settled body should be looking after a poor, foolish, shy thing like herself. But the acquaintance grew and ripened as well as it would have done environed by the strictest rules of etiquette. When at last the matter was settled, Peggy could hardly tell which she loved most, John or his mother. She was quite as proud of Mammy Honey — who had visited her with an offering of ten hanks of flax yarn, ten ells of linen and six pairs of

stockings — as of her son, " the fine settled
masther."

When the marriage ceremony was over,
John brought Peggy home in the new donkey-
cart, — the only equipage his establishment
boasted. Mammy Honey stood in the cottage
door arrayed in her best cap and gown, to
receive them, while Paddy Mannon, in his
Sunday corduroys and brogues, took the
donkey's bridle, and stood waiting to witness
Peggy's reception.

Folding the young orphan to her breast,
Mammy Honey cried out, with the eloquence of
her people, " Blissed be the God and Father
of the orphan, that has this day given ye a
mother, Peggy O'Canty! Blissed be the God
and husband of the widow, that has this day
given me a daughter, who never had a one
before! It is this old heart, jewel, that will
hide ye where trouble can never find ye; and
it's on yer lovin' breast, mavourneen, that
I'll lean and forget there's such things as old
age and wakeness in the world."

Then throwing her arms around the stalwart

form of John, she cried out, " **Ye**, darlin', are the son o' a righteous man, and have come of a long line o' them that feared God. The promise to the seed o' the righteous has been fulfilled to ye, and see now that ye 'bide in the fear o' God and seek Him henceforth with the whole heart. Look, boy," she continued, "and see what God has given ye to make your home shine 'like heaven, and to close the dying eyes o' yer old mother! God save ye, John, from ever piercing her heart with one sharp word. And now the grace o' God bide on ye both and on this house!"

Peggy was a blue-eyed, fair-haired girl, "made of love, entirely," John himself—and who should know better than he?—being witness in the case. She loved everything, from John and his mother down to the ducks and the chickens; whatever had life shared in her love or pity. She now bound up her hair under a snowy cap, saying, "As John are ten years older nor me, he'll be plazed to see me layin' off girlish ways and lookin' sober-like." She applied herself to her work with that glad spirit which changes toil to a blessing, and soon became the model wife of the region. The whitest flax, the sweetest butter and the brightest hearth-stone were hers. But such was her humility that she took none of the credit, but always spoke of " Mammy Honey's silver flax " and " Mammy Honey's golden butter ; " and wondered why John ever chose her for his wife, and how Mammy Honey could bear so patiently with her slow ways, and never weary teaching her her own " ilegant " ones !

Many a richer and wiser bride has gone to her husband's home without such a welcome as Peggy received at Daisy Farm ; many a mother has given away a son with no such return of love to cheer her declining days as that in which Mammy Honey now rejoiced, and for which she praised God in prayer and song, and thank-offerings to every beggar she could find. And the thatch, which she declared was " just full o' the prayers of centuries," sheltered a happier family than did the lofty dome and wainscoted walls of Harpley Hall, — the seat of

the gentleman who owned and neglected Killyrooke, and the region between it and his fine
mansion.

Years wore on at Daisy Farm. The family
had their sorrows, but they were hardly worth
the name. John had lost a donkey one year
and a cow the next, and Mammy Honey was
afflicted by "gapes" among her feathered
family, beside having a pet lamb mangled and
torn by the ferocious dog of the O'Gorman
boys. But Peggy's trials were the sorest,
while she had the least strength to endure
them. Her careless neighbor across the way
was constantly accusing the innocent creature
of trying to outshine her in the neatness of her
person and in the order of her household; — a
thing easily done by any one. The neglected
little ones, catching the spirit of their mother,
felt at liberty to annoy her also. The big boys
stoned her ducks, stole her Christmas turkeys,
and turned their half-famished pigs into her
cherished cabbage garden. But, according to
her first resolution, she returned good for evil,
and, with the sympathy of Mammy Honey,

bore their insults with meekness and patience. Once, sorely annoyed, she shed tears, when that old philosopher said, in soothing tones, "It's yer ould mammy that knows, mavourneen, how hard all this is to the flesh, for she's gone through it for nigh half a cent'ry with the O'Gormans in the grave and them alive; and I can say this for my promise-keepin' God, that so has He helped me through all these years that I never gave them back an angry word, or laid up one ha' peth o' revinge agin them, but always pitied them. And so I did, dear, till the pity turned to love, and in the end brought back love again. For when the ould mother o' this man come down to death, it was I alone must smooth her pillow and mix her drink, and I — Protestant though I was — must close her eyes in death. She remembered how patient I had borne with her, and this was all the way she had o' asking my forgiveness. And if she had not it would ha' been all the same, for *God never forgets,* jewel! Patience with them will bring heaps of heaven's gold into yer own heart, and ye'll find that even *them* is helpin' ye on in the road to glory, by-and-by."

And under such wise instructions Peggy took up the cross which the old saint was about laying down, and moved meekly on.

Now the cruel neighbor had one cause of boasting of which poor Peggy was very sensitive. She had, in her own words, "nine as bulky childer as ye could find ony day at Blarney Fair." Peggy had none, and John was fond of children even to a weakness. But the pure-hearted creature was resolved to turn even this bitter cup to one of sweetness, by her submission to God's will, and her tenderness towards all little children. So, when her careless neighbor was away from home, she would call in two or three of the youngest of the flock, and after treating them to clean faces, would feed them with her sweet bread and milk, and keep them till John's return from the field, knowing how fond he was of children's prattle.

Once when "the masther" expressed pleasure at their frolicsome ways, she said, "I'll bring them over ony day, dear, to play with ye, but neither yer mother nor myself is plazed to have ye cross the street after them, nor yet to chat with their father as ye have o' late ; " for she had noticed that for the last few weeks O'Gorman had frequently called to him to come over and hear a letter from Jim, in " Ameriky," or to smoke a pipe with him. This was an unwonted civility which John had not power to refuse — indeed, he had not power to refuse anything to anybody. He had been held in by his stern father and his resolute mother from going among evil companions, but he had never yet learned to say " no " in his own name. And no man, however old he may be, is safe till he can do that.

CHAPTER III.

MAMMY HONEY.

A DARK day comes sooner or later to every dwelling. If no other shadow falls across its sunshine, death's surely will, and sad indeed is the home over which his wing broods.

Mammy Honey was now nearing the end of her fourscore years. Her labors had been one by one relinquished; her dairy was no longer inspected daily, the music of her flax-wheel had ceased, and lastly, the bright knitting-needles had been passed through the gray ball and laid away forever. But still her heart was fresh and warm, and therefore she had not outlived her usefulness; there were yet some little acts of love which she could perform for her children.

But one night — a night never to be forgotten at Daisy Farm — she was prostrated by a sudden palsy, and became thenceforth like a helpless child in the care of Peggy.

"It's a life's load ye'a got now," cried out her hard-hearted neighbor to Peggy, the morning after this calamity. "The Sheehans will get good pay out of ye now, for all the fine living ye've had there these last years! Och, but she'll be a burden!"

"O, no, don't say that, neighbor," replied Peggy. "It's such a burden as I pray God to let me carry to the end o' my days. If He'll only spare her to me, I'll be the thankfulest child He has in all the wide world, and never weary o' her day or night — the darlin'."

"Ye know well that this is a widow's curse that has fallen on the ould body, o' course?" asked Biddy O'Gorman.

"A curse fallen on her blissed head? It can never be!" replied Peggy, turning pale.

"Yis that same," repeated Mrs. Biddy. "It was this way: When John and my husband were b'ys, there cam' along ould Bet Mighoul tellin' fortun's, and as yer kitchen was the hugest in Killyrooke, she asked might the

crowds come to her there. And Mammy
Sheehan said, ' No deeds o' darkness shall
be done benath the roof through which prayer
has risen night and morn for more nor a century.' Then Bet was sore angered, and standing in the road just fornint the door, she
pulled off her cap and let her gray locks fly to
the winds, while she prayed that Mammy
Sheehan might, afore she died, lose the
power to ask a drink o' water, and *that no
child might ever after be born in that cottage
again* — and so there hav'n't — and worse
nor all, that her heart might be broken by
the child she had that time, — that's John."

" What, not my darlin' John ? " cried
Peggy, leaning against the donkey-post for
support.

" Yis, that same," replied Biddy, " and
then she prayed, too, that the son o' them
who *did* resave her in — that's my husband —
might have as many childer as there war
moons in the year, and thim all grow to be
lords and ladies ! " and the cruel woman held
up her rosy infant before Peggy, and then

pressed it to her breast, casting, as she did so, a look of triumph at the terrified listener.

"The curse about no more childer in the cottage has come true, then; and *now* the palsy will forbid the ould body to ask water, and the other one about John, — well, well, there's no tellin' what a man will come to, till he's safe in his grave!" added she.

"O, Biddy, ye scare the life out o' me," cried Peggy, and then she rushed, pale and breathless, towards the cottage. The rasping tones of Biddy's voice had pierced the little room where Mammy Honey lay in her weakness, and she cried, as Peggy entered, "Come here, flower o' my heart! Surely, yer fear o' a sinful woman is not greater nor your trust in God! His blissing rested on this cottage long years after I smoothed the dying pillow o' poor Bet in the workhouse, and will yet rest here if ye 'bide in His love. The lack o' childer is sometimes the lack o' sorrow, and God knows best where to sind them. Then, the last evil word she spoke — about my John — O, Peggy, if he goes asthray when I'm no

longer here to hould him in, it'll be because o'
the evil in his heart, and not for her curse;
for she knew no more o' the futur' nor ye do.
He's powerful o' body, but he's wake o' will,
Peggy, and he's fearful forgetful o' his Maker.
Watch him, and pray for him, dear, when
I'm at rest. I've laid down that burden now,
and though his feet may slide sometimes, I
know he will be brought in at the last."

Harvest was drawing on, and John Sheehan
had his reapers all engaged; and an uncouth
and famished-looking set they were, gathered
from the road where they were begging for
work, as starving men beg for bread.

John was full of business, and of joy, too;
for the harvest was very heavy and the weather fine. "Peggy, dear," he said, "one pair o'
hands can never fade this host o' men, and
tind on the dairy, and wait on the Mammy
Honey. Now, dear, let us call in a nurse to
mind her, or ye'll destroy yerself before this
hard season is over."

Mammy Honey heard this from her little inner
room. Her will was as strong as ever, and so

was his obedience to it. "No, John," she
cried, "ye can niver take away the child God
sent me in my old age, to fade your men.
Ye can call in somebody to do your rough
work, and pay her for it; but I can not buy
such love and tinderness as Peggy's with
gold; and the life would just go out o' me
if I lost the sight o' her dear eyes. 'Bide
by your poor failin' mother, Peggy, dear," she
cried imploringly.

"So I will, darlin'," replied the gentle Peggy, "though the rapers should starve for it.
Better the mildew fall on the grain than *ye* be
neglected that has been every other body's
sarvant in sickness. And more nor that, it's
a small while only that I'll have ye, and I
grudges every hour that I'm losin' o' yer company. It's not an hour agone since yon bright
Nan O'Gorman sprang over the stile, begging
would I suffer her to come in and hilp me
through the harvest. She says it's a sorry
life she lades at home, betwane the abuse o'
her mother and the throuble o' the childer.
She's a fair, pleasant-voiced cretur, and it's a

pity no one takes her by the hand to save her.
I'd a mind to ax ye might I bid her in to the
kitchen for ten days; but then the thought o'
her mother, and the fearful scarin' she gave
me about you beggar's curse come over me,
and I hadn't power to be spakin' their name."

"No, no, my jewel, that will never do!" replied Mammy Honey. "There's evil blood
in the veins o' the whole race. They triumphed over me when the hand o' the Lord
touched me. The sun could not shine on the
harvest if the reapers as gathered it war fed
by an O'Gorman, nor —— "

Here Mammy Honey stopped suddenly, and
throwing up her hands as if startled by her
own words, cried, "Alas, alas, childer! what am
I saying? Is this the spirit o' Him that spint
His last breath prayin' for his inemies? Is
this all the meetness I have for the home I'm
reachin' after, and whose doors is just opening
to let me in? Is there more hatred and revinge
in my heart, now that I stand on the brink o'
Jordan and see the promised land, than when
I was far back in the highways o' life? Have

I no hungerin' after their salvation, and no longin' to meet them where *foes* cannot meet? Woe's me! Now can I cry our in spirit, ' Who shall deliver me from the body o' this death?' I thought I was done with sin; but oh, the evil one holds on to God's own with a powerful grasp! He'd triumph now could he but bring down me that he's had so many battles with; but he'll niver do it, for Him that has redeemed me has said, ' *None* shall pluck them out of my hands.' I'll show Satan that though flesh and heart is failin,' I'm yet able to withstand him, and to war agin the flesh too. John, go across the street and bid in that poor uncared for girl; and who knows but God will 'low Peggy to hape coals o' fire on their heads by making her a thrifty, modest and honest woman? She war a pretty baby — Nan — and a fair-faced child, till the brazen look o' the mother crept into her eyes. And now go awhile to your work, dears, and let me be alone with God."

The next day, the bright, careless Nan was installed in Peggy's kitchen; and although

she fell far below the good woman's standard
of neatness and modesty, she surprised her by
her quickness and her readiness to learn.

Peggy's heart was full of excuses for the
untrained child, now almost a woman, and she
checked with real kindness all grumbling and
complaints from John. Paddy Mannon, who
confessed that he hated " with most unchrist-
ian hatred every O'Gorman, dead, livin' or yet
unborn," patronizingly admitted that she was
the least vicious of the name. After awhile,
John seemed amused by her wild, sprightly
ways, and even Mammy Honey asked for little
attentions at her hand, and addressed her
gently, as, " Nanny, my child," and was grat-
ified by Peggy's forbearance with her.

CHAPTER IV.

PADDY MANNON.

THE harvest was gathered in, or "stacked," and immense heaps of peat in the yard promised light and warmth for the coming winter. The heavy work of the farm being over, Paddy Mannon was at liberty to attend "fairs" and races, and to make his annual visit to his wife, "a most ondustrious young woman, who provided for herself and child intirely by begging, and never bothered him at all no more nor if he war a young b'y without a wife."

Meg Mannon's home was a dilapidated hut on the roadside, many miles from Killyrooke. She had a field of operation too productive to leave even for a husband. Mammy Honey had offered her work when she was first married, but she declined it, saying, " I was brought up a beggar, misthress, and I understand my oon business better than another one's. 'Let the shoemaker stick to his last.' I'll just bide where I am, and visit Paddy at whiles o' leisure."

Meg's home was not as good as a thrifty farmer's cow-house. A woolen coverlet, the gift of Mammy Honey, supplied the missing door. A barrel, sawn asunder, served for chairs, and a whole one, with a rough board across it, for a table. A sack, filled with straw and covered with plenty of warm blankets, composed a bed seldom visited by care for the morrow. The walls, through which the light peeped, were ornamented by pictures; one of the Virgin and Holy Child, another representing the benevolent St. Patrick banishing serpents from Ireland, and a third, portraying a fat monk, bareheaded and barefooted, beating, most unmercifully, some half-dozen sinners, whose race and sex must remain forever a mystery.

Meg Mannon was a fine specimen of a prosperous Irish beggar, and was, on the whole, a proud and happy woman, having nothing to do but to walk from parish to parish, followed by little Pat, and receive the gifts of those who " owed her a living." She carried her treasures all with her, and so had no keys to turn and no robbers to fear. To add to her happiness, Peggy always sent her a little supply of luxuries by Paddy, and Mammy Honey never forgot warm stockings for her boy. Paddy presented her with a bright calico gown once a year, and took her, arrayed in it, to a " fair." Meg never felt any degradation from her business, but on the contrary was proud and boastful, saying that she was young and strong, and could walk on a wager with any woman in Ireland, and had " the lovingest husband and the rosiest child " in it; and then asked, " Is it any wonder that I'm a contint and happy woman ? "

Two or three times a year, her business arrangements brought her to Killyrooke, whither, as the way was long, she bore little Pat on her back. At these times she was allowed to " keep house " for a week in an old cow-shed of " Masther Sheehan," on condition that no fire was lighted and no pipe smoked within five rods of it. And with such a life Meg was satisfied, and looked no more into the realities of the future than if she had not been an immortal being. She paid her fees to the church, went to mass when she had any thing new to exhibit, and confessed her sins once a year to secure a christian burial. After that she was easy, throwing all responsibility on the priest. Nor was Meg alone in this; with the same stupidity does Rome curse all her lowly children. She blindfolds them, that they do not see the light; and those of a purer faith look on and cry, " The bandages can never be removed from their eyes." But few, alas, take hold with vigorous hand to try what can be done. While, however, the mass of the people in that corrupt church are at ease in their bonds, there are some there struggling in their fetters, and reaching out for the light of life.

Paddy and Meg had one only ambition unfulfilled — it was to go to America, where they fancied beggars laid up fortunes and lived in

fine stone houses. They were always planning
a fund to pay their passage. The first farthing,
however, had never been laid aside for it,
although Paddy talked of the " passage-money "
as if it were all ready in the bank, waiting to
be called for. He enjoyed the dream of future
grandeur more than most men do the reality;
and neither toil, poverty, nor yet separation
from those he loved, had power to dim the sunshine in his light heart. He had as little care
for the morrow as the birds of the air or the
lilies of the field. But this was not the result
of faith; for, after all the labor dear Mammy
Honey had expended on him from childhood
up, she was forced to confess at last that " poor,
foolish Paddy lived like the beast o' the field,
forgetting that there was a God above him."

When this saint-like old woman lay on her
bed and felt that her work for souls was nearly
done, she called Paddy to her and recounted
the mercies of God to him during the long
years he had dwelt under her roof, begging
him to be wise and repent while it was called
to-day, lest he should be cut off in his sins.

" Whist, noo, misthress dear," he replied;
" it will do for ye, whose time is yer own, to be
readin' and prayin' half yer daylight. The
likes o' me has to do it all up of a Sunday.
When I puts on a clane shirt and shaves me,
then I says my prayers as well as the best o'
thim Noo, dear, there's scores o' boys about
here that tells their beads twice a day, and yet
them same will swear, and drink, and steal,
and lie. And yersilf knows that poor Paddy,
that prays only of a Sunday, is as sober, and
honest, and loving as the daylight aboove us.
Noo what better would I be if I was confissing
to the priest and mutterin' over the beads half
my time ? "

" Paddy, Paddy, my poor lad ! it's not con-
fessing to *man*, nor yet counting yer beads that
will save yer soul. What will ye do when
death comes ? "

" Och, dear heart, *thin* I'll pray as fast as
any o' thim ! I always *does* whin I'm in
trouble. Don't ye mind the night my ould
granny died at the workhouse, how I prayed?
I had the beads in my hand all night, and if

I'd be to fall asleep for a minute, sure I'd spring up and go at it again, fear her ghost would come to me!"

Mammy Honey groaned. "Oh, Paddy, it's nigh quarter a cent'ry since I took ye in hand, and this is all I've accomplished for ye! Sure I'm aither a blind lader o' the blind, or a most unprofitable sarvant!"

"Och, no, Misthress Honey, ye're nather o' them; the fault o' my not heedin' yer religion is on the head o' his riverence, for he watches me as the cat watches the mouse, and tells me if I'm a 'turn-coat,' that the ghosts o' all my Catholic anchesters will come down upon me and tear me to pieces, and I'll lose my soul then — sure!"

"Paddy, my poor man," replied his mistress, "ye are fast in the net o' Satan, and how can I die and leave ye there?"

"Don't tell me *that;* I'll be 'feared to go to my bed alone for a month; for I'm e'en more scared o' you Satan, nor o' the ghosts thimselves! But keep ye aisy, dear heart, for I've no doubt I'll get into heaven *some way.* If his riverence is chating me, I'll be let in for *yer* sake. Ye've done good enough to get yersilf and Masther John, and mesilf all safe through; and as for the young misthress — there could be no excuse for keeping her out at all, at all; for she's as hooly now as any in it."

Such were the low ideas Paddy entertained of heaven and the way of life, after all the efforts which had been made to enlighten his darkness. Nor was his a solitary case; he was surrounded by men and women who lived as they listed, and who trusted for eternal happiness to their own good works — a poor array —, and in the prayers of the saints and the Virgin, while they were as ignorant of the plan of salvation as are the far-off heathen.

"Oh, Paddy," said his mistress, "I could lay down my life for the salvation o' poor, blind Killyrooke, includin' John and yersilf! But *that* wouldn't save ye. Ye must repent o' yer sins and believe in the Lord Jesus for yerselves. I can no more do it for you than the priest, for I'm a poor sinner, like himself and ye."

"Well, dear," replied Paddy, a little piqued; "as to bein' such a *fearful* sinner — ivery one must spake for hisself — and I'm just sure *I'm* not quite evil yet. Lookin' at mysilf beside the other boys, I'm a raal dacent-behaved lad, and desarve as respictable a funeral as ony o' thim — yis, and respictabler too!" This last sentence was uttered with some sharpness, as if his funeral arrangements were being then made, and did not meet his approbation. But suddenly remembering that in this one item of expenditure, if in no other, he was independent of his master, he added, with a smart toss of the head, "I desarves a fine wake and a funeral, and I'll get them too; for Meg and me has made a promish together, that whichever of the twos dies first shall be buried fine, if it takes the livin' one the rest o' her days to pay for it! Then ye think, mis-thress, that not a Catholic body will be let in to heaven at all?" he added, returning to the first subject.

"No, Paddy, I think no such thing. I belave if ever my eyes see 'the King in His beauty,' I shall see beside him poor Dennis Burke, who bore his sufferings so patient, and blissed God in the furnace, and died with the name o' Jesus on his lips. In a dark place Dennis had spied a great light, and made after it, and walked in it. But the cloud was so thick about him he did not see how to get clear out o' the Romish church on earth. But he's all right now, where the name o' a church is o' no avail, but where Jesus has saved all who trusted in Him, from the errors and blindness of arth. And more than ould Dennis is safe in Christ, while havin' a name in yer church. There's good Mammy Crogin, that spun for me last fall; the two o' us had just a little heaven together a talkin' o' the love o' God, and a wishin new days for poor Ireland. And some o' the holiest of men lived and died in the Catholic church."

"Och, then, sure *I'm* safe in it!" cried Paddy, quite relieved to find his mistress had sympathy with any of his faith.

"Oh, no, for ye are not like them ones, Paddy. They saw the errors of Rome, though they saw not the way of deliverance from her, but came themselves into the gospel road, the only one that can lade us to God. Even the pope hasn't power to bar the way from his children, if they seek it with a true heart. But go now to yer work, lad. I can only pray for ye and yer masther, as I have iver done, that ye may be drawn by an iverlasting love; for ye will never come o' yerselves; John is too wise in his own eyes to take a guide, and ye are too ignorant to know yer need o' one! Heaven help ye both, poor lads!"

This old saint seemed one born out of place and out of season; one who, had she been placed with hands unfettered, where she had helpers, would have done a mighty work among the lowly. She was a Bible saint, having as her only other books, Pilgrim's Progress, Boston's Fourfold State, and Baxter's

Saints' Rest. She had none of the appliances of our day and our land, wherewith to bring the truth before men. No books, no tracts, no prayer-meetings; but, for all this, she kept the enemy at bay in her own hamlet, and foiled his efforts many a time at Cloynmally.

CHAPTER V.

A CLOUD OVER DAISY FARM.

WHEN the autumn winds brought the sere leaves from the branches, the strong staff and the beautiful rod on which the honor of the Sheehans had leaned so long was broken. The setting of Mammy Honey's sun was marked by a brilliancy and beauty surpassing even that of her pure and glowing every-day life. The peace of heaven shone through her clear eyes, and her brow, long deeply lined, grew smooth and fair like that of a child. Her blanched locks fell from beneath the broad frill of her cap in waves of silver, as she sat pillowed in her rude easy chair before the little glass window. Her soul had seemed for days floating on a sea of peace. No fear of death, no desire for life cast a shadow over

51

her joy. Her voice, long unstrung, had regained its old melody, and she cheered her
heart with hymns and snatches of the Psalms as
paraphrased for the Scottish church. Her children, while they moved about their toil, heard
her singing, as she neared the cold river, —

> " The hour of my departure's come,
> I hear the voice that calls me home ;
> And now, O Lord, let sorrow cease,
> And let Thy servant die in peace ! "

Yet if the Holy One felt the tempter's power
in His mortal conflict, is it strange that some
of His followers are forced to cry with Him,
" This is the hour and the power of darkness " ? Is it not enough that the disciple
be as his Master ; that the same thorns pierce
his feet ; that the same spear wound his heart ;
and that the same vinegar, mingled with gall,
be put to his lips ? Blessed be fellowship with
Jesus, even though it be the fellowship of
suffering !

Need we, then, wonder that a transient cloud
shadowed the peace of this blessed old saint ?

It disturbed her vision of her children's future and her hopes of Ireland, leaving her own prospects still glorious. What true mother can be satisfied with heaven for herself alone? Mammy Honey was going to her Father's kingdom; but she wanted John, and Paddy, and all Ireland, and indeed, the whole world, to follow her there. For Peggy she had no fears, as she said, "Heaven would not be complate without *her*."

"Mavourneen," she called to Peggy, on the last day of her life, "come now and let me lane my head on yer lovin' bussum. Call John, too, darlin', for this is the wakeness o' failin' natur'! I'm just now puttin' foot into the cold waters, but I see the horses and the chariots waitin' me beyond; so I know that I shall sup ere break o' day with Him I'm sick o' heart to see! True, the arrow is in my breast; but like Christiana's token, it is pinted with love. I hears the bells beginnin' to ring in heaven, rejoicin' over another poor sinner come off conqueror through grace. But I've a partin' word on the bank of Jordan for ye

twos — my darlins'. I would be to warn ye
that *the divil's not dead*, but still goes roarin'
about; and if iver he strives to damage ye,
it'll be by putting a space between yer two
hearts! I've no fears o' ye' Peggy, my jewel,
for ye have even now the meek and lowly
sperit o' the lovin' Master. But Oh, John,
John! *ye* are all taken up with the grain,
and the peat, and the pratees, and the dear
bastes, and the powltry! I'm afeared ye'll let
the very mercies o' God lade ye astray from
Him till ye lose yer soul! Peggy, love,
watch him every hour and keep a fast hould
on him, and bring him safe to me at last!
I'll expect that o' ye, darlin'. And now I'd be
to give my partin' orders. I had a vision,
dears, days agone, that drank up my sperit
with anguish; and I must tell it ye afore the
trumpet sounds for me, that I may put ye on
yer guard."

" No evil can come on this house while the
thatch hangs to the ruff, Mammy," sobbed
Peggy; " there's been that many prayers sent
to Heaven from it! "

" Peggy, the righteousness of the father will niver avail for the son! John must make no trust in that, or he will lose his soul. I fear, I fear he is dead while he has a name to live! But now aboot you vision : I had the wakeness in me head for a bit, and then I saw crawlin' slowly over the floor o' the kitchen a sarpint! Betimes it sprung up and thrust its pizen tooth into Peggy's heart o' love! And worse nor all, John, I thought ye looked on and niver lifted a hand to give it a blow. Then it turned to go, and I saw it had a human face,— shall I tell ye? — the face o' the O'Gorman gerl! Me heart died within me, and I hadn't the power left in me to scream out to ye. But I thought Paddy Mannon — poor, foolish, lovin' Paddy — struck it a blow with his huge fist and killed it ontirely."

" It war only a drame, darlin,' and no vision at all," cried Peggy, trembling and turning pale. " John's all love and full o' care o' me!"

" Do ye think," said John, " that yer son would iver stand by and see the light o' his eyes touched by a sarpint or ony other onholy thing? Indade no! There's nather man nor thing in all Killyrooke would dare give her an oncivil word; for betwane Paddy and mesilf we'd soon make an eend o' him! Ye're throubled now, dear; sthrive to rest a bit."

"There's a long rest just beyont for me, John; I must give my last breath to ye and Peggy in counsel. Now promise me, ye son o' a hooly man, that ye'll go no more across to the O'Gormans', as I've seen ye doin' o' late. There's too much whisky and too many evil words there. Ye cannot walk into the fire without bein' burned, lad."

"It's only the prattle o' the childer that takes me there at all, mammy," replied John. "*It's so lone and silent here!*"

"And aren't silence better nor brawlin', man?" asked the mother. "If God has sent no childer to comfort ye, thank Him He's sent none to break yer hearts. And heed ye my words, John; don't ye fly in the face o' the Almighty, for if ye do ye'll be sorely baten in the contist. Send Nanny — Heaven pity

the child — home when I'm gone, and live
yersilves like two **tartle-doves** till I see ye
again."

For a little time Mammy Honey lay as if
done with all below. Then she cried out, " Oh,
that God would pity Ireland, — poor, swate
Ireland, bound in chains and darkness! The
men of God go to the far-off hathen, to **the**
black man and the red man ; but who o' them
all pities my people, ground under the heel o'
the Man o' Sin! How can **I die** and leave
them thus!" Then **a smile** passed over her
pale face, and she whispered, " **When the isles
of the sea shall be converted unto Thee, the**
dearest and the greenest o' them all *shall not be
forgotten!* **Good** night, jewels." And she
was not, for God had taken her.

When **the form** of Mammy Honey was borne
from the cottage to the little Presbyterian
church in Cloynmally, all Killyrooke followed
it. Many who had never entered a Protestant
church before stole in there ; **and** such as
dared not enter lest they might thereby lose
their souls, stood without, wringing their

hands, and howling out lamentations for her
who had " left a huge spot impty, and carried
the heart o' Killyrooke to the grave with
her!"

When the coffin had been lowered into the
grave, the pastor of the little flock in Cloynmally seized this rare opportunity of explaining to the poor people the way of salvation
through Christ alone. He spoke of the holy
life by which their dead friend had honored
her faith among them, and through which she
had now entered into rest. While he was yet
speaking, a simple youth from Killyrooke,
known there by no other name than " the poor
fool," and who had a reputation for second
sight, mounted the wall, and uttered a succes-
sion of the most unearthly howls, till every
eye was turned on him. " Oohoul! Oohoul!
Oohoul! Bats, and owls and ravens; the air
is full o' 'um! This is the evil day for Daisy
Farm and the Sheehans! I seed a white
dove perched on the coffin o' Mammy Honey,
and it followed her here; and it'll bide on her
grave whin we's are gone hoom; and then it'll

die on the turf above her, and never go back more to hover in peace over the cottage! But owls, and bats and ravens will bide there, and clap their wings and hoot, and croak through the long black night that 'll never be lifted off the place!"

Then he clapped his hands and laughed loud and long, as he looked up to the heavens. " Och, och!" he cried, " but this same is the blessed day for herself that fed the beggars, and knit warm stockin's for mesilf these nine years agone! She shuk off her heresy like a varmint with her last brith, and bid John to tell o't. I sees her now passin' through the fires o' purgatory, the first Sheehan that ever got through since heaven war built. 'And now, look! look! she's let in among the hooly — the only Protestant body in the hape!"

The people stood as if turned to stone by the ravings of the idiot, who was really more knave than fool. But John, whose pride was touched by this reflection on his family and his faith, forgot the decorum incumbent on him as a mourner. He stepped out from among the people, and cried, "Hoot, there, poor crack-brain! Go home and tell him that bid ye do this onchristian dade to broken hearts, that not a Sheehan ever lived on arth — mesilf excepted — but's in heaven to day! and tell him that whiles I'm the respictable man I am, nather owls, bats nor ravens shall get lave to bide above my hoom, nor yet will ye ever be. fed there again. Away with ye!"

Poor Peggy, who could not endure angry words, fell fainting with exhaustion and fear. Kind women gathered about her, saying, "Well may she sink now, poor body! Her bist friend's in the grave. Did ever man's mother get love like this from his wife!"

What hour in life so sad as the evening after the funeral of one beloved? John and Peggy sat in the deep shadow of the broad clay chimney-place, where the peat was smoking and smouldering, but neither spoke. She was nursing her grief, he laying plans to punish the poor fool. At length Nan O'Gorman rose from the little casement where she had been sitting with her chin resting on her chubby hands, gazing at the passers-by. She fell upon her knees before the fire, and began blowing the peat to light it. A sudden gleam fell across her face, and Peggy cried out, "Quit blowing, Nanny, for I cannot bear ony light on my eyes this night, when Mammy Honey is lying 'in the dark, cold grave. I believe my own heart lies with her, for I feel the damp and cold o' the grave all aboot me;" and she shuddered fearfully.

"It's a huge cold ye've taken standin' so long on the fresh-tarned arth, dear," said John. He rose and took down a coarse frieze cloak from the peg on which it hung, and was wrapping it about her, when she cried, "O, John, that is her cloak! How can ye touch it with thoughtless hands!" And burying her face in its folds, she kissed it again and again with floods of tears. "Who'll help me on to heaven now?" she sobbed.

"Don't be breakin' yer heart this way, jewel. Sure you've got me left," said John tenderly.

Peggy made no reply, but with a deep groan, she closed her eyes, and laid her pallid cheek against the cold clay chimney, and clasping her hands, whispered, "O, God of Mammy Honey! will Ye not pity her child?"

A heavy step was now heard on the door-stone, and a merry well-known voice cried out, "Safe hoom again and wilcome to ye, Paddy Mannon!" and that gentleman, with a bundle on a stick over his shoulder, leaped in with a whoop and a comical grimace. He had just returned from his yearly visit to Meg, and was wholly ignorant of the great sorrow at the cottage. He stepped on tip-toe to the inner door, and peeped in, hoping to cheer Mammy Honey with the sight of his honest face. All was quiet there, and in perfect order. Paddy turned round, and seeing Peggy's ever busy hands folded helplessly on her lap, the truth burst upon his mind, and he cried out, "It's surely not dead that she is!"

"Yis, yis, Paddy, dead and alone in the churchyard; and why didn't God let me go with her when the heart o' me is dead too?" cried Peggy, with a fresh burst of tears. Paddy dropped the stick and bundle, and fall-

ing down between John and Peggy on his
knees, covered his face with his great rough
hands, and gave way also to a flood of tears.
Soon he broke out into a wild Irish wail, and
chanted the praise of his lost mistress in a sort
of rhyme, for which he **was very famous in the**
region, often **being sent** for to "howl out
varses" over the dead whose relatives were no
poets. He ran over her history and her vir-
tues, from her childhood till the day she took
possession of him at the work-house. As a
specimen of **Paddy's** poetical genius we will
give the portion of the wail referring to himself : —

> " And from the workhouse once she tuk
> Poor Paddy Mannon — that was luck!
> And rared him up a splindid youth,
> Haped full o' vartue and o' truth ;
> Until he'd be to marry Meg,
> Who — rather far than work — would beg;
> She tached her how to spin and knit,
> But work she wouldn't, not a bit!
> And when that silver mornin' dawned
> On which my little Pat was borned,
> She filled poor Paddy's heart with joy,
> By askin' God to bliss the boy."

He told of her holy life, in which she " fed beggars, sought after peace, and loved her inimies better nor herself; " and how, when " the old masther " was taken from her she " thanked God still that Himself was left to her; " he told how " she walked down quite contint into the grave, satisfied that she'd find hiven beyont," which, he added, " she did, too, and is there to-night." Each sentence ended with a wild howl peculiar to himself, which no one could imitate.

This duty over, poor, thoughtless Paddy seated himself, and was soon doubly comforted by a bowl of bread and milk, and by the announcement that Mammy Honey had bequeathed him the blue deal chest containing the wardrobe of the deceased Daddy Sheehan.

" Och ! but I wish this same had happened afore I wint; Meg would ha' been that proud to go with me, dressed up in that honest man's Sunday coat, to Blarney Fair," he exclaimed.

" O, Paddy, Paddy ! " cried Peggy, mournfully, " ye surely did not wish her sooner

gone ? Lave yer foolish talking now, and go
to bed like a good lad."

"To bed in the loft is it, misthress dear?"
cried Paddy. "Sure there's not gold enough
in all Ireland to timpt me up there alone.
She'll be coming back oot o' her grave to
watch do I say my prayers. 'Deed, I'll sit
in this chair till the marciful daylight comes,
with the peat fire for protiction." He started
suddenly, and turned towards the inner door,
which, being on a crack, creaked on its hinges.
"Och, but I think I saw her there now,
shakin' her head at me for the small drop o'
whisky I drank with Mike Troobrig on my
way home from the Fair. I'm that scared o'
her that I'll niver touch another drop while
the life's in me! I've heard often that dead
people sees ivery thing a body does," and casting another cautious glance at the door, he
cried, "Hooly Mother Mary, protict me!"

"If the blissed saint could come back and
sit down here beside us, you surely would not
be afeared o' her," said Peggy. "When she
did only good on this sinful arth, she'd do

no evil now that she's seen God and is like
Him. If I could but see the shadow of her
here, my poor sick heart would lape up for joy.
But I'll never, never see her more — unless,
please God, I grow holy enough to go where
she's singin' to-night. But O, John, how can
she sing there if she knows that her Peggy's
heart is breaking down here? John, John,
will you strive to help me on and to seek God
yerself?"

"Ay, will I, darlin', and ye'll see we'll get
on well in the way. I'll set out anew, dear;
I'll give two pound ten — "

"Cease telling what ye'll do, and think on
what's been done for ye, darlin'. Ye never
did a thing in yer life that would help ye on to
heaven. What is our poor righteousness,
John, to recommind us to God? Let us not
be like the Papists, to trust in our own
deeds."

Paddy sat with his beads in his hand, and
nodded in the chair by the fire all night, occasionally calling out, "Are you there, Masther
John?" and being assured that protection was

at hand, he would doze again. After that John hired a neighbor's boy to sleep with him for weeks in the loft.

CHAPTER VI.

CONFLICT AND VICTORY

WHEN the cottage was again restored to its old order and quiet — that order and quiet so painful to a bereaved heart — Peggy had "not work enough to keep the grief down." When she folded her hands to rest, she suffered "such a hunger after the blissed one" that she grew nearly wild. She felt a constant impulse to run to Cloynmally and lie down on the grave; and her prayer was not that God would sanctify her bereavement, but that He would take her "jist now and without delay to Himself and to the darlin' one."

"Come, jewel," said John, one day, "ye've wept the full o' a bucket o' tears; now cheer up and see if ye can't fill the place o' Mammy Honey in Killyrooke. Ye've always been a great sheep," he added, looking at her proudly,

" and it did well to have ye so when there was a strong mother in the cottage; but now that ye are the mistress o' the house, ye must put on a brave face or I'll be left without a woman at all ! "

So Peggy — poor, faithful heart — set out in real earnest to keep her sorrow down, that she might be a good, obedient and cheerful wife. She now, according to Mammy Honey's request, called Nannie to her and told her as gently as possible that she had no further need of her services, and soothed her disappointment — for Nan thought herself settled for life — by giving her a little silver brooch which Mammy Honey had worn in her maidenhood. " Nannie, child," she said, " remember when you go from me that there's a God aboove ye; and so never let one onpure thought 'bide in the heart that beats under Mammy Honey's brooch. None but a hooly heart iver yet throbbed beneath it; and only for its reminding ye o' her, and so, may be, ladin' ye to her God, makes me part with it at all." And she kissed the little pin tenderly.

Nan grasped the trifle eagerly, expressed regret that there was not a red stone in it, fastened it into the bosom of her linsey-woolsey gown, and stepped up to Peggy's nine-by-twelve looking-glass to admire herself.

Turning her head this way and that to get a full view of her comeliness, she replied, " One thing is sure ; if ye won't keep me here I'll go over to Mike Crogan's, for he wants a barmaid. He says my red cheeks is just the things to draw in guests o' market days, and he'll give me ten shillings a year more nor the last one had. She's destroyed entirely by the small pox, ye know."

" Don't go there, Nannie. It's but a rough place at best, and what with fightin', and pitchin' coppers, and bettin' on donkeys o' market days, it's growin' to be a curse to the town it's in. Take a place at sarvice, or else 'bide at home, knitting and mending for the childer," said Peggy.

"I'll do nather one nor yet the other," replied Nan, pertly, "for I'm my own masther now."

With several other gifts and words of advice, which were thrown away on Nan, Peggy parted with her the next day, and saw her set off — without crossing the road to speak to her mother — for Drougally, where Mike Crogan kept a poor inn for drovers, under the style of "The Bull's-horn's Inn."

Once more alone, Peggy sat down to Mammy Honey's little flax-wheel. But the wheel caught and would not turn, and the thread knotted and snarled so that she could make no progress. Ah, it takes a happy, or at least an easy heart, to do effectually the lowliest work! She put the wheel away in the inner room and seated herself, knitting in hand. She looked around the kitchen which had been for years so like a palace to her; but now the smoky rafters frowned on her, and the whole place looked poor, empty and gloomy. She glanced within her own heart, but all there was blackness and darkness. Dropping her hands helplessly at her side, she cried, "Hivenly Father, had ye no pity left for yer poor orphant Peggy, when ye took the blissed Mammy Honey away where ye had millions more like her, and left the world without a one, and my heart broke in two pieces? Sure, ye can niver love me, or ye would ha' spared me this, by takin' me along with her!"

And then the hitherto patient and submissive woman cherished hard thoughts of God, and doubted not only His mercy but His power. She was for a season in the hands of the tempter and left to buffet with him alone. Awful thoughts, of which she had never before dreamed, came rushing madly over her hitherto placid mind, like deafening torrents. "Perhaps, after all," she thought, "there is no God and no immortality. Perhaps Mammy Honey, and the minister, and all the church have been deceived, and the dear heart has slipped out of life — like her own pet lamb that died in the spring — to lie sinseless forever!" The bare suspicion against God filled her soul with anguish; and falling on her knees she shrieked out, " I'm undone, undone! I've grieved the Holy Spirit by castin' away my confidence, which hath great recompense o' reward; and now I've lost God as well as Mammy Honey, and I'm goin' wild!"

Just then the words of the dying saint came to mind, " Remember, dears, the divil is not dead yet;". and she realized his presence, tempting her to curse God and die, and trembled as a young lamb in the fangs of a wolf. Waving her hand behind her, she cried out in her agony, "' Get thee behind me, Satan,' for I have not the power o' Him ye trifled with and lied to on the mountain! I cannot fast forty days and forty nights; Lord, bind him hand and foot, that he do not destroy me!"

John was repairing ditches a little way from the cottage, and hearing Peggy's cries, went in and found her prostrate on the cold floor. " Rise up, there, darlin'," he said. " Do ye pray all yer time? Why can't ye let the dear jewel rest in her grave now, and be aisy?"

" Och, John, Mammy Honey's loss is a small thing now! I've got a huger throuble nor that on me!" she cried, turning her pale face up to him imploringly.

" What on arth can it be?" asked John, running to the door, and looking, involuntarily, toward the cow-house and the sheepfold, where his treasures were. " Have we lost any body else?"

" Yes, John; I've lost God!" cried the tempted woman. " My soul's in the dark, and the divil, that Mammy Honey had such sore battles with, is standin' afore me and hiding Him — if He's here at all."

" You're losin' yer sinse, dear!" cried John. " Cheer up, now, and I'll get the donkey-cart and we'll have a ride over to the widow Doane's, and ye'll carry her some o' yer new honey; and ye'll come back bright eno'!"

" John, I'll never go to see any friend till I first find the Lord; and if ye love me, lave me to myself till then. Could ye and Paddy do without me after dinner? I'd fain spend the

lavin's o' this day alone in her room in fastin'
and prayer."

"Fastin'? Sure, yer not turnin' Papist,
are ye?" asked John.

"Och, no, dear, but I'm seekin' my lost
Lord — Him whom my soul loveth; and sure,
dear, eatin' is o' small account beside such
business as that!" replied Peggy, solemnly.

John looked at her wonderingly. His
mother's conflicts and triumphs had been
matters of constant conversation, her religion
being so woven in with her every-day life that
the fruits of it, charity and patience, were
visible to all about her. But Peggy had lived
within herself, being always reserved on matters of a spiritual nature, so that her speaking
thus freely amazed him.

"Well, take yer own way, wife," he replied;
"only don't give yerself so to religion as to
neglect the dairy and the poultry. The piousest
time our mother ever had, she was as arnest
about her business as ever. She said that
livin' near the Lord helped her better with her

duty. And for that, itself, if no other, religion would be a fine thing in the world."

Peggy prepared the humble meal and served it as one whose spirit was far away. All being restored to neatness in the kitchen, she withdrew to the inner room, where the time-worn Bible lay on a rude little stand, covered with a clean linen towel; and she was seen no more in the kitchen that night.

In the morning John was wakened from a deep sleep by the voice of singing in the kitchen, where his good wife was busy preparing the morning meal.

> " Oh, for this love let rocks and hills
> Their lasting silence break;
> And all harmonious human tongues
> The Saviour's praises speak! "

" Sure, that can never be ye, Peggy, tunin' up this joyful way," he said, as he entered the kitchen, over whose smooth clay floor the sun was now shining cheerily.

" Och, dear heart!" cried Peggy, coming forward to meet him and taking both his hands

in her own; " come and sit down till I ask ye
a question. Did ye ever hear Mammy Honey
say that a body could be 'born again' more
than once?"

" Well, noo, I don't mind that I did,"
replied John, with an air of surprise, as he
looked at Peggy's face, which shone like an
angel's. " Why, dear, what if she did?"

" Why, then, if that can be so, I've been
twice ' born again;' once when I was a lonely
orphant at dear Farmer D'oane's, and now this
last night again. And, John, look at me, and
tell me if I'm the same Peggy ye saw breakin'
her heart these last days because God didn't
give up the ruic o' all things — even life and
death — into her foolish hands?"

" I was niver great on thaology," replied
John, " and if ye'd like, I'll drive ye to Cloynmally to ask you question o' the minister to-
morrow."

" To-morrow! I must walk the two miles
as soon as my work is over, and call upon him,
and good elder Peter, and them all, to bless
and praise His holy name that He has revealed

Himself to me above all my **sins o'** doubt and distrust, and sent the divil off ashamed to his own place — ashamed o' the mane sperit that **bid him to pass by the strong soldiers o' the** cross to **fight with a** poor, weak and ignorant child like mesilf."

"**And will ye** go alone, yerself, to the minister's house?" asked John; for that was a stretch of courage in her for which **he was not** prepared.

"Indade will **I, though I** never made that bold before. Why, **John, I** would go into his pulpit if **God bid me,** to tell o' **His wondrous** love — how He revaled Himself to me as the altogether lovely, the last night, when all the world but **me** was sleepin'. I think I'll never have time to sleep more while **I** live, John; a whole life o' wakin' hours is far too short to praise Him in! **Och, but** blissed be His name, I'll have a whole etarnity to finish in — but finished my praise can niver, niver be."

Paddy Mannon's appetite was the token to him that breakfast was ready. He had drawn near the cottage and stood at the door, amazed

at the joyful animation of his mistress, usually
so calm and silent. He entered and took his seat
at the table, before the snowy potatoes and the
savory herring. "She's been convarted into a
new Misthress Honey," he said to John.
"Sure, I never heerd her say the like o' you
afore. What's coome over her, that the tears
is all dried and she a psalm singing?"

"Whist, Paddy," said John. "She's got
peace to her soul that ye could niver understand if I should strive to explain to ye." Alas,
the poor man did not himself understand
Peggy's sudden transition from anguish to joy;
but he did not tell Paddy this. "This cooms
in the way o' our religion," he added. "And,
dear," said he to Peggy; "be sure ye take the
darlin' mammy's little egg basket to the minister's, and till his lady we'll keep up the gift
o' herself as long as we have a hin to cackle
aboot the doors! For I'll be sorry the minister
should think there weren't a Christian left in
the cottage to fade the Lord's sarvants, now
my mother's gone!"

CHAPTER VII.

VISIT TO THE MINISTER.

THE soft breeze of the bright autumnal afternoon was playing among the leaves of the luxuriant woodbine which overhung the porch of the unpretending house of Mr. Murray, the excellent minister of Cloynmally, when Peggy tapped at the door. She asked the maid, " Do ye think the minister would be at leisure to spake a few words to me ? "

She was ushered into the little parlor, where Mrs. Murray sat reading to her boys, and was kindly received. Before she was seated, Mr. Murray entered, and holding out his hand, spoke in very gentle tones, as is natural when we address one in deep affliction.

" My good friend," he said, " I'm sorry you should have to come after me in your sorrow. I was going down to Killyrooke in an hour or

two, to see you. I met John and heard how
crushed you were by your great loss — and our
loss, too, Peggy; for we are all mourners in
Cloynmally."

Peggy dropped a low courtesy and looked up
to him with a beaming face. "Dear Mr.
Murray," she began, "it's not to talk o' death
or sorrow I've come; but to tell ye something
that's wonderful and glorious — more like a
message from heaven than of arth. I don't
know where to begin nor what to say."

Mr. Murray saw the unnatural light in the
mild blue eye, and said, "As you are so shy,
Peggy, perhaps you'd feel more free to talk
with me alone in my study."

"O, dear heart, no!" cried Peggy. "I
want the whole of Cloynmally and Killyrooke
— the whole world, to know what God has
done for me, a poor, rebillious, weak, shy
thing, unworth his care or notice! Do ye
think, sir, that iver a body was 'born again'
twice?"

"I believe, Peggy, that many who have been
truly renewed in heart are afterward brought

6

into a fuller light and joy, which seems to them almost like a new birth," replied Mr. Murray.

"Well, dear Mr. Murray, ye know well what a weak child I have been — in sperit — always holding on to Mammy Honey's skirt to keep my hope up. I've been years a hungerin' and a thirstin' after righteousness. But mind what blindness I was in! When I'd pray, I'd say, 'Make me holy like Mammy Honey,' and not, 'as He is holy.' I made that blissed saint my pattern, and was iver strivin' to be like her and to plaze her. If God helped me to forgive my poor neighbors and to retarn them good for evil, I rejoiced, and thought, 'That is like her and will plaze her.'

"When the fear o' death would come over me I was in great trouble because I'd be parted from her, and I used to pray that God would take us two at one time, havin' a kind o' dim hope that her strength and courage would help to uphold me. But God.came and took her from me, and I'd fallen into sin and doubted his mercy; and woe's me, I charged

God with forgettin' to be gracious and not
keepin' His covenant with the orphant!
Satan then came and brought with him blackness and horrible darkness; and I lost God
and hope, as well as her! Och, ye would ha'
pitied me, dear sir, for I'd none to speak to —
for John didn't understand me. I prayed for
hours, till I sank exhausted on my pillow and
fell asleep. Then I dramed that I was walkin'
weary and lame through huge bogs full o'
holes and pits, and it black night about me.
I dropped my staff and feared to go on without
it, and stood cryin'. All of a suddent it grew
light, and there before me stood the two
shinin' ones that Bunyan saw, and they bid me
have good heart and walk bravely homeward.
I told them I was hurted and could not go
alone. Then said one o' them, ' Ye are niver
alone; for though ye see him not for yer
blindness, the Saviour is beside ye always, and
benath ye are the everlasting arms. It is this
which has kept ye so that ye could not, and
that ye will not fall — foriver!' I looked at
my right hand, and there stood one like unto

the Son o' man, and all the time I'd been held
up by Him and didn't know it. He turned
His lovin' eyes on me and spake; but the
words I can niver tell, for they're gone from
me; but they left my soul haped full o' joy,
and now there's room for nothing else there!
I'm just flyin' to go and be foriver with Him,
and yit I'm quite contint to 'bide here tin
thousand years if by that same I could add a
whit to His glory or bring one poor soul to
taste His love. And my heart is that full o'
love to my neighbors that I could take them
all into my arms: they are no longer miserable
'Papists' to me, but dear sinners that I must
get saved with this great salvation! Did ye
iver hear the like o' this before, sir? I
walked all the way to ask ye."

"Yes, my good woman," replied the minister, looking in wonder at the radiant face over
which tears of joy were freely coursing. "I
know two persons who have enjoyed such
wondrous revelations of God's mercy. One of
them was a godly Scotch minister in Dundee.
He told me that he once had a season of such

perfect and conscious union with Christ that
he had no will of his own left. He felt his
whole being, for time and eternity, swallowed
up in God. His glorious perfections and attri-
butes were revealed to him in a way that led
him to realize something of the glory of heaven,
where He is all and in all. But I'll tell you,
my dear friend, what else he said — not to discourage you, but so that, should his words
come true, you will see that no strange thing is
befalling you. He said that in all the cases he
had known of this wondrous revelation, God
was thus preparing the soul either for some
great work or some great sorrow. Immedi-
ately after his own triumphant view of God,
there was such an outpouring of the Spirit as
had not been in that city for a half century;
and he was thus fitted to gather in the lambs
and to edify the saints. A worthy old saint,
named Carmichal, experienced, years ago, much
the same displays of God's power in his soul,
leading him to make a new and fuller sur-
render of himself and his all to Christ. Not
long after this a fearful distemper prevailed,

and his three children were smitten down and his house left unto him desolate. And he said that he gave them up with joy in his soul — that he could not refrain from falling on his knees before his neighbors, and thanking God that He had accepted those whom he had so often committed to His care."

"And so, dear Mr. Murray, them two had a heaven as well as mysilf on arth. But what could labor be but joy, after one has had a look at the Saviour's face? I can't see what could come that one would have the boldness to call 'throuble,' after yon vision o' heaven in the soul."

"Why, Peggy, death must ever remain a curse, for it separates us from those we love, you know, even if they and we are prepared to meet again," said the minister.

"But it can never be a curse to me, dear heart, after this day. If I had twenty Mammy Honeys I'd give them all to Him, though I'd not a one beside, in all the world, to love me. What could I hold back from one who gave Himself for me?"

"Ah, Peggy, my good woman, you have reached a height your minister has not yet caught sight of. The King has held out His sceptre to you and suffered you to speak in His presence chamber. Go home and ask Him to reveal Himself to me — His weary servant who has long toiled for souls in darkness here — as He has done to you. And may the God of peace abide with you."

All this time Peggy had held Mammy Honey's little egg-basket on her arm, and now, recollecting herself, she gave it with John's message to Mrs. Murray, and said, "The sun is sinking, and I must go to look after my milk when poor Paddy brings it in. And I must take a step into the church-yard as I go, to look at the swate, paceful grave where my darlin' is sleepin." And with a courtesy she departed.

As she passed through the little flower-garden on her way to the road, Peggy stooped to look at a little flower "Pluck as many as you please, my dear friend," said the minister, who stood in the door watching her. She gathered a few sprigs of mignonette and heart's-ease, and, curtseying her thanks, went on. As Mr. Murray closed the door, he saw her press them to her lips. "Ah, look at her!" he said to his wife. "Her heart is so full of love to-day that she is forced to pour it out on the smallest things that God has made! Oh, for her exceeding great joy!"

When Peggy reached the little church-yard, she stood a moment looking over the hedge which surrounded it; then she passed in, and up a path to the new-made grave. A workman was there trimming the hedge; two little boys were wandering about hand-in-hand in solemn curiosity, whispering their questions and answers to each other; a score of merry birds were trilling and twittering — they had no fear of death. But Peggy heeded neither sight nor sound. She was alone with God. "Sure," she said, "this can never be the awful place we left so late! all here is calm and holy and homelike! and she, the mother o' my heart, is but slapin' after the wary day.

This is but the open door to hiven, my Father's house, where herself is a waitin' me! But whin I reach the place, my heart will be that full o' Himself, that it'll be a space ere I run to her! He is to me, as niver till this day, the altogether lovely! He makes death aisy and the grave blissed. O, death! where is thy. sting, O, grave! where is thy victory? They are both gone; and we, when we is risen with Christ, will be conquerors, and shall wear the crown! Oh, the love o' God in Christ Jesus! How iver shall I show it to the world, and bring them all to taste it!"

She sat on the new-laid sod, smoothing it gently with her hand. "I must away now, darlin', home to my duties; the roughest o' thim all looks jist lovely to me now! I'll never again ask to bring ye back from the joy o' the Lord; never weep more for ye, and never cast reflections on God, by sayin'—'I've *lost* my mother;' for I've not! I have her still, far safer and surer nor before, in the bosom o' the Lord. Farewell, darlin' dust!

for there's nothing here but that!" And with a placid face, the loving creature pressed a fervent kiss on " the dear arth that covered the darlin'," laid the little flowers upon it, and went on her homeward way.

CHAPTER VIII.

SINGING AND WORKING.

WHEN Peggy returned to her labors, a light seemed to shine over every homely thing she touched, and toil was changed from a curse to a blessing. When the dairy work was over, she stirred up the peat, which usually supplied her with light, and brought out once more the little wheel. The flax flew as if by magic under her fingers, and the threads ran from it like silver wires in the changing firelight; and before she knew it, she was singing at her work. That she had rarely done in her happiest day, for, as John said, "she was such a quiet-like mousie ye'd niver know she was in the world but only for the power o' work she tarned off her two hands." It had been Mammy Honey's wont to cheer labor with song, and Peggy had now resolved to be as

91

nearly like her as possible, in all things. John joined her song, and at the end of the first verse Peggy turned to Paddy, who was sitting cross-legged on the floor beside her, mending the donkey's harness. He always insisted that "though it was manners ontirely to sit in a cheer, if it was *rest* a lad was afther, there was nothing like a smooth clay floor for that." " Paddy," said his mistress, " ye've got a swate voice whin ye sing yon heap o' nonsinse ; why can't ye use it, dear man, to praise the Lord with ?"

" I'm afeared o' that cudgel o' his riverence's, misthress dear. I've felt the weight o't moor nor once; and one time warn't my shoulders black and blue with the knocks I got o't for larnin' the 'Simbly's Catechism ? I promished him that day I'd hear no' more prayers here, and forgit that same catechism — sure I know it so well now that I can say ivery blissed word o't and count at the same time ! Whin Misthress Honey wint and asked him what her b'y had ben doin' that desarved imbraces like you, didn't he tell her I'd been stalin' pears out o' his garden? It nigh broke her heart thinkin' that I, a well-fed lad, would be that mean and vicious! And *niver a pear* did he raise in that ould garden!

"Well, thin she put me to larnin' the commandmint, 'Thou shalt not stale;' and the first time I confissed, didn't he draw *that* out o' me and give me another batin'? So betwixt the twos o' 'em poor Paddy had a sorry life o't, and the wise conclusion I come to was jist this: to belave my dear misthress' religion, and to *pretind* that I belaved his. So that ways I gets on quite asy. No, no, I'll not be caught by any neighbor that'll chance in, a singing hums, but I'll listen; that's all ye can expect o' me."

"There, there, Paddy, don't hinder the swate singin' all night with yer talk, foolish man. Keep quiet while we sing, and try to praise God in yer heart," said John.

"Ay," replied Paddy, "I wull. Don't ye think, masther, the lather o' thim reins war rotten ontirely whin we bought em? I was tellin' Jack Garin ——"

" Whist, Paddy," cried John, sharply, " and listen to the singin'."

" I wull, thin," answered Paddy, bending over his work, and pressing his lips together so tightly that no word could slip through unawares.

When Peggy had finished her spinning and her singing for the night, she brought out two large bags filled with yarn, carded and spun by the hands now folded forever. She poured out the hanks on the table, and looking proudly at the high mound they made, said, " Look, John and Paddy! It's little o' this ye'll need, for she left ye both supplied with warm stockings for five years. So the nady will get it; and I've had jist a lovely thought come to me, like it had come from herself in heaven."

" May be ; but it wouldn't need come so far, for yer own heart's full o' as good and pure thoughts as is to be found any where ; " replied John ; " but let us hear this one."

" Whin I was wonderin' what more lovin' work I could do in the world, this came to my mind, that I was young and strong, and didn't nade all the slape I'm takin'; and that if I'd rise one hour arlier and go to slape one hour later, addin' that time to the hours I could give to her old work for the nady, it would atone a bit for the loss o' her, and it would make me that glad to feel that myself was honored by fillin' her place in the poor's hearts;" and parcelling out thé yarn she continued, "Thim skeins will be enough for Teddy Byrns, and thim for old Davie Loon. These will knit four pairs for the poor babies o' careless Kate Connor, and these for lame Jerry, and them for the poor fool, and ———"

"Quit, Peggy, woman," cried John, starting up, and manifesting a temper that she had seldom seen before; "would ye be turnin' yer back on yer husband's honor and on the rispictability o' all the race o' Sheehan by covering the feet o' you vile scapegrace? I hope the toes will freeze off his two feet, and that he'll starve to death with the cold afore spring laughs on the fields agin — to disgrace a fine rispictable funeral as he did you day, — the villyan!"

" Mammy Honey both clothed and faded her inimies, John, and it's no more nor the Masther bids us all do. Sure, there'd be a great tarnin' up o' things if Himself should cease to fade ony but His friends! O, dear man, mind He's sent His rain on our fields mony the time when we war livin' forgetful enough o' Him, and has had an eye on every cratur' in herd or fold while we war slapin' warm in our bed."

" Peggy, woman, ye're a great sheep. I belave if one should slap ye in the face ye'd offer him bread and milk to pay him for his attintions! Now mind what I say — that seldom bids ye agin yer will, as other husbands does — let no mouthful that I arns iver go betwane the teeth o' yon fool, and let no wool off my sheep's backs ever cover his old feet! I'm plannin' yet how I'll punish him for yon onreligious insult, and ye'd be knittin' stockin's for him the manewhile! Indade ! "

Peggy made no reply; but Paddy's ready tongue filled up the gap which would otherwise have been left in the conversation.

" Masther, dear," he cried, eagerly, " will ye
lave his punishment in my hands? I'll hide
ahind the hedge when I sees him comin', all
dressed in a shate wid horns on my head, and
hug him in my two arms. He's the cowardest
cratur' in Killyrooke, and that would tarmint
him far more nor the hugest batin ! "

" Och, John, dear, don't let Paddy taze him,
for he's one o' the Lord's stricken ones, and
we'd surely grieve Him if we'd be to scare
away the bit o' sinse he has. Shame on ye,
Paddy Mannon ! Ye that are so afeared o'
ghosts and the Evil One that ye daren't go to
yer bed alone, and has to be coaxed up to the
kitchen fire like a froze lamb ; ye to be plot-
tin' torture like you for a poor thing that's
witless enough to do ony man's biddin' ! "

" Well, noo, both o' ye do *my biddin'*," said
John. " Paddy, ye lave you fool in yer masther's hand ; and, Peggy, let me see no
stockin's goin' out o' the cottage to him."

This resolute tone was so unlike the yielding
John that Peggy looked up in alarm, and
made no reply. Remembering, as she never

ceased to do, that all there belonged to John, and that she came to him a poor orphan with her worldly all in a little blue trunk that Paddy had carried into the cottage in one hand, she submitted to his will.

CHAPTER IX.

AN UNWELCOME GUEST.

THE winter, long and dreary, wore away, and the first whisperings of spring were heard among the branches around the cottage. Cheerfully as the fond Peggy had yielded up her mother to God, she yet suffered at times an unutterable longing for her, and an undefined dread lest the swallows might not come back to build under the thatch, and that the hawthorn and honeysuckle would forget to bloom. It seemed impossible that the birds could come, now that the hand which had fed them was gone, or that the vines could creep upward in their silent strength when her hand was not there to train them; or that the shamrock and the daisy could peep above the cold sod, when she who had so loved their lowly beauty was no longer there to smile on them.

Nature is not retarded in her progress by
any changes in our homes, but moves on in
her noiseless work to cheer the hearts and provide for the wants of the living.

Fruits succeeded the blossoms, and again
the grain waved with its ripened burden in the
fields of Daisy Farm. The reapers were busy
with John and Paddy at a distance from the
house. Peggy felt keenly the loss, which
seemed renewed by this commemorative season. The stillness of the cottage impressed
her so painfully, one day, that she was glad
when the sinking sun shone aslant the door-
stone, reminding her that it was time to go to
her milking. The shadows had begun to fall
before she had finished her work in the barn-
yard; and being sad, she was not as brave as
usual. As she took up her stool in one hand
and her shining pail in the other, and turned to
go towards " Maid o' Longford," the last cow,
she was not a little startled at seeing a tall,
thin-figure close behind her in the garb of a
beggar. The famine was just then beginning
to cast its shadow over poor Ireland, and

beggars were becoming not only plenty, but insolent, often threatening and cursing those who did not meet all their demands.

Always timid, Peggy was really terrified as the close, black hood was not lifted from the face of the silent beggar.

" And what is it I can do for ye, poor thing ? " she asked, in a tremulous voice.

" Peggy," replied the woman, " it's a shelter and a bit o' bread I wants. For the love o' God and Mammy Honey take me in, for I'm dying with hunger and wakeness."

The voice struck Peggy with a sudden faintness, and she exclaimed, " Sure, Nanny, this is never ye, lookin' thus miserable ? "

" It's no other," replied the girl, throwing back her hood, and showing her wan face. " Peggy, Mammy Honey never refused shelter even to a dumb brute."

" No more will her child do it," replied Peggy. " I'll give ye all ye nade."

" Well, thin, I nades a home more nor any thing else. I've been tindin' bar ilsewhere since I left ould Crogan, who niver paid me a ha' pith, and I was sick the last three months in a hospital, and have walked all the road home, and am dyin'."

"Why not go to yer own father's house, child? Where else would one go in throuble?" asked Peggy.

"They're angered with me for lavin' thim that suddent. My mother sint word she'd murther me if iver I come aboot here agin."

"And why thin did ye come, child?" asked Peggy.

"To find marcy at yer hand, ye happy woman. Let me 'bide under yer marciful ruff," she answered, in an imploring tone.

Peggy's heart sank within her, but her kindness triumphed over her fears, and she replied, "Ye may 'bide here, Nanny, till ye're warmed and fed, but if they'd give me Harpley Hall I could never give ye a home. Mammy Honey bid us two live by ourselves, with her last brith. But come with me now into the cottage;" and Peggy took the little red shawl from off her own shoulders, and wrapped it around the girl, who was shivering, for the dew was falling, and led the way to the cottage. Here she stirred the peat till the waiting kettle puffed out anew its steam, and then, taking down from a high shelf the tiny canister, mixed a cup of tea.

When Nan was well warmed and revived by a good supper, her old assurance returned.

"Come, Peggy," she said, coaxingly, "give a poor, disappointed and abused girl a home in yer cottage, and I'll spin and wave for ye from daybreak till midnight."

"Nanny," replied Peggy, summoning all her courage, "I'll do ye good ony way but this. *Ye can niver 'bide* in this house. John made me misthress o't the day God took the darlin' mother to Himself; and while I remain *that* ye can never slape under this thatch."

Nan gave a low, derisive laugh, which made her wan face terrible, and said, "If I war a Protestant ye'd kape me. But take yer own way; there's poor luck follows them as tarns the homeless oot o' doors."

"Ye are not homeless, child, and nather am I thrustin' ye out; but doin' my bist for ye," replied Peggy. "Paddy Mannon, that's o' yer own religion, has often declared he'd not 'bide under the same ruff with ye, for he's heard evil tales o' ye, child, since ye left me. So, when ye're well rested, go over to the father's house and get forgiveness, and be a good girl. There come my rapers now over the field, and I must take up their supper. Here's a crown, if ye'd be wantin' any little comforts."

Nan rose feebly, took the proffered crown, turned her deep blue eyes sorrowfully on the good woman, and said in a hollow tone, which struck to her heart, "Ye may see the day, Peg O'Canty, when ye'll cross this door-stone with a sorrowfuller heart nor I do now!"

Peggy was startled by her wild manner, and cried, "Och, Nanny, child, don't be cursin' yer bist friend! I'm ony mindin' Mammy Honey's biddin', and yet I must tell ye that I'm more afeared o' ye nor o' death itself."

"And well ye may be," cried Nan, as with another stare at the timid woman she departed for her home.

Peggy was in an agony. She could then
have given her the cottage and all it contained, so great was her fear of Nan's designs
on her peace of mind. The serpent's tooth had
entered Peggy's heart, and she could scarcely
wait till the reapers had gone out to smoke by
the roadside, to cry, " Tell me once for all,
John, that ye love me more nor all else in the
world."

John laughed and asked, " Who other have
I to love, jewel ? "

When Peggy told the story of Nan's visit, he
said, " Ye did well, for she's not fit company
for ye, and I'll not suffer her aboot the place
after the word o' our mother." And Peggy
was satisfied, and laughed at her own fears
and those of Paddy, roused by Nan's boast,
which had reached their ears that though John
was her father's playmate, she would be his
second wife, and have that fine cottage and
dairy yet.

CHAPTER X.

FAMINE AND DEATH.

THE fever which followed in the wake of starvation in Ireland some twenty years ago, had been sweeping off its victims in the surrounding region, but had not hitherto reached Killyrooke, nor yet had the potatoes there suffered to any great extent. The people listened with white lips to any account of "the sickness," and if a person came from an infected region they fled from him as if he had the plague. The stoutest hearts quailed before the dreadful scourge, and men were afraid even to be merciful to the starving, lest the next day their own little ones might be crying for bread.

Meg Mannon had extended her begging excursion unwittingly into a village where the fever had just broken out. The half-starved and poorly sheltered people were flying, panic-stricken, in every direction. Here she fell sick, and gave a pauper two shillings to walk three miles to Killyrooke for Paddy, who ran all the way there, howling piteously, talking to her and crying real tears, and not the mock ones he got up for strangers. He reached the workhouse "just in time to see her die without a word o' love to the fine b'y who had been layin' down his very life for her all the years she war his wife."

Oh, the overflowing anguish of that poor, foolish heart in that bitter hour, with none to speak a soothing word, and the gruff beadle giving his orders impatiently to have Meg buried before her form was cold !

Paddy grasped this dignitary by the arm ; and while his tears ran like a summer shower, he cried, "Oh, if yer honor has the heart o' a hoosband beneath his waistcoat, I imploores him to give me the swate clay o' my lovely wife till I gets it waked and buried in holy ground at Killyrooke — the only place in all the wide world worth bein' buried in."

The hard heart of the beadle was moved by Paddy's deep grief, and he finally promised to let the body remain in an out-building till the devoted husband could make his arrangements at home, and return for it with the donkey-cart.

So, carrying the frightened little Pat in his arms, Paddy ran back at the top of his speed — he had won a fine pipe and a steel tobacco-box once at a foot race — and rushed breathless into the cottage.

"Och — masther — John — and Peggy, ye angel o' a woman — I've a great honor — to ask o' ye. For the sake o' — Mammy Honey — that niver denied me an honor — for the sake o' the Virgin — Mary — and all the saints ontirely — would ye let me — bring Meg — the dear dead jewel — to the ould cow-house fernint the bog to-night to be waked, and thin to be buried the morrow ? "

Terrified as they were by the very name of the sickness by which Meg had died, and by the sight of Paddy and his boy from an infected house, they had not the heart to deny his request. But the prudent John dared not trust his donkey in the infected region, and told Paddy so. He, nothing daunted, replied, sobbing bitterly, "Och, masther, heart o' love, if ye'd be to lend me the loan o' the dray we drags water with from the loch, I'm quite willin' to be a donkey mesilf, for the sake o' kapin' my word to the dead jewel, that I'd give her a fine funeral. Och! och! But it's black night ontirely in my soul now and will iver be till the day when I lies down beside her. I'll never ate, drink or smoke more; why would I when she's dead? Och! och! oo, hoo!" It really seemed to Peggy that Paddy's heart would break through its strong breast-works with its tremendous throes.

Peggy wept too, not that she cared much for the beggar-woman, but from sympathy with him. She told Paddy to take poor little Pat into the cow-house and feed him well, and put him to rest in the hay till his return, for John was not willing either father or child should remain in the cottage a moment. Having done this,

and in a marvelously short time returned with
his melancholy burden on the dray, he went
off to spend his quarter's wages in ginger-
bread, whisky and tobacco, and to invite his
friends to the melancholy feast. But the news
had preceded him, and they all fled from him
with screams of terror. So he returned home
and shouted to his mistress from the stile:
" Sure, I've lost my quarter's wages, for not a
one will come to the wake ; the fools is all
afeard o' Meg, as harmless a cretur' as iver
begged bread. But she'll get a prayer said for
the repowse o' her sowl, as good a one as if she
war the lady o' Harpley Hall, and I'll settle
with his riverence at the end o' my nixt
quarter."

And Paddy, who was so afraid of death
that he ran off a few months before and stayed
away two days when the oldest donkey died,
sat alone in the cow-house all night beside his
dead, singing a dirge, or howling and crying.
Now and then he consoled himself with his
pipe, but he dared not even cast a sly glance

at the whisky jug, lest that might bring up
Mammy Honey, who was a sworn foe to every
thing like it.

Some mourners plant rare flowers and rear
costly monuments over their beloved dead; but
it costs them nothing compared with what
Paddy endured before he thus rose triumphant
over inborn cowardice and natural superstition.
Had he believed that his doing so would have
helped Meg's unshriven soul to slip more easily
through purgatory, he would have lain down
and been buried beside her.

In the gray light of the morning, while
little Pat was sleeping soundly in the hay,
Paddy drew poor Meg to the little Catholic
churchyard and, lowered her gently into a grave
he had dug there the night before, talking to
her all the time amid bursts of tears, " It's yer
own Paddy, dear, that's puttin' ye to rist. It
war him made yer bed, and only for little Pat
he'd come and lie down aside ye. Sure I'd
niver let ould Murtagh dig yer grave with his
dirty hands. No, darlin', mesilf did it with me
best Sunday clothes on, — thim as was Daddy

Sheehan's — though they're a trifle too big — for he was a huge man, ye mind. Good-by to ye, Meg, ye fine ombitious gerl. The sun shines not on yer like, and it's a short space Paddy can live in the world ahind ye."

The " holy father " now came up according to appointment, and, standing at a respectful distance, read a service of which Paddy could not understand a word ; and it was just as well it was in Latin, for had it been in English, his reverence was too far off to be heard.

All being over, Paddy returned to the old cow-house, the same in which he and Meg had kept house occasionally, and prepared breakfast out of doors for himself and his child, Peggy having set a jug of milk half way between them and the cottage.

After Paddy and his boy had been quarantined for several days in the old cow-house without showing any symptoms of the dreaded fever, Peggy allowed them to come to the cottage one evening, and eat their bread and milk on the door-stone. Standing in the farthest corner of the kitchen, she said, " Paddy, yer

masther and me is both wonderful taken up
with yon curly-headed lamb o' yours; and he
bids ye not take him back to the workhouse,
for he's to 'bide with us and be our child, as
we niver had one o' our own. And who can
tell, Paddy, but God took Meg away that the
poor lambie might be spared a beggar's life,
and grow up a holy man to fear God and to
sarve his gineration."

"Very like He did, thin," replied Paddy,
"and if so, it war a great stroke o' luck that
sint her to that town the very day the faver
began!"

"Don't say that, Paddy, o' the poor mother;
for whativer failin's Meg had, she was tinder
o' the boy—niver lavin' him about among
neighbors, as the half o' them do, but draggin'
him weary miles on her back!"

"That's true, indade! But for all, it was
luck to little Pat, that tuk her off, if therebys
he's to be rared the son o' a fine, rispectable
farmer, place o' bein' reared a beggar. It's
fine luck for little Pat, though it's murther for

me, poor distracted lad that I am, without a heart in me bussum! Ohoo! hoo! hoo!"

"And who can tell, Paddy, but the child's innocent prattle may win yer masther away from his frolics with thim ontidy urchins across the road? He's such a loon about childer, the poor, foolish man! We'll kape the boy that swate and clane that the very minister himself could take him on his knee and kiss him."

"Dade will ye," replied Paddy, looking proudly at the pretty, bright boy. "But what about the religion, though?" he asked, as the disadvantages of the offer began to suggest themselves. "His riverence will bate the life out o' me if I suffer him to be tached yon 'Simbly's Catechism and the ten Protestant commandmints."

"Paddy, if we takes him for our child, he'll be named Johnny Sheehan, and the priest will have no more to say aboot him nor he does aboot Mr. Murray's boys. And Paddy, I belave yer bearin' false witness agin Father

Clakey. Yer masther will tell him whin nixt he goes by, that we've taken little Pat for our child, and had him new named."

So little Pat was stripped of his beggar's garb, dressed like a farmer's child, and placed on a high stool of John's manufacture, at the table. He at once began to call Peggy "mammy," and John "daddy;" and being almost a stranger to his father, he now called him "Paddy Mannon," as every body else did. Whenever John came in from the field the little fellow would run to meet him; and when he was seated in the cottage, he would climb on his knee, and putting his arms round his neck, call him "pretty daddy," and ask, "May me ride donkey? What did old donkey say?" Then John would tell long stories of what the donkeys, cows and ducks asked about "the new little lambie that had come to the cottage, with black wool on his head and red roses on his cheeks!" John taught him to count, and to tell the names of coin, and to whistle; Peggy taught him the commandments, and the words of Jesus, "Suffer the little children to come unto Me, for of such is the kingdom of heaven." Before he had been there a week, whistles, tin carts, a jumping-jack and a drum, — trifles which had never before found their way to Killyrooke, were scattered over Peggy's kitchen-floor, and John never went to town but he brought home some toy, about as new and surprising to him and Paddy as to the boy. All three agreed that a child was a wonderful thing for making sunshine in a cottage.

One day, before poor Meg had been a week in her grave, Peggy went out of the cottage, leading little Johnny by the hand, to feed the poultry. As she neared the stile which led from the garden into a barley-field, she saw Paddy mounted on the topmost rail, mending his corduroy breeches with a darning needle and twine, and singing, with the full power of his lungs — and that is saying a great deal —

> " Norra is a fine gerl,
> Chakes like the rose,
> People think she is the quane,
> Every where she goes!
> O, the flower of Tipperary!"

"O, Paddy, Paddy," cried Peggy, "that's surely not ye, singing yon foolish song! What were ye and the priest doin' but a few days agone in the churchyard?"

"Hooly mother!" cried Paddy, springing from the stile and throwing up both hands in surprise, "Sure I'd forgot ontirely that Meg was dead at all! Ye don't think, dear misthress, that she'll come back to haunt me for singin' aboot the 'Flower o' Tipperary'? Belave me that I've not at all made up me mind aboot another wife yet, or even whether I'll take one or not; and why would I, miserable man that I am, when the wide warld hasn't another like her? Where would I iver find one so strong as she, that would niver ask me for the price o' a peck o' male in the year, but take all the care o' hersilf and her boy, and buy all my tobaccy beside! Oohoo! Oohoo! How'll I iver live in the arth without me jewel Meg?" and he wrung his hands, and wept and groaned piteously.

His grief, however, was soon spent, and he sprang up on the stile again and resumed his mending with as much **spirit as if no great** sorrow was on him. Paddy loved his friends while they **were** with him, but "out of sight" they were **soon** "out of mind," and he was as **jolly and contented as if he had** never known them.

Peggy suffered some anxiety about the com- panions with whom little Johnny would mingle when he **could no longer be kept at her** side. Her heart shrank from his hearing an oath or witnessing the brawls **of** the neigh- boring children. Nan, who had not **yet been** murdered **by her parents, as she had** predicted she would be, often brought over her **mother's baby, a** bright, plump creature, neat **to a marvel, for him,** to play **with Johnny,** and **occasionally took her seat, uninvited, at** the supper-table. **This, of course,** vexed Peggy, **but she bore it meekly, being too** much afraid **of Nan to** forbid her visits.

The good woman's **fears for little Johnny's** future were **all needless. For one short year** he made sunshine in **the cottage, and then** came a sickness which **gave no** alarm till too late for help, and soon his prattle was hushed in death. And again the cottage was silent.

Peggy wept as if her heart would break; and yet she blamed John for his boisterous grief, saying, "Don't let yer neighbors say, dear, that ye wail louder for a beggar's baby nor for yer own holy mother! Thank God with me, John, that the little darlin's safe with Himself, rather than us taken and him left in the hands o' poor, careless Paddy. Heaven will be more like our home, John, now that we've both our mother and our child there."

Heaven was to John a place very far off; and he gave little thought to it — or, indeed, to any thing beyond his home-work and his crops. So, after a sad week or two, he was the same as before he had found and lost the child.

While John and Peggy were weeping over the little cold form lying on Mammy Honey's bed — now a sacred place — Paddy was flying about with an excited business air, making arrangements for the funeral, and comforting

Peggy and John as if he himself had no part in the affliction. He had given the child away, therefore his death was nothing which particularly concerned him.

CHAPTER XI.

A GREAT SORROW.

NOT a week had passed, after the death of little Johnny, when Paddy saw his master tossing coppers among the little O'Gormans, and stepping up behind him, said, "Ye'd better quit that, Marsther John. Remember what ye promised by the deathbed o' yer mother, and kape clare o' the villyans altogether."

"Yer right, Paddy, I'll do that," replied John, "and not grieve poor Peggy, that likes the whole race so ill."

Peggy had had but little time to weep for Johnny, when a message came by the post chaise that Mammy Honey's sister, an aged and friendless woman, lay on her deathbed; and begging that Peggy would come to her at

once. Seventy miles away! It seemed to her
as far, and attended with as many dangers, as
a voyage round the world would to us. But
duty called; and so the timid woman prepared
to face the world, and make her way to Bal-
dorgan.

John and Paddy both promised her to
attend faithfully to the kitchen and the dairy
till her return; and, with some misgivings as
to the fate of the poultry, Peggy set off, weeping at the thought of leaving her "ilegant
home and John," even for a few weeks.

"Now, Paddy," she said, as he grasped her
hand at parting, " mind I bid ye be tinder and
respictful to all the cows when ye're a milkin',
but partic'lar to the Maid o' Longford; for ye
know that ye're often impatient when she lifts
her foot, and spakes in ways that hurts her
feelin's."

"I'll bear that in mind, thin," said Paddy,
" and good luck go with ye and bring ye spady
home."

For four weeks Peggy ministered to her
aged friend before she died, and then followed

her to the grave, a solitary mourner. She
almost flew at the thought of home, now that
she was released. She could not wait twenty-
four hours for the post-chaise that passed
through the village where she was, but walked
five hours to meet one which went sooner from
the next town. All the way along the dusty
road she was drawing bright pictures of her
home, which never seemed so beautiful to her
as when absent from it; and her heart beat
proudly at the thought of the welcome awaiting her. The post-chaise stopped at Cloynmally, and she had then a long walk to Killyrooke, for no letter had announced her
coming. It was late in the afternoon when
she opened the rude gate that led into the
garden; and, seeing the cottage door open, she
concluded that John was at home, and stepped
very lightly, hoping to give him a joyful surprise. She was suddenly startled by what she
fancied to be the hum of Mammy Honey's flax
wheel! She stopped, and whispered, "Can it
be that she's come back to watch over him she
loved, when I'm away? But there's the voice

o' song! Not the holy song o' heaven,
though! Och, my heart! my heart!"

Entering the cottage, she saw a spectacle
which sent the blood from her cheek and lips
back to her heart; and, almost fainting, she
sank into the nearest chair and dropped her
hands helplessly at her sides.

There, at " yon blissed little flax-wheel," sat
Nan O'Gorman, spinning, and singing —

> " The world's a bid o' roses,
> With niver a thorn for me."

Peggy only groaned; for the power of utterance was gone. She fixed her eyes on Nan,
and had not strength to remove them, much as
she strove to do so.

The brazen face flushed under her gaze, and
Nan said, " Don't be goin' wild, now, Peggy,
because a poor abused girl has taken shelter
beneath the ruff where ye've had years o'
plinty. Ye hadn't a home always; and the
copy-book o' the schoolmasther says, ' Turn
aboot is fair play.' And don't be blamin'
John, ather, for it's not by his askin' but o'
my own will that I'm here kapin' his house

and cookin' his food in yer absince. Indade, he bid me away at the first, but yerself knows I'm not aisy disposed of" — and she laughed. "Paddy Mannon, that loves ye more nor he does the Virgin, has refused to ate what I cooks, and biles his own porridge beside the old cow-house. So it's none o' his doin's, but all my own. I'll work under your hand, Peggy, and let ye still be the misthress; but *I'm to bide here;* that's settled, and it's not in yer power to drive me off! Are ye turned to stone, Peggy? Ye scare me with yer wild eyes and yer white face."

"Nan," replied Peggy, faintly, "the same thatch can niver cover ye and me! May God forgive ye as free as He pities me this day!"

She then rose, and with an unsteady step passed through the garden towards the old cow-house, where she found Paddy making a peat fire on a pile of stones, to cook his supper.

When he saw her, he turned away his face as if he could not meet her eyes; and bursting into tears, he sobbed out, "Och, och! that

was an evil day when ye left us and quit
watchin' him! The sarpint with the human
face is crawlin' round yer kitchen; but as sure
as I'm Paddy Mannon I'll give it a blow that'll
send it out, if ye'll bide aisy till I does it!"

"No, Paddy, if she do not depart this night,
I will on the morrow. Why ever did God
take Mammy Honey to heaven when she was
so sore naded on arth! But He's wilcome to
her, for all. I'll not grudge her to Him, nor
yet will I resist the rod in His hand! O,
Paddy, it was well this didn't come afore I got
the great light in my soul! Himself was despised and rejicted o' men, and why not me,
His unworthy disciple? Himself hadn't a
where to lay His head, and why should I have
this lovely home? I remembers how he drank
the vinegar and gall, and I'll just drink it too,
'stead o' demandin' the swate milk I've had so
long. Dear Mr. Murray said God was fillin'
my soul with Himself to prepare me for some
great thing—little I dreamed o' this! If
John was dead and lyin' beside the darlin'
mother, what joy would fill my heart, aside o'

losin' him this way — soul and all. But He opened not His mouth, and nather will I. I'll not add sin to sorrow by holding words with any aboot it; but strive to lane my soul on God, who is the husband o' the widow — and I'm a widow, now, Paddy!"

Still Paddy sobbed, but managed to tell his mistress how he had abused the usurper, taunting her with all the evil he had ever heard of her race, "from her great-grandfather, who was a poacher, to her uncle, who was 'migrated off to Australy." He told how he, in virtue of his prophetic office as serpent-slayer, had taken Nan by the shoulder the day she came, and put her out o' doors, and got his eyes nearly scratched out in return, which convinced him that he could do nothing at present but "make up grimaces behind her back — which same was a relief to himself, though no harm to her."

Not a tear moistened Peggy's eye, but her anguish betrayed itself in her pallid face and her hoarse, tremulous tones. Looking at the sinking sun, she said, "Paddy, I'll sit down in

the cow-house till yer supper's done. Then go
ye for the cows, for I'm homesick to see the
dear craturs — them, without the light o' reason or holy tachin', is faithful to me still."

To show his devotion, the weeping Paddy
threw his supper violently on the ground, declaring that he was "not the man to ate contint when the life was bein' crushed out o' his
misthress!" And taking a great shilalah,
which he carried to fight imaginary foes, he
set off for the pasture. Peggy remained motionless, as if bound by a fearful spell, save
that now and then she lifted her eyes heavenward, and whispered a prayer for support and
comfort.

Peggy was aroused from the stupor of
anguish by heavy foot-falls on the sward, as
Paddy drew near with his charge. He was
still weeping bitterly and telling the cows,
between his sobs, that a black cloud had fallen
on Daisy Farm, and that the saints were all
forsakin' it and lavin' it in the hands o' a sarpint o' a woman and a goose o' a man. " And
only for ye, dear cows," he said, " I'd go too,

and follow the kind misthress all over the world, and arn her bread for her. She's afeared to look at a stranger, but Paddy Mannon is not — nor a hundred o' 'em."

Peggy rose up as the cows approached her, and throwing her arms around the neck of a silver-gray cow, the "Maid o' Longford," which had been Mammy Honey's last gift to her, she burst into a flood of blessed tears. She pressed her cheek against the silvery neck and said, " Och, little ye knows, innocent thing, o' my sorrow! I, that has fed ye so free, has nothing to ate myself! I, that has loved ye so tinderly, has not a one in all the world to love me! Ye don't know that ye are no longer mine — that ye'll see me no more, nor hear my soft voice that niver give ye a hasty word, — Och, my poor heart!"

" Will ye tak' a stool and milk her ? " asked Paddy.

" No, Paddy, there's nather power in my hand nor yet in my heart for that," Peggy replied; " but I'll look at ye doin' it, and say what I'd like while we're alone. Ye have iver

been a faithful boy to me, and niver once gave
me an onrispictful word. I'd wish to thank ye
for all yer love in the past. Ye're the only
friend I have now, Paddy, that I can spake to.
Yer masther promised God and his mother that
he'd stand 'twixt me and throuble while he had
life in him. But now it is himself that's put a
spear in my heart! Peggy Sheehan's not the
woman to 'bide in a house and quarrel; and
nather is she the one to stand silent and see
her husband's heart stole from her and his
honor destroyed ontirely! Ye can do me one
more service, Paddy dear," — she had never
addressed him thus before — " and may be it'll
be the last yer poor friend will ever ask."

" And what's that, misthress, darlin'? I hope
it's to murther Nan, and then fly off to Ameriky
or some other pagan country!"

" No, Paddy; do her no evil; lave her with
God," answered Peggy. " I'd wish ye to be
at the gate to-morrow morning afore the sun
peeps over the bog, to meet me. And mind,
ye're niver to spake my name to himself till the
day comes when his heart is broke for his sins

agin God and his poor lovin' wife. Mind what I say, Paddy, my name is a forbidden word! I'd wish ye to do yer duty to yer masther and to the craturs; but it'll be a great comfort to me if ye'll still 'bide in the cow-house and not countenance you cruel woman when I'm gone."

"I'll starve first! But where are ye goin'? Ye've not a friend or a kin left that ye can make free with, now that the old Doanes is dead," replied Paddy.

"I have health yet, and can toil even with a broken heart, Paddy. I'll seek a sarvice place, for I could niver live where John war not honored and rispected. And now I must gather heart to go into the cottage, for I must turn keys on a few things not to be touched by on-holy hands."

"Keys!" cried Paddy, scornfully. "What's thim good for when the likes o' her's about? Didn't she wear Mammy Honey's best shawl to Ned Givin's wake the last week? And hasn't the old mother the duffel gray cloak over there now!"

Peggy threw up her hands and uttered a

sharp cry; then clasping them tightly over her heart she said imploringly, "Please, dear man, tell me no more, or I'll be driven wild and lose my hold on God! It's all over with my happiness in this world; but I'm a small cretur' to be thinkin' of, when John's soul is at stake, and all Killyrooke setting this great sin down agin our blissed religion and stumbling over it!"

Peggy rose to go into the cottage. As she turned the corner of the cow-house, she saw John standing there as if waiting for her. She did not raise her eyes; but he joined her, and after a moment's silence said, "Ye're welcome home, Peggy."

Still she did not speak, but her deathly countenance betrayed the struggle going on within. "Jewel," he said, after a great effort, "this is none o' my doin's. She came into the cottage the day after ye left, for shelter from the abuse o' her mother. And once here, she took all into her hands! She would nather go for my beggin' nor yet for Paddy's abuse; but now ye are come back to us as are the misthress, ye can send her off yerself. Ye know, Peggy, I'm a great sheep, and could never spake a rough word to a woman — though she were an evil one."

Peggy found breath to say, " No, John, I shall never bid her away! My neighbors shall not see me doing what my husband should do, and then taunt me with it! And more nor that, I doubt if even ye can drive her out now. She tells me ye have promised her a home, whinever she wills to 'bide here! And the same thatch couldn't cover us two! · O, John, John, why did Mammy Honey lay that fearful charge on me, when she said, ' Bring him to me at last; I'll expect that of ye, Peggy.' "

And saying this, she closed her eyes and passed through the kitchen, where Nan was singing as she spread the simple board for supper, into her mother's little room, and drew the wooden bolt behind her. She threw herself into the rude oaken chair, laid her cheek on the pillow, and gave way to a flood of tears, mingled with prayers to Heaven for strength. Her plaintive tones, echoing through the low rooms of the cottage, were enough to melt a heart of stone.

John followed her to the door; but he was too great a coward,—sin makes even the bravest men cowards,—to ask her pardon, and thrust the intruder forth. He stood there weeping; and when called, he refused to eat his supper. He spoke harshly to Nan, asking her if she were not ashamed to turn a pure-hearted wife out of her own house. But she only laughed in his face, and replied that she was quite willing to allow Peggy back, and had even offered to let her be mistress still!

All night John sat in the kitchen or walked the floor, listening to the sobs and prayers of his wife, planning reforms to begin with the light, and promising to atone with redoubled kindness for his faithlessness and cruelty. Alas, poor, irresolute man! He did not take into account his own weakness, nor the strength of the foe; nor yet was he prepared for the courage with which Christian principle and womanly pride had armed the timid creature he had so deeply wronged.

CHAPTER XII.

HOMELESS.

AT break of day Peggy looked out of the little glass window, — the pride of the cottage, — and saw Paddy leaning against the gate, awaiting her. She waved her handkerchief to him, and he approached her with swollen eyes, which told how little he had slept and how much he had wept. She passed to him her little blue box or trunk, the only thing she had brought with her to her new home when a bride. It now contained the few articles of clothing she had bought with her own spinning-money; for she shrank from taking any thing given her by John, now that he had suffered the serpent with a human face to " put a space between their two hearts."

This done, the meek creature passed through the kitchen, — where John still sat

sleeping, — without stirring the air. She
dared not look at him, lest her strength might
fail her.

Before she joined Paddy at the gate, she
went round to the glass window and plucked a
sprig of the sweet brier that overhung it.
This she pressed for a moment to her lips, and
then laid it in the folds of a fresh handkerchief and hid it in her bosom like a " charm."

As Peggy looked at her poor friend, an in-
voluntary smile passed over her pale face. He
had dressed himself in **Daddy** Sheehan's
clothes, to honor the occasion, and was almost
buried in them. " Dear man," she exclaimed,
" why do ye make such a figure o' yersilf
when I cannot laugh as I once did at ye!
I've told ye a score o' times to take yon
clothes to Jock, the tailor, and have them
made to fit ye. Ye look like a harlequin!"
And so he did ; for the tails of the blue coat
barely cleared the ground, and the pockets
behind, graced with huge brass buttons, were
a foot and a half below their proper place.
The breeches were pushed up in great heavy

folds to make them short enough to buckle at the knee, and the sleeves were rolled half way to the elbow. " Why don't ye do my biddin' about the clothes ? " she repeated.

" Because it would be a great refliction on the old masther; the same as sayin' he didn't have them made right at first! And more; if they fitted me, people would only say, ' See Paddy Mannon's new shute !', and never think o' the honor that was haped on me by gittin' them willed to me. Now they say, ' See Paddy Mannon in the fine ould masther's Sunday shute. How yon family honors that lad!' 'Dade I'll just wear them *as they is*, for his sake and my own," answered Paddy.

Paddy shouldered the blue box, remarking, " It's a dale lighter than it war the day ye came first to us, and I lifted it out o' the new donkey-cart."

" Yes, poor man," replied Peggy, " I'm like Naomi o' old ; I came in here full o' prosperity and blissed with hapes o' love, but I go forth empty of arthly good ! But I'm rich for all this, Paddy ! I feel just now as I did the

day I gave Mammy Honey and every thing
else up for Christ's sake! The great peace
has come on me again with new **power**. **I can**
not only give up mother, and house, **and land,**
but even *him that's dearer nor all*, at the
Master's biddin'. And **I'm** quite contint in
belavin' that the Judge o' **the whole arth** will
do right, though one poor heart may break by
the way He does it."

"Well, misthress, **darlin',**" sobbed Paddy,
"I'm glad yer not ravin' wild with the **throu-**
ble, but I'd be better plazed if ye'd show a
little more sperit! Sperit is a fine thing in a
woman. I'd hoped that ye'd be roused **up a**
little afore ye left, so that ye'd break the lookin' glass, and the windy, **and** the red and
white dishes, and burn up the **linen** that them
blissed **hands spun** and wove, afore **she'd en-**
joy thim."

"No, Paddy, **there's** no revinge in my
heart; but only sorrow and shame **for the**
masther; and for Nan — well, **Heaven pity**
her, and bring her to repintance afore death
comes."

"What! and so she be let into heaven?" exclaimed Paddy. "I'll not put a foot into it myself if she's there! 'Dade I'll not! I thinks too much o' myself to be in ony place where she'll be!"

Peggy had no time now for either instruction or controversy, for she was in haste to reach Cloynmally, where a wagoner stopped on his way to the distant city. She chose to ride on the high seat with him, rather than in the post-chaise, where she would have to look strangers in the face, and hear conversation which might distract her mind.

As they came up to the little Presbyterian church and burying-ground, Peggy said, "Ye sit down on the roadside till I pluck a shamrock blossom off the grave, and thank God that He tuk her to Himself from the evil to come. O, Paddy, how lovely the grave looks! And, dear man, I'll trust ye to bring me back and lay me beside her if I dies away."

"I'll do that same, even if ye'd 'migrate to Ameriky, and I'd have to wade the Atlantic

ocean and bring ye back in my arms — I'd do
it — would I! But where'll I ever find ye?"

"Paddy, a lady that Mammy Honey's old
sister nursed when a baby, came to see her,
and to bring the pension the family 'lowed her,
when I was there. They always looked after
her and loved her, though they had removed
far away. The lady was that thankful for my
tinderness that she asked me would I go to the
great city with her and mind her fable ould
mother? I told her I had no nade o' sarvice,
but was the richest, and proudest, and happiest wife in our town. She'd be to make me
take a guinea as a keepsake, and that, with
three Mammy Honey gave me seven years
agone to keep agin a rainy day, is what I has
for my journey now. This lady, Miss Grey,
said, at partin', ' Well, Misthress Sheehan, I'm
glad ye're so comfortable; but none knows
what's afore 'em in life. If ye should iver
nade a friend, come to me.' And she gave
me a bit o' card with her name on't, and it's
to her I'm goin'."

" Give me the name o' her place ; and after the next harvest I'll call and find ye out, and spind a week with ye. May be there might be a horse-race or a ' fair' aboot that time ; and if so, I'll kill two birds with one stone," exclaimed Paddy, with animation.

Peggy could not help smiling at such folly.

" I'm to be a sarvant there, Paddy, and will have nather room nor wilcome for guests. I'll tell ye where Miss Grey is, if ye nade me ; but mind, it's to be buried in yer own heart ; for I'd not wish another one to know where I be."

" Nor will they, ather. Hasn't ye sint word to Mr. Murray ? " asked Paddy.

" How could I revale to him the disgrace o' this son o' the righteous ? If he asks for me, make my respicts to him, and tell him the peace o' God, that he'd so often implored on us all, was 'bidin' on me when I left home," said Peggy.

" He came to the cottage when you were gone, to inquire into the evil reports he'd heerd ; but the coward o' a man saw him, and run off into the farthest barley-field, and wasn't to be found; and so did Father Clakey come to the gate. Nan went to the door and dropt a low curshey, and asked, ' Will yer riverence come in?'

" ''Deed I will not, ye brazen-faced maid,' says he. ' I'll not put my consecrated feet into a house where ye are like a thafe and a robber! Go off to sarvice and arn yer honest bread, afore ye break a kind woman's heart. I'm to rade ye out o' the church next day; and I've sore work to keep my cane off yer shoulders!' So himself doesn't countenance her no more nor Mr. Murray," said Paddy.

" No; he's a dacent oold man, and does as well as he knows, may be," replied Peggy. " Now mind, I've trusted the powltry and the craturs all with ye, and be faithful, and spake soft to thim. But, Oh me, there'll be no prayer in the cottage! Ye and Nan may mumble over yer beads; but John will not dare to pray, sore as he nades marcy. I'd bid *ye* lave, were it not that John has a soul. Ye watch for the first sigh o' penitence, and manewhiles I'll pray day and night that God will take his

PEGGY'S GOOD-BYE TO PADDY.

feet out o' the net afore he die ; and if so be, who knows but He'll let me bring him safe to her at last, as she bid me."

" There's poor tokens on't," replied Paddy.

" But what a lovin' father God is, that He tuk little Johnny to Himself afore this," said Peggy.

" So He is, too," answered Paddy ; " but I hears the great, lumberin' whales o' the carrier."

The wagon now rolled heavily up the road, and was stopped in answer to the call of Paddy, who reached up the blue box to the driver.

Giving Peggy his hand to assist her to a seat beside him, the man said, " Yer for an early start, good wife ;" and then looked in amazement at her, as, leaning down from her perch, she grasped the rough hand of her poor friend, and exclaimed, " May the Lord reward ye for yer love and pity to me with the salvation o' yer soul, dear man. God in heaven bliss ye, Paddy Mannon ! "

"Am I takin' a body to the 'Lunatics'?" asked the wagoner.

"'Dade ye're not, but to a fine lady's house, as a nurse, my man! But she's a dale throubled about laving her ilegant home. So do ye be tinder o' her, or I'll take yer life next day," said Paddy.

The man rolled out a rough oath, and laid the lash heartily on the backs of his heavily-laden horses.

"Dear man," cried Peggy, "don't give an onnadeful pang to any thing God has made. We and the dumb craturs is all His work, and all sufferers, too, under the hand o' man. Be marciful to thim as He is marciful to us."

And they drove off, leaving Paddy wailing and sobbing on the roadside.

CHAPTER XIII.

SOWING BY THE WAYSIDE.

"IT'S heavy whaling the day, misthress," said the wagoner, by way of opening a conversation with his passenger; "and I fear we'll not see Baldargie, where I halts for the night, till the moon be riz."

Turning to receive an answer, he saw Peggy wiping the tears from her pale cheek, and his kind heart was touched.

"You've lost yer sarvice place, poor thing!" he said; "but I'm just sure by yer looks it was no fault o' yer own; ye must keep up heart, for all will turn out for the best in the end. There's a better place waitin' ye nor the one ye've lost, and a kinder and feeliner misthress. I've lived more years by a dozen than ye, and my experience is, that there's a sartain amount o' luck for each one o' us. Some gets it all in a hape and has hard fare afterward; and some gets it sprinkled along through life. The last's been my lot. I've had hard work from a lad up, till my back's been nigh broke at times; but when I took a wife, then came luck to my door, for I got one that made the most o' the little I arned, and always met me with a smile, whether my hand was empty or full. By-and-by more luck come in the shape o' little folk; they came faster than the bread did, but they never lacked. If any went hungry, it was Molly and me. In them days I saw nobody I envied; but agin, our luck turned two ways at once. I got this team o' horses to drive, and fine pay. But when bread was plenty, the mouths grew scarce. The little darlin's dropped off, one followin' the other, till we counted four graves in the churchyard. Now we're alone, and sorrowful enough too. But as we've had a share o' good luck, we mustn't grumble. Your luck will turn with this journey, take my word for it! Why, dry yer eyes there; don't yer know its luck to ride with Barney's horses? and if yer purse is low, my good girl, it will niver be a farthing lower for me. I'll give ye the ride and wilcome and say a good word for ye at the end o' the journey, where I puts up these seven year."

"Yer too kind, friend," replied Peggy. "If I was nady I'd accept yer offer as if ye was my brother; but I've several guineas o' money, and a place to go into when I arrive in the great town."

"Then I can't see what on arth makes ye cry. If yer a maid, ye cannot have buried husband or child," said the wagoner kindly.

"Ah, sir, I've lost both. I first buried the swatest mother God iver gave a poor girl, and then a dear lambie o' a boy that I tuk motherless to my bussum. But them was small loss, because it was so asy to see God's hand in their goin'. I've lost *the other now*, but not in the grave. Yer too kind to ask me more. Listen patient now, while I tell ye the idee I has about *luck*. I calls it ' Providence,' and whether it comes in sunshine or in black

cloud, I sees **God's face in it. I can** say, with
you holy **David, 'Goodness and marcy have**
followed me *all the days* o' my life,' for when
God tuk all the others from me, He left Him-
self. And, dear man, nobody can be poor or
desolate **as has** Him in his soul, — Him that
sticketh closer nor a brother. **When I**
was livin' at my ase, Him that sees **the end**
from the beginning was preparin' **a** table afore
me in presence **o' my** inimies. And He it was
that led ye, **too,** through **both bog and pastur',**
that ye might see His hand and come and taste
o' His love. He gave yer wife and babies in
marcy, and He tuk the lambies in the same
marcy, to draw the parents' heart after them.
Don't, then, call yer joys and throubles ' luck,'
like a hathen, but call them the dalins' **o' God**
with **ye.**"

" Why, **my** good woman, ye're a **Methodis,**
sure. I niver heerd the like talk from another
but thim!" cried the wagoner, looking in surprise at Peggy.

" I never seed **a one o' them,**" she replied,
" though I've heerd tell **o' the Wesleys, and**

knows a lovely hymn that one o' them writ about Jesus."

And thus Peggy beguiled the way, talking in a manner almost miraculous for her, and leading the mind of her rough companion up to God. Before night fell she had heard his history and given him hers, — all save the one sore point on which he was too delicate to question her. She had heard of the few praying Methodists in his native town, who, he said, " were parsecutin' every body to be convarted like themselves, and goin' on as if religion was the importantist thing in the world. They had won little Billy over to their school, and Jerry too, afore they died, and had filled up their small heads with varses and hymns that came out in their dyin' breath; and now they are tarned to parsecutin' me and my wife the same way, and she's a' most one o' 'em, — goin' to their prayers, and their sing-ings, and the like. But I never tuk much to thim things; all the religion iver I had," he added, " was hathred o' the Catholics, and holdin' up my head with pride that I warn't born among them. Why, good woman, thim Methodises belave that Papists may all be turned yet; and they prays and prays for that, but they can't know the power o' the Pope and the priests."

" Dear man, thim poor craturs, whose brith is in their nostrils, is no more in God's hand nor the stubble afore the fire, and it's as asy for Him to bring the Pope off his throne into the dust, where he'll plade for mercy, as it would be to soften yer kind heart and bow it to His will," said Peggy.

Then she told him of Mammy Honey's dying prayers, and of her faith for poor Ireland; and while on this theme, the wagon rolled up heavily into the paved yard of the " O'Connor's Arms Inn," where they were to rest for the night.

Another day's ride brought them to the city whither they were bound. The wagoner refused to give the little blue box and its owner into any stranger's care. After attending to the animals, which he dignified by the name of " harses," but which bore a remarkable

resemblance to the mule family, he shouldered
the box, and, followed by Peggy, made his way
to Berkely Terrace, with Miss Grey's card in
his hand.

When they reached the door and Peggy read
" Grey " on the thin, broad brass plate, she
said, " And now we must part, friend. I
thank ye for yer goodness, so unlike what I
looked for at the startin', when I heerd an oath
and saw the blow ye give the craturs ! Niver an
oath did I hear from ye, nor yet a blow but that
one. If ye don't love nor fear the Lord for His
own sake, plaze, for my sake, niver sware more.
Look after yer soul, dear man ; and if iver ye
or yer wife nade a friend, Miss Grey will know
where ye'll find Peggy Sheehan. Farewell."

Poor Miss Grey, herself far from young or
strong, was engaged in her never-failing task
of settling disputes between her feeble and
childish mother and an impatient nurse, when
Peggy was announced as " a queer, dressed
body with a blue wood box in her arms."

Entering her sitting-room, the lady was
amazed to see a stranger standing there on a

pocket-handkerchief, holding a trunk in her arms, afraid to set it down lest she might injure the carpet, never having trod on one before. When the lady recognized her, she said, "O, Peggy, have you changed your mind and left that elegant home and that good husband to help me a little while? You've come in an hour of need. Your visit is like an angel's. How long can you stay?"

"While ye nades me, dear lady, and I'll sarve the feeble one day and night, only don't ax me a question till I tell ye what's happened that sent me here."

"Peggy, I have not left my mother's room for seven nights," said Miss Grey. "Her nurse has no patience and I must see that all are gentle with her."

"Och, but I'll have hapes o' patience, and ye may now slape asy, sure that I'll be as tinder o' her as if she was the gentlest lady in the world," said Peggy.

And she fulfilled her promise a thousand-fold. She became a nurse to the mother, a comforter to the daughter, an example and a teacher to the servants, — a blessing to the whole house; in which we leave her for the present, striving to be faithful over a few things.

CHAPTER XIV

MISERY IN THE COTTAGE

O N Paddy's return to the cottage, after parting with his mistress on the wagon, breakfast was still waiting, although the hour was
late. As he sprang over the stile he heard Nan
call out from the door, "Yer breakfast is all
coolin', John." John returned her no answer,
but followed Paddy to his own quarters without
raising his head or speaking.

"A'n't ye for ony breakfast this morning,
masther?" asked Paddy, assuming an air of
jocoseness.

"Not yet, Paddy; I'll wait till Peggy comes,"
he replied.

"Will ye? Och, then, ye'll shtarve to dith,
I can promise ye that," replied Paddy, with a
smart nod of his head.

"Do ye know where she is?" asked John.

" 'Dade I do," was the answer.

John looked at him, expecting to hear that she had taken refuge with Mrs. Murray, or some of her other friends in Cloynmally. But Paddy began to whistle carelessly, and to prepare his humble breakfast.

The wretched man groaned aloud, but still Paddy whistled a gay tune, as if to make him as miserable as possible by contrast with his own mirth.

" Where *is* yer misthress, then, if ye know ? " asked John, in a sharp tone.

" She's where ye can't find her! Nobody knows where but thim that's got her, and poor Paddy, that loves her faithful, *though he never tuk' oath to do it afore God's altar!* Now ! " cried Paddy, triumphantly.

" Whist, man ! " exclaimed John. " Do ye know who ye're talkin' to ? "

" To *yersilf*, masther. Do *ye* know who ye're talkin' to ? Becase I can tell ye it's a small excuse will take me off Daisy Farm now ! My riputation's at stake, and as I've always lived with dacent people, I'm resalved to do so still! Mind, I'm not tied down by a family now, and I'may turn out a great traveller yet. Who knows?"

Again John groaned. He felt that the poor, simple work-house boy, whom he had from boyhood both despised and patronized, was now his superior and his master, looking down on him with contempt. He knew, also, that Paddy was possessed of a secret which he had not power to extort from him; and, with his head bowed and his hands clasped behind him, he went to his work in the field without breaking his fast.

At nightfall, when Paddy returned from the peat-bog where he had been all day at work, he seated himself on the door-stone of the cottage, to wait for his milk. His heart was gladdened by sounds of discord from within, and not being remarkably delicate on points of honor, he placed himself where he could hear without being seen.

"Nannie, I'd beg ye on my bended knees

to go to yer mother, or off where ye plaze,
and let the broken-hearted jewel back to her
home."

"The cottage is big enough for us both,"
replied Nan ; " but she's that selfish that she'll
have the whole or none ; so she's tuk the last.
She'll run back when the first strange man
looks her in the face ! "

" It would take more than that to frighten
ye, then ! " exclaimed John, tartly.

" 'Deed it would ; a hundred o' em couldn't do
it ! " said Nan, bravely.

"Ye are a bould woman, and I *bid* ye to
depart at once out o' my house. Ye'll ruin
my riputation in Killyrooke," cried John.

" Ye've none left to be hurted," she said.
" Only this morning I heerd two lads say o' ye,
'There's the Protestant church of Killyrooke.'
Yer character is gone, but a man may live
without *that*, if he has enough to ate. Keep
ye asy now, and I'll tind to yer cottage and
dairy, for Peg gave me all her nate ways."

" I will niver 'bide ye ! " cried John, resolutely. " I'll put an end to my life, or I'll run

off to Ameriky, to be rid of ye. I hates ye,
and yer whole race, for the evil ye've brought
on this house and on my name."

By this time Nan, deaf to his words, was
singing in a merry voice a snatch of a nonsen-
sical song, as if he was not worth replying to.

Poor, miserable, irresolute dupe that John
was! He saw that his wife was heart-broken
and gone, and his character ruined, and he gave
up all for lost. Before the sun set that day it
spread through the village, — all alive with indignation before, — that Peggy had returned to
her cottage, and finding Nan installed as mistress, had fled for ever; and there were few of
either church so heartless as not to pity the
suffering wife, and to censure those who had
so cruelly wronged her. And very few women
were sunk so low as to cross the threshold to
speak with Nan.

Poor, ruined John sank into a settled melancholy. He walked about the farm with his hat
drawn over his eyes, and turned away from
every neighbor he met, without saluting him.
He forsook his seat in God's house, and cast

aside even the forms of religion. He would not go to market, but trusted **Paddy** with his business and his money. He felt his degradation not only when former friends turned from him, but more so when the very beggars, who had always found a welcome at the cottage, passed it by without a glance. His only visitors now were the family and the hoyden companions of Nan, who all made as free at the cottage as if it were their own. The only peace John had now, was when Nan went off with these friends, as she often did, to merry-makings for a week or more at a time. Then Paddy would return to the table and to his old bed in the loft; and John would grow strong, and prophesy that she would never return. But when her money was gone, and she was weary with tramping about, back she would come, causing John to turn pale, and Paddy to flee, as if she were a phantom of the pestilence.

But through all those long days and years, although Paddy had heard frequently of his mistress and had seen her once, he had never spoken her name to John, and if his master uttered it, he would say, " Take care! ye'll burn yer tongue if ye spake o' yon one." Seeing how the name of his mother stung him, Paddy took a savage delight in calling up her memory and her instructions, whenever they were at work together. " Will, will!" he would say, in irony, " but it was fine tachin' she gave us both in religion, sure, and a good use we're makin' o't! I'm thinkin' o' tarnin' Protestint mysilf, when I sees what ilegant Christians that church makes! Yis, yis, we're makin' good headway, you and me, masther, to where *she* is now. It's a strange thing, indade, that the whole town do not all lave Father Clakey in the lurch, and run to Mr. Murray, when they sees what angils he makes out o' men. Say, masther, do ye belave that the saints aboove — Misthress Honey, and the like o' her — looks down and sees what's goin' on below ?"

No matter how insolent or how tantalizing Paddy was, John dared not rebuke him, lest he might take it into his head to go off·on

" the travels " he was constantly holding up as a threat, and the poor, erring man felt that there he would not have a mortal to speak to.

Just before Paddy went, at Mr. Murray's request, to carry a letter of comfort to his mistress, he took occasion to irritate his master beyond endurance ; and when rebuked for his insolence, he packed up his all in bundles, which he hung on pegs in the cow-house, donned " the ould masther's Sunday shute," shouldered his oaken staff, and set off apparently in high dudgeon. When at the end of a week " he came back for his bundles," John went to the cow-house and implored him not to forsake him. By some cunning on Paddy's part, and an offer of higher wages on John's, the matter was adjusted ; and thenceforth the master took good care not to give farther occasion for a separation, fully believing that Paddy had been off to look for a new place.

CHAPTER XV.

ON THE MOUNT.

THERE is a high point in the Christian's
upward journey whence he may look down
on all below as on the playthings of childhood,
or the vain pleasures of youth. Even the
things which belong to himself lose their size
and their importance in the distance, and fade
into nothingness, in comparison with the calm
glories by which he is surrounded on the
mount. The home that once he called his
own, but from which misfortunes have driven
him, no longer seems the one only spot where
he can live or die. Whether it be palace or
cottage, it sinks into insignificance beside the
home of "many mansions," with a glimpse of
which he has been favored. The treasures
of gold, or merchandise, or harvest, all grow
poor in the eyes of him who has the earnest of

162

heaven and its eternal wealth already in his soul. Sorrows, as well as joys, are regarded with other eyes than of yore. The grave where the beloved were hidden when torn from the bleeding heart, is now only a peaceful bed; and the dear sleepers are not dead, but living and loving still.

> " Hope then lifts her radiant finger,
>   Pointing to the eternal home,
> On whose portals they yet linger,
>   Looking back for us to come."

Even the erring among his heart's dear treasures, — those who have wandered far from God, and for whose salvation he would lay down his life, — their case seems not so utterly hopeless when seen from this hight, as when he walked on the low ground beside them. As he learns more of God's power, he sees also the weakness of Satan's chain. As he learns more of His holiness and mercy, he casts away his fears, and trusts the wanderers with Him. Even if their sun may seem to set in darkness, he still sees " light in His light," and bows to His will, sure that the Judge of the whole earth will do right.

That there is such a hight as this in Christian experience, we know from the testimony of those, few though they be, who have reached it, and who move among us still, while they live on the verge of heaven and breathe its peaceful air.

To this summit our humble heroine rose on that night when, after a fearful struggle, she gave up her mother to God, and kissed the rod which had so sorely smitten her. And although at times dark clouds had gathered around and obscured the light for a little season, she had never descended again to the dark valley where before she had walked and stumbled like a weak and timid child. The littleness of earth and the greatness of all beyond were so deeply impressed on her mind, that life thenceforth became to her of vast value. Every moment was consecrated to useful toil, and in this blessed activity she forgot, in a measure, her own sorrows. Love to others, and earnest efforts to carry that love out into action, are sovereign balms for the wounded spirit.

Peggy possessed that rare faculty of lightening every body's burdens while seeming to do but little. Without any bustle or stir she had become sole nurse for the poor failing mother of Miss Grey.

The servants were not slow to see how their own toil was lessened ; and so, from selfish motives if from no other, they treated her with that respect which they hoped would keep her long there. Miss Grey had at first spoken of her in the house as a connection of her old nurse, whose presence would be a great comfort to them all, and had bidden the servants to address her as " Misthress Sheehan ;" and they were always civil to one for whom their mistress manifested so much regard, and who was such a comfort to her in her own weakness and trouble.

Miss Grey was herself one of the pure in heart, but she was encompassed with trials, and was the subject of nervous depression which at times cast shadows over her mind, and left her to grope in the darkness and to write bitter things against herself. Her earlier life had been one of health and of activity in all that was good; but the confinement of years in a sick room had broken down both health and spirits, and had forced her to relinquish every work but that of giving. And now, forgetting the great labor and sacrifice she had been making at home, she looked upon herself as an idler in the vineyard, a cumberer of the ground.

When quiet and order were restored to the house after the death of Mrs. Grey, Peggy thought her work was done in Berkeley Terrace. One day, after many thanks to Miss Grey for her kindness, she opened the subject of a new place, saying, "And now, dear lady, as I'll be but an idler here, I've thought well to look about me for work. But I'd like it to be work that would call for not only strong arms, but a lovin' heart and hapes o' patience. If I could go into some hospital or 'sylum, where old people war to be humored like childer, or where little ones war to be tinded and rared up, I'd like it well. My heart's that full o' desire for work, that I be draming o' nights that I'm gatherin' flocks o' little childer in my arms and coverin' 'em up with my shawl from the wind and the storm. I'd be glad to make sunshine in some place like o' them, and so, may be, I might lade some wanderer, great or small, to the heaven that seems just at my hand. Dear lady, it is so near my sperit, that when I shuts my eyes I feels that I'm in it a'ready!"

"Well, Misthress Sheehan," replied Miss Grey, "I have an hospital and an asylum all ready for you. I'm ' patient ' enough to begin with. I need all your care and skill for the present; and when my health is improved so that I can return to my old labors, we will look after my poor people and friendless little children. I am not asking you to remain here for your sake, but for mine. If you leave me, I must have some one in your place ; and who can be such a nurse for both body and mind? I shall call you my friend and companion, and while you help me, I may be able to help you."

"Och, but that would be work for the heart, indade! But I'm afeard I'd grow idle with such an asy life," said Peggy.

"Make it as toilsome as you please," replied Miss Grey. "I have eight or ten poor people for whose comfort I once felt myself responsible. Of late years I have done nothing for them but to send their little pittance weekly. We will look them all up again and see to their wants. One of them is blind; to her you can read the Bible she loves so much."

"Och, dear lady, but ye knows well how I stumbles at the long words. Ye mind what work I made with the hard names the day the poor old lady, yer mother, would have me read about the handwritin' on the wall."

"Well, pass over those parts till you practice more," said Miss Grey. "There are many beautiful chapters and psalms without a hard word in them."

"I've thought o' that same many times, dear lady; and what a marcy it is to the ignorant bodies like me. All about the Lord Jesus and His salvation is as plain as the sun. One that could but only spell his words could make out, 'I am the way, the truth and the life;' or, 'Come unto Me all ye that labor and are hivy laden, and I will give you rest.' It's just the very book for the poor and simple; and I'll strive to read it better, that I may get a hearin' for it whenever I goes among yer poor and sick ones."

"Misthress Sheehan," replied Miss Grey, "I have a work for little children on my heart, if I knew how to accomplish it. We had for many years a housekeeper with a little child. Fanny Bond was taught to read, and write, and sew; and my mother, being very fond of her, resolved to give her an easier life than a servant's; to have her taught a trade, perhaps. She and her mother ate at a table by themselves, and Fanny, who never associated with the servants in the kitchen, nor learned their ways, grew up an amiable and interesting girl.

"My brother's regiment, was recalled from

India some years ago, and he brought home
with him a young Englishman as his at-
tendant, who had been one of his subordin-
ate officers. He was very amusing, and had
curious arts for killing time in the camp,
which made him a great favorite, not only
with his comrades but also with the officers.
But he had not the art of making a living, and
thought no more of preparing for the future
than if he were not a reasoning man. Being
now discharged from the army, he lived on
from day to day, always proposing to leave the
house to begin some work, but not doing so
for months.

"Against the advice and entreaty of her
mother and the commands of mine, Fanny
married this Sam Wells and went with him to
England, where he admitted he had neither
home nor prospects. Well, like many other
simple girls, she found out her error when too
late. She came back to her mother three or
four years afterward, with two pretty babies,
saying that he had gone to look for work, and
would soon come for her.

"We provided a room for her in a house near by, and did all in our power to rouse her to do something for herself. But she was always looking for her husband, and getting ready to follow him at a moment's notice. We could not learn that he had been unkind to her, but felt sure he would never provide for her; and so we strove to keep her where we could see that her children were cared for. One day, after long and anxious waiting, she came to my mother, almost wild with hope deferred. She had an impression that Sam was in danger of being pressed into the service again, and begged for a guinea to take her to the seaport where the men-of-war were lying. Leaving her little ones with a kind widow who lived in the house with her, she set off, and was never heard of afterward. We feared at first that she had met her husband, and with him had deserted the children; but we finally decided, from her excited manner when she left us, that she had destroyed herself in a fit of discouragement. Her poor old mother paid out all her wages for the board of the little

girls, and I clothed them. But Betty Bond's
heart broke under the dreadful suspense of
watching and waiting for the return of her
only child ; and then the little ones were left
alone in the world. My brother felt some
compunctions of conscience for having brought
the young man to the house, and he paid their
board while he lived. Since his death, I have
done so, but I fear they are sadly neglected for
all that. Previous to my mother's sickness we
had discussed several plans for their benefit,
none of which could be carried out then. I
have thought that, perhaps, after we are all
a little rested, you would take the care of
them. We shall have this large house to ourselves, and can easily spare two rooms for
them. Their table could be spread with yours,
and you could teach and train them as you
please — you may have them for your children,
if you like, and I will bear all their expenses."

Peggy threw up her hands in amazement,
and then clasped them tightly, and raised her
eyes in thankfulness toward heaven.

"Och, but there would be work for a

quane!" she said, "and I'd niver weary o'
lovin' and laborin' for the poor lambies. And,
dear lady, I'd be more grateful than I can iver
tell, both to God and to ye, for the lovely work
and the peaceful home, without even goin'
abroad to seek ather."

Miss Grey soon changed Peggy's peasant-like
appearance into that of a comely matron, by
exchanging the coarse cotton gowns she had
brought with her and which she had worn in
the sick-room, for neat black dresses. The
thick cambric caps, with full, broad frills, were
exchanged for those of thin muslin, while a
kerchief of the same material was crossed
under the half-open waist, over her bosom.
Her hair though turning grey was still abund-
ant; but her face was far paler and thinner
than that of the Peggy of other days.

Not long after the conversation just repeated,
Miss Grey brought little Bessie and Marion
Wells to the pleasant upper rooms she had had
prepared for them, and which she playfully
called, "The Orphan Asylum."

At the first sight of their sad little faces,
Peggy took them both to her heart. They wore
that depressed look which told there had been
no play for them, and they moved about as if
fearful of the sound of their own footfalls. The
poor things had been well fed and clothed and
sheltered by Miss Grey's generosity; but they
had not been loved or petted; and these are as
important items in the training of a merry,
happy child as are food and clothing. If they
had been defrauded of this hitherto, they were
to be fully repaid in the future.

Bessie Wells was a tall, thin child of six
years, whose sad blue eyes were always swim-
ming in tears that were never shed, and overhung by lashes so long and dark that they
seemed not to belong by right to blue eyes and
fair hair. Marion, four years and a half old,
who called herself "Madie," was a sweet,
curly-headed child, who seemed ever craving
the lost attentions which are the just due of
babyhood. She had not been ten minutes in
the house; before she had climbed on Peggy's

knee to stroke her motherly face, and to say,
" Pretty, kind lady ; Madie loves you, and will
be a good child."

A happy and useful life was now begun in earnest by this faithful woman. God had sent work
to her hand in answer to her prayers, and she
had accepted it as a great honor. She devoted
her first morning hours to Miss Grey, and then
fled to her little charge, who watched eagerly
for her foot-steps on the stair. When their real
wants were all supplied for the day, she applied
herself to making little garments for them,
under Miss Grey's direction ; and while she
sewed or knitted, she told them stories from the
Bible, and taught them verses from " Watts'
Hymns for the Infant Mind," as well as the
pleasant old stories in verse by Jane Taylor.
When they grew weary, she took first one and
then the other on her knee, and sang to them,
or amused them with the toys and pictures
Miss Grey had provided. This sudden transit
from a gloomy room in a tenement, where were
three or four baby boarders younger than
themselves, who must never be wakened by a

laugh or a cry, was like passing from a cheer-
less and silent cave into a blooming paradise.

And Peggy stood on this high mount with
" the great peace " still in her soul unbroken.
While she prayed without ceasing for the lost
one far away, she always added, " I lave him
in Thy hand, and where could be a safer
place ? "

CHAPTER XVI.

AN AWAKENED CONSCIENCE.

FOR four long years the black cloud hung over Daisy Farm; for four long years the serpent with a human face moved through the rooms of the cottage; for four long years its poisoned sting rankled and festered in the heart of the exiled wife, who was patient in her tribulation, but in tribulation still.

Great changes had now taken place in the humble little hamlet of Killyrooke, both by death and emigration.

The poor, useless head of the family over the way from Daisy Farm, who had long been too indolent to do any thing but breathe, had lost the energy required even for that small effort, and so, one day, without any other apparent cause, he slipped out of life.

A year previous to this event, his two eldest

boys, who had long been impatient to get off
to Australia, but could never get money
enough for their passage, were unexpectedly
treated to the voyage at the expense of a gener-
ous Government. The haste in the case was
owing to some little " irregularities" in their
business — the deer-trade ; in which they were
accused by the owner of Harpley Hall, of
living on his venison rather than on their own
potatoes.

The younger boys who were large enough
to work were put out by the parish officers, and
the improvident mother and her small children
were glad of a shelter in the workhouse. They
were scarcely gone, when one night, not long
afterward, a bonfire swept away all traces of
that poor home of sin and sorrow.

The intruder at Daisy Farm had been stoutly
affirming for two years past that Peggy was
dead, and that she herself was married to John.
Some believed her, and regarded her as now the
rightful mistress of the cottage. But the most
respectable among the people kept aloof from
her, and Father Clakey had twice ordered her

out of the church. This caused her great uneasiness, as she feared she might die without absolution, and be denied a Christian burial. She tried to buy the old man's favor with gifts of butter and eggs, but he was inexorable, and sent them back to her with many bitter reproofs.

Paddy had well nigh lost heart; he had certainly lost all patience. His "grimaces" at the object of his hatred; his faithfulness — John called it "insolence" — to his master; and his prayers to the Virgin had all failed to right matters at the cottage.

One day, having been reproved for carelessness in trimming a hedge, he turned upon John, saying, "Don't ye be rebukin' me for an onfaithful sarvant! I'm honest and upright, and can look every man in Ireland square in the eye, and that's more nor my masther can do! My sperit's fearful roused, and I warn ye it's dangerous triflin' with an angered lion! Some day ye'll find ather yersilf murdered, or poor Paddy drownded in the lough. So ye'll add murder to yer other sins."

John groaned, and walked away a few steps. Then he turned back, and said, " Och, Paddy, Paddy, if ye but knew the anguish o' my heart ye'd pity me place o' 'torturin' me thus ! If ye, or Mr. Murray, or any other one thinks I'm at ase, ye're sore mistaken. I'd lay down my life this hour to make my peace with God and poor dear —— "   .

" Hi, there ! " cried Paddy, " don't let me hear that name. Why don't ye lay down yer life, then, or do somethin' else ? "

" What shall I do ? " exclaimed John.

" Say yer prayers," replied Paddy.

" Paddy, I can't pray. When I tries to spake to God, that poor white face, wet with patient tears, comes atween me and heaven," replied John.

" O' course it does ! " cried the poor fellow. " Did ye think God would hear ye and sind ye pace till ye first make a turn o' things at the cottage ? That would be like a poacher askin' pardon o' the gintleman at the Hall, at the same time he was loadin' his gun to shoot more deer."

John leaned against the stile where Paddy was sitting, pipe in mouth, taking his evening rest; and the tears ran down his cheeks.

"I wish I'd never been born!" he cried.

"I wish ye hadn't," answered his reprover.

"I dramed last night that ye drove off the sarpint, and that then the black cloud rolled away, and the sun shone aboove us all, and that Mammy Honey came back to 'bide with us, and to watch us that we'd never fall into sin more," said John, mournfully.

"Tush!" cried Paddy, scornfully. "A man more nor six feet high, weighin' two hundred pound, might behave himself civil without his blissed mother lavin' heaven, where she's so comfortable, to come and look after him! But I'm glad to see yer heart gettin' a bit soft, aven at this late day, and if it hadn't been made o' flint it would ha' melted long ago. Think o' the holy tachin' o' yer mother, and the fine example o' *myself*."

"What shall I do?" cried John again, in his anguish and indecision.

"Do ye remember the old fable o' the rat

that was **caught in a** trap? She ate her own head off rather than give the waitin' **cat the** satisfaction o' doin' it! Now if ye can **think** o' no better way o' escape, jump into the **lough** and **drown** yerself," remarked Paddy, composedly.

"But I have a *soul*, man!" cried **John**.

"Och, have ye? I thought ye hadn't," was the reply. "Sure, it's a strange soul **for a** Christian, **ony way."**

"I'm not a Christian and niver was, Paddy."

"Indade! Are ye **a** hathen, then?" The simple man knew of no middle ground **between** the two conditions.

"Not just quite a hathen," replied his master.

"What are ye, then?"

"I'm a great sinner, Paddy."

"Ye niver spoke a **truer** word, **masther, and** yet I can't **just comprehend how ye were niver** a Christian in yer best days?"

"No, never, in heart, like **them** two we loved, and heaps like them **in Cloynmally.**

"**I'd give all I have in the world, Paddy, to**

hear Mr. Murray's voice again in the church, and to get a kind word from his lips," said John, mournfully.

" Well, the church door is open and his tongue is not palsied yit, I belave," replied Paddy. " But if ye'd like a sarmon from one that's nather priest nor parson, ye'll get it by goin' to the lough on Sunday next. There's a fine young jintleman stoppin' at Mr. Murray's, that has a mind to spake on religion to thim as niver goes to that church ; and he's given word that as the young men gathers by the water to fish and to skip stones and the like, that he'll be there among thim. He's been at games with the Cloynmally boys the week gone, pitchin' quoits ; and they say he's a fine hand at a game."

" We'll go to hear him, Paddy," said John, " and may be he'll put a bit o' strength into me."

" He ? Ye could take him up in one hand and hould him out at arm's lingth ! " cried Paddy.

"Och, but he may have a bigger and stronger heart nor I," said John.

"Very like he has, or it's a poor one," returned the reprover, in language more faithful than delicate.

"Paddy, lad, why can ye not show me some marcy?" cried John.

"Because the Protestant Bible taches to show marcy to the marciful only. And on thim grounds what right have ye to ask or ixpect tinder regards from a vartuous and onerable man like mesilf!"

"Yer mistaken, Paddy. It says, ' Blissed are the marciful, for they shall obtain marcy ; ' but it does not say others shall not find it. The world is full o' proofs o' God's pity and marcy to many that's gone asthray from him. But none ever got so far wrong as mesilf, after such lovely trainin' from the cradle up ;" said John.

"Will, thin, I'm not as larned as Mr. Murray, to instruct nor yet to condimn ye ; so I'll kape ye waitin' for consolation till ye sees

this new-come jintleman ; I thin will fall on
him with puzzlin' questions on religian, and
see what he's made on ! If there's ony pluck
in him to stand his ground agin my church, as
if he knew the difference in the two, we'll
trust him with yer case, — though it's a
shameful and disgraceful and onrispictable one
to intertain company with ! We'll be first at
the lough, masther, on Sunday, waitin' him
there."

CHAPTER XVII.

LAY-PREACHING AT THE LOUGH.

ON the following Sunday afternoon a crowd gathered around the lough, the usual rallying-place when mass and dinner were over. They had been warned against listening to heresy; but curiosity was stronger than fear. Some came to hear about games in England; some to look at the strange gentleman; and others to watch for heresy and put a stop to its utterance. John and Paddy were there among the rest. Presently there was a stir; and those who were fishing drew in their lines and wound them up. All pressed towards a grassy bank overhung by four old willows; for there the Murray boys appeared with their guest, a "boyish jintleman" of twenty-one or two, with a very slender frame, and a face as fair and delicate as a girl's. I'

held a book in his hand, the sight of which
caused alarm at once.

"Now, boys," muttered an old man, "it's
just as ye war warned! He's one o' thim
artful Methodises — a Bible reader — a fearful,
dangerous fellow!"

The words caught the young man's ear, but
not letting that be known, he said, "Good-day,
friends. What a beautiful place you have
here for rest and exercise! I never saw a
lovelier sheet of water than this, nor a more
beautiful playground; and as I've been great
at games, I've looked well to the grounds. I
heard at Cloynmally that you always met here
on Sunday, and so I've come to see you, and
talk a little to you about things that we all believe. I'm no minister, and can't preach.
I'm only going to talk; and you have as good
a right to talk here as I have. So any of you
may speak out and ask questions, or contradict
me, if I say what's not right."

"What book's yon in your hand?" asked
the old schoolmaster, who had better been

styled " the village child's-nurse," as his ten pupils were too young to learn from books.

" This book, friend, is the Douay version of the Bible, prepared by a Catholic priest and used in your church. I will not open it unless you wish. I've not come here to argue, but to talk on things that you and I agree in. We will let other things go."

" But ye're a Protestant ? " asked a voice from the crowd.

" Yes, I am."

" Then in what can ye agree with us ? " asked the schoolmaster, who regarded himself as the spy and watchman of the hour.

" Oh, in many things, friend," replied the youth. " You believe in a God who made the world and all who dwell in it, and who sends the sun and the rain to ripen our harvests, that we may have bread, and so live ? "

" Oh, sure, we believe in him ! "

" Och, yes, yes ! " replied many voices.

" And so do I, friends. You believe that God sent His Son, Jesus Christ, into the

world, and that He died on the cross to save
all who trust in Him, don't you ? "

" O' course we belaves that."

" Yes, yes."   " Indade we does ! " were the
varied replies.

" And so do I. And you believe in the
Virgin Mary, too, don't you ? "

" Ay, do we ; but ye don't," said a man.

" You're mistaken, friend ; I do believe in
her and I honor her.   She was ' blessed among
women.'   God honored her above all women
ever born before or after her, in making her
the mother of His Son, the Redeemer of the
world."

" I thought all the Protestants despised
Mary," said one.

" None but a great scoffer could despise her
whom God so greatly honored," said the
young man.

" But you don't pray to her ? " said the
schoolmaster.

" No, I pray only to God, the Father, Son
and Holy Spirit; but this is a point on which
we disagree ; and we were to talk of those only

on which we think alike. **You believe in** Peter, don't **you ? "**

" **Peter ?** Oh, sure we do ; he it is as **holds** the keys."

" **Y**ou believe that **he** wrought miracles ? "

" Surely ; all the saints do that."

" Would you like to hear from your own Bible how Peter and John healed the lame man at the gate of the temple ? "

" Are you just *sure* it's not the Protestant Bible ? " asked **a** timid-looking man **in** the crowd.

" Quite sure, friend. You may take it and show **it** to Father Clakey, and if he **says it is** not the one he uses, but a Protestant version, you may **do** what you please with it."

So they all sat motionless while **he** read the **narratives of** the healing of the lame man, and of Christ's walking **on the** water, **stilling the** tempest, and **feeding the multitude. When** he closed the **book, he said, " You notice, friends,** that when Jesus saw the multitude He had **compassion on them. It** is not on them alone, but on us here, and on all who are in want and sorrow. His compassion has not failed now that He has returned to His glory. He still hears and sees, and is ready to grant what we need. That multitude were hungry. Is there any one here who ever knew what it was to be hungry, when there's no food in the cottage and no money to buy any?"

"Ay!" "'Deed there is!" "Few but has known it, sir!" "Ye've heard, in England, o' the famine we had here when the potatoes failed, and the great sickness came?" These were among the many answers to his question.

"Yes, I've heard all that."

"I wonder if there's one here hungry to-day?" he asked.

"I bees, yer honor," said a trembling old woman, who sat on the grass near him, "and not a handful o' meal in the house!"

"Then here's a crown for you, poor friend," said the young man. "Jesus has compassion on you, and perhaps He sent me here to tell you so."

An old man rose to his feet, but sat down again, as if too modest to make his plea.

" Who's that, boys?" asked the gentleman.

"It's ould Jemmy Flynn, a real dacent body!" cried several at once.

" Then here's a crown for him too, and I've still another for any one that's poor or sick. But I'm sure all that can work have too much honor to take what should be given to the needy." Strange as it may seem, among a class proverbial as beggars, no one else applied for help.

" Hunger is not the greatest sorrow," continued the young man. "If there is any one here with other troubles, remember Jesus is among us, and He has compassion on you."

" Plase, sir, I lost my baby, and my heart's broke, and I can't ate nor slape I'm that hungry for him. My arms is so empty they aches all day and all night," said a pale woman, pressing through the crowd.

" Jesus' own mother had her heart broken too, when the cruel Jews were crucifying her Son. He pitied her, and He told John to take her for his mother, and to comfort her, and he did so. He will comfort you too, if you ask

Him, and fill your soul with His love, so that you can think with joy of your baby, and of the time when you shall take it again in those poor aching arms," said the stranger, with pity in his voice.

The people, finding he had a word for all, pressed around him and began telling him their sorrows, half a dozen speaking at once.

At last he said, " Let me say to each one of you, no matter what your sorrow is, — or your sins, either, — Jesus has compassion on you."

All this time John and Paddy had been sitting under a willow behind the stranger. Paddy now touched his elbow and said, " 'Dade, sir, if I should till ye *my* throubles, ye'd niver belave me. Ye'd think I was makin' up lies to amuse ye ! " The young man probably saw that it would be like letting loose a torrent, if he began to talk with one who bore so little resemblance to a mourner ; so he just bade him remember what he had said to the others ; and, thanking them for their civility and bidding them good-day, he was about leaving, when one of the young men called

out, "But, sir, we heard **you** was to tell **us**
about the games ye have in England. **Will**
ye stop **a** bit and **try a** hand at pitchin'
quoits?"

"**Not** to-day, my good fellow; God gives us
six days to ourselves, but on this one, the first
day of the week, on which the Saviour rose
from the dead, He commands us **not to do our
own** works **nor** think our own thoughts,
but **to** keep it holy unto Him. Come here at
sunset on Tuesday, and **I** will meet you as a
boy, at healthful sport. To-day **I** came as **a**
Christian, to tell **you of Him** whom my soul
loveth, and whom I want the whole world **to**
love. Take this Bible, schoolmaster, and make
sure **I** have not deceived you."

As he turned to **go,** John rose and followed
him. "**You** don't think, sir," he said to him
in **a low** tone, "that He could have compassion
on *me.* I'm **such a** fearful sinner! I've been
a hypocrite, and a Pharisee, and **all** that's evil.
O' course you've heard o' *me*— John Sheehan."

"**No, never,**" replied the young man.

"Ye haven't? Why, I thought the whole world had heerd o' me and was cursin' me by this time! Didn't Mr. Murray tell ye o' me, and o' the disolation I had made in the church and the home?"

"Not a word, friend; but unless your sins are redder than scarlet and deeper than crimson, Jesus has compassion on you, and will forgive you."

"Well, sir, will ye ask Mr. Murray if he thinks there is power enough in Heaven to. forgive me, without destroying the justice of God?"

"I will ask him, my poor man, and he will say, 'Yes,' and Jesus will say unto you, 'Thy sins are forgiven thee; go and sin no more.'"

Had Protestants built a church in Killyrooke and sent a minister to preach in it, they could not thus have accomplished as much for the people as did that almost boy, with his heart full of love for Christ and of zeal in His service. The Bible was pronounced a "Catholic" one by the priest, and so the stranger's word was verified.

The compassion of **Jesus** and the miracles by which **He** proved it were the themes in many a poor home that Sunday night; and during the three or **four** weeks of his college vacation, that young lay-preacher did a great work for those cottagers.   He broke down the barriers, **so** that after that, any man whom they respected **could** get an audience at the lough, while he read portions of Scripture from the Douay version and made comments on it; care being used not to arouse prejudice or fear by openly assailing the Romish church.

CHAPTER XVIII.

A VISIT OF MERCY.

WHEN the young stranger returned to the parsonage, he reported his doings to Mr. Murray, who had been too wise to accompany him. When he delivered John Sheehan's message, a shadow passed over the minister's face.

"He has indeed made desolation in both church and home," he said, "and only for the abounding mercy and grace of God I should have no hope for him! He ran well when none hindered, but he was a poor, weak creature, without Christian principle. His parents were pillars in the church, though poor and unlettered folk. His mother was as nearly a saint as any mortal who ever walked the earth. They held him up, perhaps too much.

"If one was kept in a standing-stool till he

was fully grown, without ever using his own limbs, I think he would fall as soon as he attempted to stand alone ; at all events, the first thrust from a foe would lay him low ; and once down, he would not know how to rise again.

"This man's case has lain heavily on my heart. Such has been the good name they bore, that we always pointed the cotters to that family as an example of consistent walk, and of the power of the Gospel to keep men pure even when surrounded by all that is ungodly. The course this last one of the race has pursued, has outraged the feelings of even the rude and ignorant Papists about him, and brought contempt on the Protestant faith. I went three times to pull him, if might be, out of the fire, but he made off and would not see me at all, as if well pleased with the fetters in which Satan had bound him. If he is ever humbled and needs help, he will have to come to me for it!"

The young gentleman remained silent, and Mr. Murray saw that the last remark did not meet his approbation.

" You may think I am severe," he continued,
" but you never saw the happy home he has
made desolate, nor the saint-like woman who
has meekly forsaken it without a word of censure, or even a farewell to the minister and the
church, who regarded her as a bright and shining light among them, and who felt drawn
heavenward by her quiet faith and humble zeal.
No, I shall never go after him!"

" And yet," said the young man, " after all
this, he has a soul! It was sinners, and not
the righteous, that Jesus came to save; to *seek*
as well as to save."

" That is true, and we must be careful not
to stand on our small dignity when He stooped
so low," replied the good minister, rebuked by
the faith of his friend.

" You know brands have to be *plucked* from
the burning, sir. They cannot walk forth
from the flames themselves," continued the
guest.

" True; and Sheehan seems to have been
bound hand and foot by the enemy, that he
might not only lose his own soul, but be also a

cause of stumbling to many. Perhaps he ought to have a helping hand, but if I should go to him it might heal the wound too slightly. I care not how sorely he suffers, nor how long. As he opened his mind to you, how would it do for you to take his case in hand, and learn whether he is really repentant, or only longing for his old peace and respectability again ?"

"If you will trust me, sir, I will talk with the poor man gladly, for his pale face has haunted me ever since he whispered those words in my ear," replied the young man.

"Well, as you have promised to meet the boys at the lough on Tuesday, take the cottage on your way home, sending my boys on before you," said Mr. Murray.

"Would it not be a good work to close this Sabbath with, sir ? To-morrow or Tuesday he may be off in his fields, or at market, or — or — one of us may be in eternity ! For my own part, sir, I feel that I'm working by the hour for my Master, and may be called in from the field at any moment. I have hardly dared to speak the word 'to-morrow' for six months past, in reference to work for souls," replied the youth, solemnly.

Mr. Murray looked up in surprise at "the boy," as he called him, and replied, "Yes, if you are not too weary, go now, and forget what I have said calculated to discourage you, remembering only that He will not break the bruised reed nor quench the smoking flax. If you see one spark of repentance, fan it; but warn him not to feign sorrow for sin, under a desire to regain his character and his home. If he speaks of seeing me, advise him rather to go to Elder Peter. I'm too easily touched by the sight of sorrow to deal with the like of him. Elder Peter is a son of thunder, and will be faithful without being too merciful."

"You are sure he will not 'smite off the right ear' instead of saying, 'Go and sin no more'?" asked the young man. "I fear that old man, with his stern sense of justice, may lack the charity that covers a multitude of sins."

"Well, then, my dear boy, send Sheehan to

me, if he desires help; and I will strive to read his case," replied the minister.

Mr. Murray took his hat and cane, and walked on with his friend as far as the little churchyard which surrounded his chapel. They went in among the beds of the lowly sleepers, just as the last streak of the golden light was fading in the west. Very near the chapel door Mr. Murray laid his hand on a plain slate headstone, saying, "Here sleeps the mother of this man — a woman of whom the world was not worthy."

And then in a few words he told the story of her strong, pure life, and ended by a recital of her son's indignation over her open grave, because a half-idiot had pronounced her safe in heaven — the only one there of the race or name! "And yet, see what he has done for her honor," he said. "Now go on, my boy; you will have the moon for your company home, and may God go with you, and put words into your mouth."

The young stranger stooped and plucked a briar twig and three shamrock blossoms from the mound where Mammy Honey was sleeping, and then passed down the solitary road which lay between the village of Cloynmally and the hamlet of Killyrooke.

He knew the cottage, — which had been described to him, — by the little glass window, which glistened through the vines in the moonlight. With one bound he sprang over the stile, and with a few steps reached the open door. The room was lighted by a single rush taper, making the figures within very indistinct. Before he had time to knock, he heard Paddy say, "But, Masther, the young jintleman said, ' All manner of sins' would be forgive to people, and I'm sure that ye — vile as ye are — haven't committed them *all!* Ye niver stole a ha'peth from any body; ye niver warshipped gods o' wood and stone; ye niver worked on the Sabbath day, — ye, nor yer donkey, nor yer manservant, nor the sthranger that war within yer gates; nor ye niver invied Harpley Hall, nor the fine things in it, to the owner, nor —— "

" Hark, there, Paddy! there's some neighbor knockin'," interrupted John. " Come in ! "

"Surely," he continued, rising to meet the stranger, on whose uncovered head the moon was shining, "this is not the young jintleman, come to visit the sperit in prison? Did ye give my message to dear, dear Mr. Murray, sir?" asked John, looking earnestly in his face.

"Yes."

"And what said he? — that there was one ray of hope for me in the world to come? In this world I do not look for peace!"

"He said, my friend, that but for the abounding mercy and the free grace of God he should look on your case as a hopeless one; but that if you truly repent of your sin against God — not merely feel sorrow for the wreck of your own happiness — there is hope."

John took the gentleman's hand in both his own, and leading him to a chair, exclaimed, "I will lay my heart bare before ye and tell ye all; and thin if ye think God can listen, I'll ask ye that has a hearin' at the marcy-seat, to plead with Him for me."

"I do not want to hear of your sins, poor

man. I only want to know that you've forsaken them, and are penitent before God. He came not to call the righteous, but sinners to repentance; and the greater your sins, the greater your need of Him, and the greater Saviour he will be to you."

" Will, will, thin there's a fine chance for him, for a huger sinner ye'll not find in Killyrooke!" cried Paddy, who had been sitting unnoticed in a dark corner of the kitchen.

" Whist, Paddy," said his master, " and listen to the jintleman while he talks to us."

" What is it, friend, that troubles you? Is it that your respectability and peace are gone, or that your soul is in danger?"

" It is that I have sinned against a holy God, whom I once thought I loved and honored, and have brought shame on His name among His foes; that I have disgraced the dead, and broke the heart o' the livin', and ruined myself ontirely. This last is sorrow enough; but when I remembers God, all that fades away. I can't pray. Och, it is a fearful thing to be shut out from the presence o' God and not be able even to call upon Him."

"You must pray or you are lost; no man can do that for you."

"Ay, you is jist what I'm always tillin' him —to say his prayers," said Paddy. "O' course he won't be forgive till he does— "what's worth the takin' is worth the askin'!"

"If I could get a ray o' hope, sir," said John, without paying the least regard to Paddy's speech, "I'd lave my lovely home and go forth among strangers and toil at any work for a crust. I'd not ask a shelter by day or night, nor a smile from mortal, nor even ase from pain o' body!"

"Ah. you'd buy peace with God by penance, like your poor neighbors, would you? But it can not be done. The blood of Jesus Christ, and that alone, cleanseth from *all sin*. Do you believe that?"

"Ay, I have believed it from my cradle up; but *my* sin, sir"——

"Is it greater than all sin, so great that it

outweighs the promise and the power of God? Take care, my friend, how you limit the ability of Him who said, 'All power is Mine in heaven and earth,'" said the visitor.

"It never entered my head that I was a sinner, sir, till late years. I thought myself an example to all, for vartue and piety."

"Och, *that ye did*," responded Paddy from his dark corner, "and the blissed one in hiven war always warnin' ye agin the 'liven o' the Pharisees,' and tellin' ye that ye war all buried up in yer crops and yer cattle! Well do I remember in those last days how she said, 'Beware, boy, o' self-rightcousness; let him that standeth take hade list he fall.' Poor Paddy remembers her holy tachin', if her own son don't, and I only a poor workhouse lad and a Papisht beside. I'd be under great compliment to ye, young jintleman if ye'd say yer prayers here, seein' that he'll not say his. I'll sit still and listen, though I daren't for the life o' me go onto my knees."

"I hope you will not forget your own soul,

my poor man, in your care for your master," said the gentleman.

" Och, but I'm safe, sir ; I'm a Catholic and quite in favor with father Clakey these days, 'count o' the fine way I've behaved myself in the throubles at Daisy Farm ; though he's a bit angered with all the boys for listening to ye at the lough, the day. He's quite sure that ye are ather a clergy or the makin's o' one, — a Methodis like, that's come out o' England to lade us asthray. He's comin' to the play-ground a Tuesday to spy ye."

" I hope he will ; I'd be glad to see him ; but at present we have to do with this one ques-tion, ' What must I do to be saved ? ' " said the gentleman.

And far into the night he talked with John, and prayed for him, and encouraged him to accept the offered pardon, while poor Paddy slept in his chair.

CHAPTER XIX.

ELDER PETER.

WHEN John Sheehan parted with the young man, in the darkness, at the gate of his cottage; he said, " I'll take yer advice, sir, even though the only way to loose the hopples from my feet be to go forth into the world penniless, to arn my bread as a farm servant. Many thanks to ye for yer condescinsion and yer marcy to a poor sinful, sorrowful man."

When he entered the cottage again, he roused the sleeping Paddy, who started to his feet as if in great alarm. After looking about him wildly for some seconds, he remembered the circumstances under which he had fallen asleep, and exclaimed, " Have I been that oncivil that I let the stranger go without a bow from me or a ' God bliss **ye,'** after all **the pains** he's took about gettin' our sins forgiven!' "

Paddy took the sins as well as the **honors of** the Sheehans all to himself; and **he now felt** as grateful to the gentleman as if he had been the especial object **of** his visit.

" Sit down **now** and rouse yoursilf like **a man** and listen to me," said John, in a solemn tone. " I've promised this night that I'll lade a new life from this hour. I've resolved to break the hateful fetters."

" And ye'll break yer *resolve* when you one comes back from the fair and abuses ye, — as ye have done a hoondered times afore," **replied** Paddy, rubbing his sleepy eyes.

" No, Paddy; ye and **me is free** from this **hour,** even if we have to lave the darlin' cottage **and** all in it. I care no more for all this land, nor the crops, than for the dust in the road, — these treasures that has well nigh cost me my soul," said his master.

" And where'll we go ? " asked Paddy.

" **We'll go** where's work **to be had, and hire**

out as farm servants, may be; but I must think first," replied John.

"I'll not lave this lovely cottage to *yon one!*" exclaimed Paddy. "I'll set fire to it and burn it up, and then I'll drive off the craturs and sell them to some marciful body as will love them tinder."

"But the cottage is not ours, it belongs to the estate o' Harpley Hall, and we'd be transported for burnin' it down. We'll do right at any rate, and not get out o' one sin by lapin' into another," replied John.

"Let's ask advice o' Elder Peter, for though he'll not buy eggs of sinners, — as if the innocent hins were to blame for the ill doin' o' their masther, — he's quite ready to *give them advice*," said Paddy.

"I can go to Mr. Murray, but I'm afeareder o' Elder Peter nor of death itself," replied John. "He's a man o' very holy life, Paddy; and never havin' fallen himself, he knows not how to pity the sinner. He goes half a mile out o' his way to the Hall, o' rent day, rather than pass Daisy Farm; and once when I met

him in the road, he sprang over a thorn hedge
rather than go by me."

"Och! he'd made a poor hand at kapin'
company with the Son o' Mary when He was
on arth! Didn't the ould misthress read us
fine lessons about Him ating with publicans
and sinners and the like villyans? And ye
mind yon Mary that He let wash His holy feet,
and the poor body He spoke tinder to, whin
the grand folk brought her to Him for punishment in the timple. If Elder Peter had been
there, he would ha' been the dith o' all thim
sinners."

"Well, Paddy, when the darkness falls the
morrow night, I'll slip up to Mr. Murray's, and
humble myself before him as I have before the
Lord; and I'll do just what he bids me, if it's
to leave all here and flee like a beggar. But
ye have a work to do for me, Paddy, as well as
the minister. In the vision o' Mammy Honey,
— by which I should ha' taken warnin', — ye
it was that drew the pizen tooth out o' the
heart o' love."

"I'll soon do *that,* with yer lave, and like no

better business," replied Paddy, springing to his feet and rubbing his hands together impatiently.

"Don't ye move a foot, Paddy, without Mr. Murray's biddin', for ye've not the judgment o' a child," replied John.

"Och, hasn't I? And where would Daisy Farm be to-day, weren't it for my judgment in buyin' and sellin' at the market these last years?" replied Paddy, with offended dignity.

The young stranger made his way home in the darkness, for the moon had set long before he left the cottage. As he passed the few poor hovels on his way to Cloynmally, the sleepers within were startled by hearing a low, sweet voice singing in the road, —

"The dying thief rejoiced to see
  That fountain in his day :
  O, may I there, though vile as he,
  Wash all my sins away."

While this earnest young disciple had been striving to lead the wanderer to God, Elder Peter, the village stone-cutter, had been closeted with the minister, looking as hard as the ma-

terial he wrought on. " Well, sir," he said, as
he took the offered seat in Mrs. Murray's
modest little parlor, " I've been hearin' strange
things from my 'printice lads, o' the doin's
of this young lad that's stoppin' with ye,
— such a doin's for the Lord's day as I would
not belave till I'd first ask yersilf. What's this
he's doing ? "

" No evil, I'm sure," said Mr. Murray, returning the stony gaze of Elder Peter very
calmly.

" Well I heered that he'd been at the Killyrooke lough consorting with Papist boys, telling them about pitchin' quoits and ball-playin',
and that he belaved in the Virgin Mary and
every thing else they belaved ; and that there
was just no differ at all betwixt the two reli-
gions. And he passed silver about, like a fool,
among the crowd, — it will all go for whisky
and tobacco, — and worse nor all, who do you
think he walked off in company with ? Who
but John Sheehan ! "

Elder Peter's righteous indignation had well
nigh taken away his breath before he got

through this description of the modest youth's effort at the play-ground. Mr. Murray went into a labored defense of his friend, pledging himself that no evil should be done through him to Protestantism in the town.

But "though vanquished," Elder Peter "could argue still." He expressed great surprise that his minister should have trusted a mere boy on such an errand as that on which he was now gone.

"He's jist quite a novice, supposin' he's even sincere," he said. "What is he, a soft-hearted lad, to set the terrors of the law before that offender? He's been at my yard tellin' me about the great awakenin' they've had in his college; and I think he's a visionary. I tried to sound him, but there was no depth, either to his experience nor yet to his Bible knowledge. He was quite thick in his views o' Daniel's vision. I could not draw him into an argument about Melchisedek; and as to the Apocalypse — why, he knew nothing of the correct interpretation of the living craturs full of eyes before and behind! He had no more opinion about the scarlet beast with the seven heads and ten horns than a babe unborn!"

"But he's a new-born soul, elder; we must not look for wisdom in a child," replied Mr. Murray.

"Ay, very good, minister; and ought we to put a strong man's work into the hands of a babe? Answer me that, will ye?"

"I have done nothing for Sheehan," replied Mr. Murray, "but I saw no reason why he might not point him to Christ when he desired to do so."

"Ye've done nothing? Didn't ye go twice or thrice to him, and he turn his back on ye?"

"But that was all I did, save to pray for him."

"Well, I've done all I could as an elder o' the church," replied Elder Peter.

"May I inquire what you have done, brother, except to pray for him?" asked the minister; "for of course, you have done that."

The elder hesitated a moment, but he was never at a loss for a passage of Scripture to suit his purpose. "Well, no, minister I have *not* prayed for John Sheehan. Do ye not mind a passage which reads, ' I say not that ye shall pray for these.' I regard him as one of ' these.' I met him once in the road, and I scathed him with my countenance. Then I refused to take my weekly supply o' eggs when he sent them ; and I've gone round the back road every time I've been up to the Hall with my rent, rather than countenance him by passing his door. My conscience is clear in his case, and I have no faith in his repentance, 'less a mericle be performed to prove it. But the night wanes; I must away.

Just as Mr. Murray, candle in hand, opened the door to let the elder out, his young guest mounted the steps.

"Oh, here he is, back from an errand which might make a very angel timid!" exclaimed Elder Peter.

The young man looked at him in surprise.

"Listen to me, lad," he continued. "Did ye ever hear o' one that ran before he was sent?"

"Yes, sir," was the answer.

" Well, and so have I ; and I've seen such an **one, too.** Good-night, minister ; **good-night, lad."** **And the elder** walked forth in all the dignity of conscious orthodoxy.

CHAPTER XX.

DELIVERANCE FROM EVIL.

AFTER Mr. Murray had talked some time with John on the following evening, he took him to the cottage of Elder Peter, who acted in all church matters as if Peter of early fame had placed " the keys " in his hand when he left the church militant behind him.

Elder Peter first denounced the wanderer with the severity of faithfulness, and then, applying all the thumb-screws and soul-screws he could invent, put him through a course of questioning to test his sincerity and his humility.

" If the church (he meant himself, for all the others were meek and tender-hearted) should bid ye stand up afore the people for a public rebukin', would ye do it ? " he asked, sharply.

"I would, sir," replied John, "before them and the Lord too."

"If they bid ye go to every Catholic house in Killyrooke, and confess that ye were never a Christian, but a hypocrite and a Pharisee, would ye do it?"

"I will do that whether I'm bid or not, sir, because I owe it to Him whose name I have disgraced," replied John, humbly.

"If they bid ye to give all yer goods to feed the poor, and lave yerself penniless, would ye do it?" And Elder Peter looked shrewdly from one corner of his eye, as if sure he had now struck the sore point.

"I would, sir, and be thankful that I had any thing to give, thus to prove my pinitence," said John.

"Would ye give yer body to be burned?"

"If God bid me do *that*, I'd ask Him for grace and strength to do it," replied John.

"Well, and if the church bid ye, would ye promise never to seek yer wife again? For it may be the desire for yer old peace, and not repentance for sin that leads yo here. Would ye promise this?"

"No, sir, not for all the churches in the world, I wouldn't. God is over all. Because I've broke my vow to Him and her, it is no reason I should keep on breakin' it. I shall seek her at once, and strive to atone for my past evil with tenfold o' love and tinderness, if she comes to me — but she never will. Forgiveness like that would be more nor mortal."

Elder Peter frowned. He was there as an inquisitor, and was not to be taught by such a sinner. "Then you make some resarve in this matter?" he asked, harshly.

"I resarve the right to cease doin' evil, and to make amends for the past," said John.

"He's right there, Elder," whispered the minister, who was the only mortal to whose opinion the rigid man would yield. "His confession is full and free, we must admit."

"Well, Sheehan, I *hope* ye're sincere, and we'll overlook the past and try to respect ye again. Ye may take yer seat in the house o' God, next Lord's day, and I'll leave the mat ter o' the public rebukin' to the minister's decision."

The minister's decision was a very merciful one, — that John should call at the parsonage, and walk through the churchyard and into the church by his side. This would show the congregation that he had been forgiven and received into favor by the minister and elders, and would secure their pardon and pity for him.

Elder Peter's sense of justice was as strong as his hatred of sin; and he said that, evil as was the heart of Nan O'Gorman, she ought not to be sent forth from the cottage penniless, — thus perchance to be led into new sin. So he ordered John, with **Mr.** Murray's approval, to place ten pounds in his hands for her, which could only be demanded by her in person.

Mr. Murray, knowing John's timidity and weakness of purpose, wanted to encourage him. He therefore requested him to remain a few days in Cloynmally to look after the men who were laying out the garden attached to the little parsonage. Matters at the cottage, and a message from Elder Peter to Nan, on her return, were left with Paddy Mannon, who by this trust was greatly elevated in his own esteem.

"God helps those who help themselves." Just as soon as John had resolved, in the fear of God, to break the chain that bound him, it was broken without a blow from his hand. The day after he left the cottage, Nan returned in high spirits, with two companions, to get her clothes, and to say "good-bye to all Killy-rooke, — the dull old place where she'd wore out her best days for nothing." She announced to Paddy that a new linen-mill had just gone into operation, about twenty-five miles away, and that she was going there to work with her friends. She was too young and too fair to spend her life milking cows and spinning flax; and so they must get on as they could without her at Daisy Farm. The message from Elder Peter was delivered, with an order to appear before him within ten days, or the money would be made over to the poor of the parish.

"Ten pounds is a power o' money!" exclaimed Nan. "But I would niver go to yon elder for it, if it war a thousand! I'll take Maid o' Longford instead, and sell her to farmer Blaney, whose wife's long wanted her; and the ten pound will pay for her."

"When ye drive Maid o' Longford off, ye'll drive the farm with her and Paddy Mannon standin' on it! My darlin' misthress' own cow, indade, that Mammy Honey give her! Away with ye, or I'll have ye 'rested for a highwayman!" cried Paddy, in a towering passion.

In an hour, she and her friends were gone, and Paddy was on his way to bear the joyful news to John, and to implore him to "send off at once for the darlin' misthress, by the b'y that knew where to find her without huntin'."

But both Mr. Murray and Elder Peter advised John to put his cottage in its old order first; for his lack of heart and Nan's lack of interest had told sadly on all within and around it. The poultry houses were almost empty; the flowers were dead, and the vines Mammy

Honey had loved and trained were tangled and broken, and disfigured with the dead leaves and stems of four summers.

When it was known in the village that the usurper was gone, and that John and Paddy were making preparations for Peggy's return — if return she would, — it gave general satisfaction. Some, in their pleasure, forgot that he had caused her exile, and took John by the hand when they met him, and said, " I wish ye joy, neighbor! Can I help ye clare the place up for her comin' ? "

The lady of Harpley Hall, herself a sad, neglected wife, knew the story of Peggy's wrongs and her quiet departure. When she heard that she was expected back, she sent a man to the cottage with a gift of two young deer for pets, — the only deer ever owned by a peasant in that region. She honored the gift by sending two blue ribbons to be tied around their necks on the day of Peggy's return, with a message that she should call at the cottage some day to see the woman who had always

15

set such good examples to the people on the
estate.

Soon after this, an old woman in the neighborhood, who had received much kindness
from both Mammy Honey and Peggy in times
of sickness, tapped at the door of the cottage.
John opened it, and looked in amazement at
the burden of life she carried in her apron, the
corners of which she held tightly in her hands.

"Neighbor John," she said, "I've heard
that the black cloud is broke over Daisy Farm
and that the sun is overhead again. I've come
with a small gift to her as is comin' back.
Here's my best hin and fourteen fine eggs laid
by herself. I'd like to *set* her in the hin-
house, that Peggy may have, at least, one little
brood to feed, — she that loves livin' creatur's
so dear."

Father Clakey, who rejoiced that Nan was
gone and thus the offence removed from his
flock, was seen, one morning, coming down
the road with a huge pot of geranium, all
aflame with flowers.

" Here, Mannon," he called over the hedge,
" set this in yer misthress' little glass window,
and till her it came with my respects. And
mind *I* bid ye clare up all this place, and trim
the vines and sort up the flower-beds before
her coming ; for she's a worthy, paceable
body, and an example to these hathen savages
that are breaking my heart with their conduct."

Paddy had scarcely done bowing to and hon-
oring his " riverence," when an infirm old
woman, who had suffered sorely for warm
stockings since Peggy's departure, came hob-
bling into the little garden where Paddy was
at work.

" I heerd, Paddy, that ivery body is sinding
gifts to the misthress but mysilf. But I've not
a ha'peth to give. Wouldn't ye suffer me to
wash the dairy or to sweep the kitchen to show
my love ? " she said.

" Och, dade I will, granny," cried the master of ceremonies. " I've got an ilegant job
for ye, and one that I offered nather to his
' riverence ' nor yet to the lady o' the Hall.

Take ye the little flax-wheel that she loved so, and a bit o' soap. Go down to the lough, and there dip the wheel tin times in the water. Thin scour it with the soap till yer arm is nigh broke. Thin dip it tin times more and wipe it dry. Burn the flax that's on it, and throw the ashes o't in the lough, and put on fresh flax that I'll give ye. And whin yer sure there's not a trace o' the evil hands on it, bring it back to its own place again."

Old Monica set about her work joyfully, and when it was accomplished, she charged Paddy to " tell the misthress, or she would never know it was done."

Cloynmally caught the spirit, and bulbs and shrubs were set out in the little flower-garden, and several good books laid on the table beside the old Bible.

But it remained for Paddy to make the most marvelous change. One day his master came into the kitchen, and found him with a hoe, minus the handle, down on his knees, scraping the clay floor, beaten hard by the wear of a century, and whose hardness and evenness were John's pride. It was now as if a plough-share had been run lightly over it in all directions, a mass of broken clay and dust.

"What are ye doing, man? Look at this destruction!" cried John, with grief in his tone.

"Kape quite asy, masther, and I'll soon make all right agin," replied Paddy. "I'm but takin' off the top o' the clay, that the darlin' may not have to walk on the same floor yon one has trod these years."

It was no easy job to smooth the floor again, but Paddy accomplished it; and in about ten days, with the approval of Mr. Murray, he set off on the errand he had been looking and hoping for, for four weary years.

John had urged Paddy to go to the city in his new working-clothes, but he disdained the thought of making so poor an appearance when he was going on such important business.

"'Dade the ould masther's Sunday shute won't be new to thim where I'm goin', for they've seen thim afore, and were well plazed

too, — for they all laughed very pleasant at me,
— from the grand lady o' the house to the
maids that fed me in the kitchen. It's no
small farmer's house, nor other workin' man's
ather, that I'm goin' to now," he added, tossing his head proudly, "but to the raal gentry's. There's a brass sign-board — nigh a
foot long, on the door, with their name on't,
showin' that it's the importantest thing in the
world for people that passes to know who lives
within. What's the good o' a lad havin' fine
clothes if he's not to wear them whin he's
among fine people? 'Dade, I'll wear no other."

John offered Paddy money to go in the post-
chaise, but he scorned it as an insinuation of
weakness.

"I've been nigh forty year boastin' that I
could keep pace with post-horses on my own
two feet, and it would be a beggarly thing to
give it up now. 'Dade, I'll be my own post-
horses," he said.

John· had given him a thousand messages
before he set off; but he accompanied him a
piece on the road repeating them.

" Mind ye tell her, Paddy, that there's niver
been a sunbame in my heart since she left it ;
that I've been hourly mournin' after her, but
was too wake to break the chain. Tell her
how I forsook God's house and shunned his
people ; and tell her all about the last sorrow
in my soul for sin ; and tell her about the
young jintleman from the college that led me
to see a ray — mind, it's but a *small, feeble ray,*
— of hope ; and say that if she will come
back, it'll be a new John Sheehan she'll find
at Daisy Farm, not the proud Pharisee she left
there, but a man humbled in the dust and
afeared to live lest he sin more agin a long-
suffering God. Can ye remember all I've said
to ye, Paddy ? "

" I'd have a bad memory if I couldn't," replied Paddy, " for ye've tould me ivery thing
tin times over. I'll make all the confissions
and promises, and I'll tell her the fine claring
up we've had at the farm, and all about the
young deer, and the priest's flowers and the
books, and then she'll just fly to get back to
the home she loved so dear."

"I'm not so sure o' that, Paddy," replied John, with a mournful shake of the head. "The fine folk will ha' learned her value by this time, and will strive to hinder her lavin' by hapin' abuses on me. And if this be so, and she refuse to come back, tell her that war what I feared and what I desarved; and tell her though I niver see her more, she may hope that her prayers and the dear dead mother's is answered, and that poor John is saved — *so as by fire.* Can ye remember that?"

The last words were evidently unintelligible to Paddy, but he did not admit it. "Oh, yes, I'll remimber it, and if I shouldn't, I'll make up something as fine as it. Now, good-day to ye, masther. May good luck go with me, and 'bide with ye; and mind ye're faithful to the cows and the rest o' the work while I'm gone, so that I'll not find all in disorder when I retarns. See, there's the sun just peepin' over the bog as he did the mornin' I conveyed her, with her blue box on my shoulder, to the wagoner at the turn o' the road. Fare ye well!"

And throwing his stick, on the end of which was a bundle, over his shoulder, the poor, faithful fellow trudged off on his long day's journey, whistling,

" Will ye go to Kelvin grove?"

CHAPTER XXI.

PADDY MANNON AT MISS GREY'S.

TWO of the sunniest chambers in the house had been assigned by Miss Grey to Peggy for the " orphan asylum." Under one of the windows was a heavy iron balcony, from which they could look into the small gardens of two old residences, and then off at the distant harbor, where white sails were always flapping impatiently, or quiet ships lying at anchor, as if resting after long and weary voyages. From this balcony, after the simple lessons of the morning were over, the humble teacher could always see something which suggested a subject of instruction to her little charge. One day she would tell them all she knew about the waters, and explain the power of Him who holds them in the hollow of His

234

hand, and who fashions and preserves the myriads of fish that fill them.

So the trees, and flowers, and birds, few though they were, seen from a city window, were turned into teachers for the unfolding minds of the thoughtful little girls.

Having noticed the delight they took in flowers, Miss Grey, who had now fully regained her health and spirits, resolved to gratify their delicate taste. So she had deep wooden boxes, filled with rich earth, fixed around the three sides of the balcony by iron rods, and stocked with potted plants in bud or bloom. The intervening spots were reserved for seeds, that the children might watch their growth from the first tender sprout to the gorgeous blossom.

On the balcony were two little chairs, with books, toys, and materials for dressing dolls, when the lessons and the half-hour's task at needle work were over. It was the summer school-room and the playhouse; a place of never failing amusement.

One morning, as Bessie sat hemming a

coarse towel, her little sister, who was on her knees gazing earnestly into the black earth in "the garden," as the boxes were called, sprung up, exclaiming, "Oh, see! God has put life into one little black seed, and given it a tiny green head, and it's just peeping up. And look, He's turned that red bud into a flower in the night!"

Miss Grey, who was in the room at the time, consulting Peggy about some of her charities, stooped to look, and then said, "Yes, that is one of the seeds you called 'black peas,' a sweet-pea. It will grow into a delicate vine, and by-and-by have fragrant flowers."

Peggy sighed heavily.

"You're not sorry the poor little pea has broken its shell and come to life, I hope, Misthress Sheehan, that you heave such a sigh as that?" asked Miss Grey.

"No, ma'am, I'm glad for it, and for the children," — Peggy had ceased saying "childer," and many other Irish words, — "but sweet peas and pinks always bring back the past to my heart. I had scores o' twigs stuck

up in my little garden, and round each one I'd
plant a ring o' sweet-peas; and they'd climb
up and cling to the twig and blossom till
they'd fall over with their own weight. And
the pinks, too, how Mammy Honey used to
love them!"

"Are the pinks and sweet-peas all there
now, and nobody to love them, mammy?"
asked little Marion.

"I don't know, darlin', but I think they're
all dead," replied Peggy.

"Is every body dead there?" she asked
again, leaning on Peggy's shoulder, and strok-
ing her cheek tenderly, as she always did when
she saw a shadow pass over her face.

"No, darlin', I hope not," answered Peggy,
lifting the child to her knee and resting her
cheek on the bright little head.

"Then why don't we go there, and plant the
peas and pinks again? Can we go some time,
mammy?"

"Perhaps, darlin', if God bids us; but we
can't tell. We've a far finer home here."

"No, Marion," said Miss Grey, "I can't

spare your mammy. What would blind Patty do if she did not visit her and read to her? And how would old Molly keep her knitting women quiet for an hour to hear about Christ, if mammy was not there to give them yarn and tea, and to get their love? I can't spare mammy when I'm sick, and tired and lonely. There's nobody in the world loves her as much as I do; and nobody shall ever have her who doesn't love her."

The children had heard stories of Killy-rooke, and of Mammy Honey, and of Paddy Mannon, but never of John. They looked on the place as a paradise of cows and calves, of hens and chickens.

" Go now to your bedroom, and sing your dolls to sleep, darlin's, till I call you," said Peggy.

When they were gone, she said in a low tone to Miss Grey, " For ten days I've been sore hindered in my prayers by Satan, o' whom I'm greatly afeared. Perhaps I've sinned, for I've long ceased to pray that I might go back to die in my own cottage. I've

looked on all of arth as lost to me, only for the
good I'd do, and I've prayed only for John's
soul, and not that he might be brought back
repinting and seek me out, and be his old self
again. O' late, when I'd be on my knees, a
question would rise, 'Can ye forgive as ye
hope to be forgiven?' And I'd say, 'Yea,
Lord.' Then I'd ask my heart, 'Could I feed
her that destroyed my peace war she hungry,
and give her a drink war she thirsty?' And
again I said, 'Yea, Lord.' Then came the
question, 'Could ye go back to yer home and
be the same lovin', true wife, and forget the
past, if God bid ye?' And the very thought
put me all a tremble. If I should but see
John's face I'd fall dead at his feet. And I
couldn't say 'yes,' to that. So I've an unbroken will yet left in me."

"I would never let you do that after the ill
usage you have had," said Miss Grey.

"Ah, dear lady, but think what a little I've
been called to bear. Scarce a harsh word
from one but the poor blind Papists over the
road, till I got this piercing o' my heart that

drove me here. And mind what Jesus Himself suffered. He war abused and insulted by the great, and deserted even by His followers that he had chosen out o' the world, that He loved with an everlasting love. And yet hear Him on the cross : 'Father, forgive them, for they know not what they do.' ''

" Well, I shall not be anxious till I hear that you're sent for — which will never be. For if ever that man repents, he will be ashamed to ask you back,'' said Miss Grey.

" I had a bit o' a dramo last night,'' said Peggy. " I thought I was standin' in a garden, when I heerd a soft voice call my name as Mary at the sepulchre ; and like her I turned me about and said, ' Master.' There stood the Master Himself, and He had my poor wanderer fast by the hand, holding him up. I took the other hand in mine, and forgot we'd ever been estranged, and as the Blessed One left us I saw His footprints like shinin' silver, and in striving to follow in His steps and to lead the wanderer on, I woke. For a little time I was troubled thinking o' the past, but before the light came in at the window the great peace was back again in my soul, and I've not thought o' the drame since till the little lambie asked, 'Can't we go there and plant the flowers again?'"

"Misthress Sheehan," said Miss Grey, "do you not think you are doing far more for the suffering here than you could do — even if all was well in your own home, — cooped up in that little hamlet among those debased Papists who will not hear you read or listen to your advice?"

"Well, perhaps, ma'am, but I can't tell. I made a happy home there, and strove to do a little outside for friend and foe. Killyrooke is a small place, but it's full o' souls; and ye can never know how Mammy Honey loved them and longed for their salvation."

The conversation might have gone on longer, but for a bustle and a sound of laughter in the hall outside the chamber door. After tapping, two maids, redolent with smiles and blushes, appeared together. Each was ambitious to tell the news first.

16

" Well, what's this trifling about now ? " asked Miss Grey, without a smile.

" Please, ma'am," they both said in a breath.

" Susan," said the lady, " be quiet, and let Mary tell what's going on."

" Please, ma'am, yon queer dressed farm-man, — the little man in the big clothes, — is come again to see Misthress Sheehan. When I opened the door at his ringin', he was sitting on the steps untying his wooden-soled brogues, and he took them in his hand and walked into the passage in his stockin's. He told us to say to Misthress Sheehan that ' one Paddy Mannon was wantin' to spake with her.' "

Miss Grey glanced at Peggy, whose face was as white as marble, and asked, " Shall the man come up ? "

" Yes, and plaze, dear lady, tarry ye too, for I'm just faintin' at thought o' what has brought him. May be his masther's dead."

" Oh, no fear of that," said Miss Grey, almost sarcastically. " This ridiculous fellow has taken the journey, as he did before, merely to see you. Here he is."

Paddy, with his shoes in one hand and his staff and bundle in the other, came a step or two into the room, very shyly; but catching a glimpse of his mistress in her black dress and her muslin cap, he was so overawed by her grandeur, that he stepped back again into the passage. Miss Grey said, "Come in," but it was not till she rose and opened the door that he ventured to do so. Then he exclaimed, in wonder, "I'd niver a knowed ye, dear. How white yer hair is gettin' with the throuble, and how grand ye look in the fine clothes! Sure, ye're dressed like Misthress Murray herself."

"Paddy," asked Peggy, in a tremulous tone, " is all well with ye?"

"'Dade it is, misthress, and better too!" exclaimed Paddy.

"Lay down yer stick and give me yer hand, my poor friend," she said.

This done, Paddy's sudden reserve gave way, and he said, looking first at one of his listeners and then at the other, "I've fine news to till ye. The O'Gormans is all dead and in the workhouse, and their cottage burned. We've been convarted at Daisy Farm, and we've confissed our sins, and re-pinted o' the same, and got back into the church again, and walked into the pew by the side o' Mr. Murray, after gettin' lave of Elder Peter, and you one's gone off to work in the mills, and the clay floor's all scraped by thim two hands" — which he held up, — "and the flax wheel scoured with soap and sand in the lough, and the flax that was on it burnt up, and the ashes thrown into the dipths of the sea, and the vines all trimmed up, and flowers growin', and a pot o' scarlets, sint by his river-ence, in the little glass windy, and two young deers, a gift from the hall, and a sittin' hin with fourteen fine eggs under her, and himself, the masther, all dressed in his bist clothes sittin' waitin' to see ye back, and I'm sint for ye."

Paddy scarcely took breath during this speech, which he delivered in such an excited manner as to lead Miss Grey to think him crazy. But by degrees, and after many ques-tions, Peggy got the whole story out of him.

" And what message did Mr. Murray send by ye, Paddy ? " she asked.

" He bid ye come back," replied Paddy ; " but here's a letter from Mr. Murray himself to Miss Grey. But I it was that complated the work, though I never told it afore. I gave Kitty Connors half my last quarter's wages to fill yon one's head with the fine time they'd have at the new mill where herself was goin' to work, and to take her over there to a dance they had afore the openin'. They war gone a week, and it was one long holiday to them, and life at the cottage looked dull beside it. So I it was that did, in the latter end, what the dead misthress said I'd do — do ye mind ? "

" Yes, Paddy, I mind, but I'm bewildered entirely now, and can not think. But why, when yer masther has caused all this sorrow — look at my white hair, and me only at middle life — if he has repinted, why didn't he come himself instead of sending ye ? "

" Because for two reasons. The first was, he was afeared·o' Miss Grey, the fine lady ;

and the sicond was that I wouldn't suffer him, but was detarmined to come mysilf, as I promised ye. Didn't yersilf till me whiniver I see my masther broke down and humbled, to come after ye mysilf?"

"Yes, Paddy, but I little dramed it would take four long years to bring him back to his sinses," replied Peggy.

"She can never go back," cried Miss Grey. "Your master does not deserve such a wife. And how could she ever live in that crazy old shieling, after passing four years amid such comforts as these?"

"O, dear heart, the comforts would niver cost me a thought," replied Peggy. "I'm bound to ye by a thousand cords o' love; but if I could know the great Masther's will I'd do it."

"But, Misthress Sheehan," said the lady, "think of the children; but for you I should never have taken this responsibility. I can leave them nothing, as this property all goes to nephews at my death. But if you remain, you can fit them to earn their bread in some respectable way. Otherwise, they will be cast on the world when I am gone."

"Dear lady," cried Peggy, "when I tuk the lambies to my heart it was for my own. I will niver cast them off. When I go, they will go too."

"You may go now, my good man," said Miss Grey, "and get your dinner at an inn. Then, if you are not too tired, you can walk about and look in the shop windows till bedtime. Here are two crowns to pay for your dinner and your lodging. You can come back to see Misthress Sheehan to-morrow."

Paddy drew his hand behind him as far as possible from the proffered silver.

"I'm not a poor man, lady!" he cried, raising his head till it came almost above the collar of his coat. "I'm a man as can command my own price, and gets thirty-five shillings a quarter! I'm not a child, to accept pence, but a man, with all the money I nades, and plinty to spare to the poor ones. And more nor that, ma'am," said Paddy, with a low bow, "if it's iver yer fortun' to walk from Killy-

rooke to this city, ye'll be glad enough o' a
bed, 'stead o' starin' in at shop windows! If I
once gets into a bed at the inn I'll bide in it a
week. I came after my misthress, and **not**
seekin' shows."

When Peggy had Paddy alone **the** next day,
she said to him, "I can not go back with ye,
poor, faithful boy. Ye see how I'm fixed here
with the little ones; I could not leave them,
nor yet could I take them with me without yer
masther's lave. Tell him, Paddy, I've long
ago forgiven him, and that I've been just sure
that God would, sooner or later, bring him to
Himself, and let me take him to Mammy
Honey at last. But tell him that after all that
has passed, himself, and not ye, ought to take
me back to my home, that my neighbors may
see that he desires me there, **and** loves me
still. And tell him, Paddy, that o' all the fine
things I've seen here there's nothing **so** beautiful to **me as** my own little cottage, and that I
can return and be the same faithful wife as I
iver was. And tell him that the peace o' God
still 'bides **with my sperit,** and that through all

my sorrow the lovin' Master has been iver at my side, — that I almost see Him by me now. And O, Paddy, don't ye be so plased about yer poor masther's bein' convarted as to forget that ye too have a soul, and that it's as worth savin' as his. Remember all this, Paddy, if I shouldn't see ye agin alone."

Notwithstanding Paddy's noble independence, he consented to stay three or four days at an inn at Miss Grey's expense. He also descended so far from his dignity as to yield the controversy he had kept up with the postchaise and horses, and to compromise matters by riding home with Barney, the wagoner. But he was sorely humbled by the result of his mission. He had gone forth proud and boastful, taking to himself all the honor of the good work at the cottage, and saying, " There's just but only one man on the round arth that can bring the jewel back, and that man's mysilf — Paddy Mannon. And look out for the day ye see us retarnin' together triumphant to Killyrooke!" Poor, crestfallen Paddy! All he had gained personally by his long tramp was sore disappointment, deep mortification and aching limbs.

When he reached "the turn of the road" where the wagoner set him down, he seated himself on a pile of stones, saying, resolutely, "Now, Paddy Marmon, sit here till ye die, afore ye enter Killyrooke alone. My heart's broke in my bussum; yis, tin times broker nor it war the day I laid my jewel Meg in the grave, intirely. Here I'll 'bide and die o' ather hunger or starvation. And then the ministher, and Elder Peter, and the miserable masther will cry tears above me, and say, 'There war a fine, faithful lad!' Farewell to ye, ilegant green arth and blue skies; farewell, craturs I've fed and housed so tinder; farewell, Masther John, that's been the dith o' poor Paddy. Dig me a grave beside Meg, and let me hide mysilf in it afore any body in Killyrooke will taunt me with the disgrace o' comin' back alone, and nobody with me! These is the last words o' Paddy Mannon, late of Killyrooke, parish o' Cloynmally, county Connaught, Ireland."

The first twinge of hunger, — the seat of that malady being the most sensitive part of Paddy's system, — drove all sentimentalism out of him; and about an hour after he had uttered his " last words," he took up his stick and bundle and made his way to Cloynmally, and delivered Miss Grey's letter to Mr. Murray. That gentleman saw no cause for such deep gloom as Paddy's, and told him that his mistress would, doubtless, be at home in a fortnight, with the two little girls.

Paddy shook his head mournfully, and said, " Ye've not seen you Miss Grey, that has the kapin' of her. To hear her talk, ye'd think the worst evil that could befall a woman was to have a husband at all. She ivident hates the whole nation of men, and was but barely civil, aven to mysilf. I'll niver face Masther John with the bad news."

Mr. Murray offered to go home with him, as Miss Grey's letter was for his master's benefit, and must be read to him. It was like the sur-

geon's lance, severe, but potent; and both decided that, **painful as it would be,** John him-
self must go for **Peggy**.

CHAPTER XXII.

A HAPPY " HOME—BRINGING."

IT was true, as Paddy had stated, that Miss Grey was no admirer of " the nation of men." She had seen poor specimens in her own family, two sisters having married men who spent their money and then broke their hearts. So she had steeled her own heart against the sex, even in her charities.

But the deep humility of poor John, and the solemn awe that marked his face and his voice, when he came for Peggy, touched her, so that the rebuke and the advice she had in store for him were all forgotten when they met. She soon ceased to think of him as the vile wretch she had almost hated, and found herself listening with tearful eye to the simple tale of his wanderings and of his conversion to God. She now acknowledged him as a

brother, and spoke of him as " poor Sheehan,"
and not as " that miserable man." She became so softened towards him that, great as
was the sacrifice, she consented cheerfully to
Peggy's departure. She promised to provide
for the little girls under her charge until they
should be able to take care of themselves.
Not to make the change too great from the
pleasant chambers where they now lived, she
insisted on sending to Killyrooke a load of
furniture, bedding, books and toys by Barney's
wagon.

" Sheehan," she said, before parting with
the family, " as you are not a poor man, I'm
going to make a request that may seem
strange to you. I don't think that cottage of
yours is good enough for such a wife as you
have. You must add a room to it, and lay a
board floor there, and put a glass window in
every room. I shall send the ' asylum ' carpet
for the new room, and the table, and the
chairs ; and do you make Misthress Sheehan
as comfortable as possible, and see that the
little girls help her in every way they can."

John expressed his gratitude, and promised to make the improvements she suggested. But Peggy's pale face flushed as she said, —

"But, dear Miss Grey, I'm afeared about the carpet. Perhaps the poor things that I'm hopin' to benefit there might think me proud, and so grow invious; and I dar'n't do any thing to drive them from me. I've great hope I'll do them good, and so must be just one o' themselves still."

"Don't tell me that!" cried Miss Grey. "I know more of human nature than you do, Mistress Shechan, and I know that the ignorant take instruction more kindly from superiors than from equals or inferiors. And, although you were not a whit above themselves, they'd listen to you with more respect in your black dress and your muslin cap than in the old linsey-woolsey and cotton. When the carpet is laid, and the new windows put in, there's no doubt you will have admirers enough. And those who come to gaze will stay to listen."

"But, ma'am, there's not a carpet in the

town only at the ' Hall,' and the priest's, and the minister's. Mrs. Murray has but one, — in her best parlor," said Peggy.

" Well, you deserve as good a carpet as Mrs. Murray, and I shall not let you go till you promise to put it down," said Miss Grey.

Peggy consented, but not without some fears for her influence in Killyrooke.

" And when ye send me garments to make for the little maids," she said, " ye'll remember that they'll be just poor people's children, and not send things too fine, to make themselves vain or others invious."

" Certainly, Mistress Sheehan, it is all important that they are taught their position now. Keep them always in neat pinafores at school, and in plain, comfortable dresses and hats at church. Train, and feed, and dress them as if they were really your children, and I will answer for their being good women," said Miss Grey.

" Ay, dear Miss Grey, they are the makin's o' lovely women by natur'," said Peggy, " and the comfort they have been to me in my sorrow is wonderful. I've just the love o' a mother to them, and many the time I've thought that all that's been allowed to come on me might yet work out for double good to them and to us."

"I believe," said Miss Grey, "you were truly sent here to school — to be fitted for future work. You have been a faithful learner. I don't believe your old neighbors will know you as the shy woman they knew four years ago. Do you remember how you suffered when my poor mother insisted on your reading the Bible aloud to her? Now you can read to half a dozen without trembling, or spelling, either."

Peggy smiled, and replied, " Yes, and not stop at the long words, ather, as I did then. I wonder ivery day how iver ye bore with my shy, stupid ways in thim days, and shall strive to return yer kindness by makin' good use o' the tachin' I've got in this blissed home. And if sickness or sorrow come to ye, remem-

ber ye've always a sarvant to bid to yer side in
me, — day or night, ma'am."

When arrangements were being made for
the journey, Peggy begged to go back in Barney's wagon, as she should feel easier there
than if crowded up among strangers. Beside
that, she wanted to see the kind man again,
and to tell him that the Providence he had
called " luck " had made all bright with her,
as he had prophesied.

As Miss Grey declined the honor of having
Barney's establishment drawn up before her
door to receive four passengers, he was ordered to take the furniture and luggage; and
the family walked on and seated themselves in
his high wagon, when he arrived at the inn
where he always put up.

The greeting between Barney and Peggy
was like that of old friends, and as soon as
they had cleared the stones of the city streets,
Peggy introduced John and the children to
him, and asked very kindly after his wife, in
whose sorrows she had felt so much sympathy.

"O, she's well," he replied. "Ye mind I was telling ye yon day what a sore heart she had about the little fellows we buried, and how taken up she war with yon Methodises in our town?"

"Yes."

"Well, when I returned home after discharging ye at the lady's door, I told her all about ye and yer throubles — the cause o' which I didn't know. I told her what ye said about 'luck' bein' the hand o' God, and about the great peace ye'd got in yer own soul, and the good advice ye gave me about my soul And what does my wife do but go tell it all to the Methodis' lader, and the next meetin' they had, they all fell to prayin' for ye, and to givin' thanks for the marcy o' God to ye in yer sorrow. They called ye right out by name, and first one prayed that yer sorrow, whatever it was, might work for yer glory, and then another that yer last days might be yer usefulest and happiest days. If ye'd been one o' thimsilves, dear heart, they couldn't made more noise about it," said Barney, who

had put the reins in John's hand, that he
might turn round and converse with Peggy.

"I am just one of themselves, dear man,"
she replied. "All who love the Lord are just
one body, and Christ is our head. When ye
go back, tell them dear saints that the Lord
has taken away my grief, and that I'm now
blessed with two darlin' little maids as war
motherless afore, and that He has given me
such a power o' courage that I can speak, and
read, and sing to as many neighbor-women as
will listen to me, about Christ. But, greater
nor all, I've got the blessings o' salvation for
my husband, the son o' the holy woman I told
ye of; and we too are now to strive for like
mercy for our neighbors. And tell me now,
how is it with yer own soul?"

"Poor enough," replied Barney, "as far as
being convarted goes. The wife talks much
like yersilf, and has joined herself to thim
Methodises, and is sore worried about me.
She confisses that I'm another man from the
one o' past days; for I've niver swore an oath
since the day I promised ye I wouldn't, and

I'm strivin' not to hate the Papists ; but that's harder nor givin' up the swarin'. I'm doin' all in my power to be a Christian, such as will suit my wife ; for beside wantin' to go to heaven at last, I'd be glad to make her happy, for she's had a sore life o't, poor thing, one way and another. But for all my tryin' it's a small headway I make, this far."

"Then stop tryin' to quit this and to do that, dear man," said Peggy. "What would ye say to a wagoner that was trying to make his journey by whippin' dead horses ? "

"I'd say he war a fool, intirely," replied the wagoner.

"And yet ye're doing just that same. Ye're dead in trespasses and sins, and ye're whipping up and cheerin' on yer dead heart and dead will, hopin' they'll get ye to heaven by-and-by. Now quit this folly, and in yer dead and helpless state go to Christ for life. It's by Him, and not by our dead selves, that we make this journey, or else we'll fall by the road and perish. Now if one promise made to me has helped ye to keep from open sin, may be another will help ye **to** Christ. Will ye cease striving to make yersilf holy, and go **to** Him just as **ye are, and** beg for **a** share in His holiness? He has plenty **o' it to** divide **among us all,** and then have **perfect** holiness left. **Will ye** go to him thus, and **not insult** Him **by expectin' to** get **credit for** not **profaning** His holy name, and **the** like wickedness ? "

" I will," said Barney, in a subdued tone.

" And give **my** love to **yer** wife, and all the Methodises, and tell them the Lord heard them for me. Perhaps the times I've been lifted above all arth, and felt like them **that** was taken **on to the mount** with himself and saw His glory, **was** just when **they was plead-in'** for me. **It's** a short road **that's** between them that's separated, when that road **lies past** the mercy-seat."

John, who had **many** times taken **the reins** in his left hand while he wiped his tears **away with** the right, **turned round now and asked Peggy,** " Couldn't **ye sing yon hymn o' Charles Wesley's to the good man ? "**

" Ay, if he'd like," said **Peggy,** " and little

Bessie may put in with her swate voice, too, for she's larned it lovely."

And they sang, in clear, sweet tones, —

> " Depth of mercy ! can there be
> Mercy still reserved for me ?
> Can my God his wrath forbear,
> Me the chief of sinners spare ? "

Before Peggy's departure from her house, Miss Grey had written to Mr. Murray asking him to receive her at the " turn o' the road," and while they were lumbering on in Barney's wagon, talking and singing, Paddy was waiting by the heap of stones where he had uttered his " last words " several days before, with the donkey wagon. When they came in sight, he, in true oriental style, lifted up his voice and wept. He took Peggy and the little girls out of the wagon in his arms, and in his foolish joy attempted to do the same for John ; but his love couldn't work miracles. After an affectionate farewell to Barney, Peggy was surprised to see Mr. Murray standing near them.

With a kind greeting, he said, " Mrs. Murray sends me to bring you all to her for a cup of tea, and then you can walk to the cottage in the evening."

This was an act of condescension which brought blushes to Peggy's cheek, but noticing how Paddy's countenance fell, she was going to decline the invitation, when Mr. Murray said, —

"And Paddy must come back when he's taken home his load and put up the donkey. Kate and Tim will be glad if he'll join them at a cup of tea in the kitchen."

Paddy's face was radiant with smiles, and bowing almost to the ground, he exclaimed, "Yer riverence is a jintleman, and I'll be back in less nor an hour — as soon as I've milked, and dacented myself up fit for the honor, in my bist shute."

A smile passed over the faces of the little group, and thus encouraged, Paddy caught off his old hat, and striking a heroic attitude, spoke the following " varses " *impromptu:*

> " When from her home the misthress wint,
> Poor Paddy howled a loud lamint ;
> And all the time she war away,
> She sarved a lady named Miss Grey.

" And in thim four long, cruel years
Paddy shed buckets full of tears;
His cheeks grew thin, his hair grew gray,
His sinses well nigh flew away.

" So often Paddy told his beads,
He wore thim down to mustard seeds;
He nather laughed, nor ate, nor slipt,
But howled, and sighed, and groaned, and wipt.

" But now the storm is passed away,
The misthress comes again to-day,
Long shine the sun on Daisy Farm !
And keep the cottage safe from harm.

" Here Paddy throws his beads away,
And from the misthress larns to pray ;
No more a Papist lad he'll be,
But Protestant, as all shall see."

And with this pledge he took aim and threw his beads as far as he could down the road, and then hastened home with his load, that he might prepare for his return to the parsonage.

When the moon rose high, shedding a silver light over the landscape, and giving a charm even to the poor cottages on the road, the little family, accompanied by their faithful minister, walked from Cloynmally to the cottage. John carried the eldest child in his arms, while Paddy brought up the rear with the other on his shoulder, galloping and occasionally neighing like a horse for her amusement.

When the neighbors saw a light twinkling from the cottage window, and heard the voice of prayer and praise ascending on the still air, they knew that old things had passed away, and that all things had become new there.

CHAPTER XXIII.

THE NEW LIFE AT DAISY FARM.

TO the little girls, who had rarely seen a green field, Killyrooke, with its acres of flax and barley, was like a picture of fairyland. The low, rude cottage was a wonder to them, and the flowers and vines about it were a source of perfect delight. The greatest charm of the place, however, was the "life" it contained. They were allowed to stroke the necks of Silverhorn and the Maid of Longford, to feed the calf and the lambs with meal from their own hands, and to ride on the donkey's back.

Before they had been many days at Daisy Farm they went to the mill with Paddy, seated on the bag of barley in the donkey-cart, and during the ride were entertained with marvelous stories and wild Irish songs. When

John asked Marion which of all his " craturs "
she liked best, the deer, or the calf, or the
lambs, or the cows, or the donkey, she replied,
innocently, " Oh, I like the funny, kind man
the best of them all, — dear Paddy Mannon."
And from the hour of their arrival at the cottage, Paddy Mannon became the nurse, the
patron and the hero of the children. He
would not go to mill or to market without
them, and insisted that the cows stood more
quietly while he was milking " if the small
bit girlies were aside thim with their soft
voices."

He soon grew so proud of them that he
overcame his fear of apostasy and of Father
Clakey, and went to the Presbyterian church
with the family, to hear what people said
about the little new-comers after service.

When Peggy began life again at the cottage,
her Bible was kept open on a little table in
her kitchen. She told her neighbors, who
dropped in one by one to welcome her back,
that she should read aloud from it every day
for an hour before sunset; and that if any

among them wished to hear the Word of the Lord they might come with their knitting at that time. If they had not yarn, she offered to supply them; and also to set up stockings for such as were not knitters, and to teach them to shape and to narrow them off.

As Miss Grey had predicted, the simple people looked on Peggy in her new attire and with her new confidence, as a lady who had seen the world, and all questions were soon referred to her for settlement. It was marvelous to see the errands which were made to the cottage just before sunset by such as were too timid to accept her invitations. One came to borrow a measure of meal or a few eggs, another to ask what would cure the toothache, and a third to inquire for the health of the two little girls; and once there, they remained to hear Peggy read. Thus, from beginning the readings with John, Paddy and the children, she soon had a dozen listeners. Sometimes they would ask her questions, which gave her opportunity to explain the passages she read — which were usually from the life

and the teachings of Jesus. She had learned
many sweet hymns, with tunes new to them,
to which they listened with great pleasure,
and not a few of them began to long for an
interest in the love which had upheld their
neighbor in her sorrows, and which now added
such charms to her simple life.

During these readings, John always sat with
his face buried in his hands, as if in prayer.
His manner was ever marked with the deepest
solemnity, like that of one who felt his own
weakness and God's power; who walked under
His eye, and feared by one trifling word to
grieve Him who had forgiven so much. He
said little; but the crops, and the " craturs,"
and all he had, were laid on the altar of the
Lord, and he was ready, at any hour of the
day or night, " to lend a helping hand in work
or in sickness to any neighbor who would con-
descend to accept his help." The proud
Pharisee was humbled in the dust, and could
barely hope that he was forgiven; he could
not rejoice in hope, and he never stood by
Peggy on the mount. Like Thomas, he

doubted, but like him, also. he could cry,
at times, " My Lord and my God." The
solemnity of eternity was impressed on his
countenance, and his old good-natured smile
had given way to a grave and thoughtful expression. His neighbors were amazed, and
watched in vain for his old boasting. He was
no longer " John Sheehan, the thriftiest farmer and the moralest Christian in Killyrooke,
giving all men their dues and feeding the
nady," but confessed himself to be " the chief
of sinners."

When Peggy strove to encourage and
strengthen his hope, she would sometimes
ask, —

> " Why should the children of a King
> Go mourning all their days ? "

" Ah, Peggy, jewel," he would reply, " what
right have I to rejoice like other saved ones ?
It is joy enough for me that I'm not in
despair ; that I've a hope o' heaven at last.
How could I be smilin' and merry, that has
crucified the Lord afresh, and put Him to an
open shame ? The wounds I gave to Him and

to ye, darlin', is iver afore my eyes, as well as
the marcy that has forgiven me. So I can
niver turn from this sight to look after what
others call joy. My joy and my crown is to
lie in the dust and cry 'Unclane, unclane,' and
to tarn from my pollution to His holiness.
With that afore me, I'm afeared to open my
lips lest I sin against God again. If I kape
near to Him and to ye I'm safe and paceful,
and that's all I'll ask till I see Him as He
is."

And yet John was just as diligent in business as when his thoughts were all centered
in the farm. He at once set himself to enlarg-
ing and repairing the cottage, a work requir-
ing little skill or little money. He and
Paddy laid the stone for the new room, and
filled the crevices with a clay mortar of their
own mixing. When this was done, the joiner
from Cloynmally came with boards and tools
to lay the floor, and to put in three new
windows,—for even Paddy was to have one
in his loft, as Miss Grey had ordered; and
over this luxury he was so jubilant that he

forgave her for being "an inimy to the whole male sict."

When all was done, John and Peggy spent days in untangling "the dear vines about Mammy Honey's window," and training them round the corner so as "to hide up the new part, which had no home look," as Peggy said. Then the carpet was laid, the chairs, and tables, and pictures which Miss Grey had sent were put into the new room. All Killyrooke came to admire, and to wonder "at the luck which had come to the mistress out of her great sorrow."

Into this little parlor the Bible and hymn-book were now removed, and here Peggy and the children sat when the labors of the cottage were over, to knit, and sew, and read; and it was into this room that the sunset visitors were hereafter to be ushered.

The lady at the Hall became deeply interested in Peggy's effort to improve her careless neighbors. She came in her carriage to visit her, and to hear the story of the little girls and of all Miss Grey's kindness. She expressed great pleasure in the success of the sunset reading and the knitting-school, and promised to send down yarn for all the little girls who would learn to knit their own stockings. " His reverence is a little stirred up, my good Peggy," she said, " about the reading. Believing, as he does, that the common people, — the ignorant, I mean, — are injured by hearing what they cannot understand, he feels that he ought to forbid the cottagers coming to you so much, and yet he knows your kindness, and is pained to interfere with you. Could you not teach these people to knit, and to be virtuous and peaceable, without reading the Bible to them, and thus not wrong the poor man, whose heart is nearly broken with the wild creatures? If not, I fear the bishop will bid him break up the ' teachings.' "

Peggy's first impulse was to tell the Catholic lady that she had no master but Christ, and that she should pay no heed either to priest or bishop. But she knew this would deprive her of all opportunity of doing the poor women good. So she wisely replied, " I could repate varses, and give advice, and sing hymns to them, my lady, without opening the lids o' my book, if that's what troubles Father Clakey."

"Do so, then, my good woman, and I will promise you shall not be interfered with," said the lady. "If you need yarn or cloth for the work, send to me; and come to the Hall now and then with your report. I will stand between you and Father Clakey in the matter."

The honor of this visit, and the memory of the fine carriage and bay horses with liveried men halting before the cottage, raised Peggy not a little in the esteem of her neighbors. They felt it a great honor to know one whom the lady of the Hall had deigned to visit. Paddy, although he saw the fine equipage frequently on the road, was so awe-stricken by its standing before the cottage door, that he ran into the cow-house and hid himself in the loft till it was gone.

Peggy sat down at her little table, and taking up her hymn-book, began to select such portions as **should** comprise **the** whole gospel.

She strove on that evening **to impress the minds of her** visitors with the sinfulness **of** their own hearts, and drew out their ideas **on the** subject. Then she sang the hymn be-ginning, —

> " How sad our state by nature is,
>   Our sin how deep its stain!
> And Satan binds our captive minds
>   Fast in his slavish chain."

After explaining to them their own helpless-ness, while thus exposed to God's wrath for having broken His laws, she told them how vain were all their penances, as well as their prayers to the Virgin and saints, which only **robbed** God of His glory. Then in her simple **way** she held **up** Jesus as the friend **and** lover of the poor, till tears fell from the eyes of her listeners, and some of them asked, " Why doesn't Father Clakey **tell us** all this ? "

When the hour was over, and the knit-ting-needles were passed through the ball to

be put away, the guests rose and stood while
Peggy and the little girls sang, —

> " Alas, and did my Saviour bleed,
>   And did my Sovereign die?
>   Would He devote that sacred head
>   For such a worm as I ? "

Although this effort of the loving creature
was anything but agreeable to the priest, and
he scolded well out of doors about it, he never
actually forbade the women to go to the cottage, but satisfied his conscience by charging
them not to listen to heresy there.

And thus, amid home cares, — which with
her had become religious duties, — and efforts
for the salvation of others, the years slipped
by far more peacefully and happily than before
" the great sorrow." John was the soul of
love and tenderness, and Paddy outdid himself in loyalty and attention.

The little maids, now strong, sensible children, went to a school in Cloynmally, which
was kept by a good sister of Elder Peter, who,
unlike him, was of a most gentle spirit.
When the weather was fine they walked,

carrying their dinner in a small wooden
bucket. When it stormed, they were driven
over by Paddy in the donkey-cart, being entertained on the way with marvelous tales of
his travels in the moon, and his sailing and
fishing in the clouds, and with merry, harmless old Irish ballads. So charming were
these rides, with such company, that they both
longed for storms.

CHAPTER XXIV.

THE ENEMY AGAIN.

WHEN Bessie and Marion were about eight and ten years old, there was to be a fair and horse-race a few miles from the cottage. The night before the races, Peggy was roused from a quiet sleep by a peal of loud laughter, which rang out wildly on the midnight air, causing her to spring from her pillow as if an arrow had .pierced her. She laid her hand on her heart to still its beating, but in vain. A company of merry-makers tramped by the cottage, singing snatches of wild songs, and chatting and shouting to each other. She was wondering why the noise should have startled her so painfully, and why she felt so wretched, when the same shrill laughter broke forth again, almost beneath her window. Then, fully awake, she knew the unhallowed voice that had **so often** rung through the low rooms of the cottage. It was **hers** who had broken **its peace.**

The light from half a dozen lanterns **flashed for a** moment across the wall, **and then the** tramping of feet **and** the **humming of voices** gradually died away in the distance. Anguish unknown since the day she first returned to her home to find an intruder there, rushed like an overwhelming billow across her heart, and seemed to swallow her **up.** She sank helplessly into a chair, and felt for a moment as if all were again lost to her. The tempter appeared for a season, and whispered that God had forgotten to be gracious, and that her enemy would yet triumph over her.

But in a moment she knew whence these suggestions came, and **she** whispered, " **No, Satan,** ye cannot beguile me !

> " ' The soul that on Jesus has leaned for repose,
>   He will not, He will not desert to His foes;
>   That soul, though all hell should endeavor to shake,
>   He'll never, no, never, no, never forsake.' "

And lifting her hands and her eyes, she

said, with a smile, "'Thou wilt keep them in
perfect peace whose minds are stayed on
Thee;' and if ever poor woman was helped to
stay herself on God, Peggy Sheehan has
been."

And again " the great peace" came over her
soul, and she was lifted above all her fears.
She returned to her pillow, and like a child
under the mother's watchful eye, fell asleep,
and only woke in time to see the sun rise over
the bog. The sudden terror of the night had
left no impression on her mind, save that of
calmness and peace, and she went about her
lowly duties in the kitchen and dairy, singing
with a thankful spirit.

The races brought a great many strangers to
the neighborhood. Some of these were very
rough characters, and Peggy resolved to keep
the little girls at home from school for a few
days, till the road should be clear of them.
They employed the first holiday in stringing
thorn-berries on long threads to decorate the
horns of the cows, and the necks of the deer
and lambs. When Bessie wearied of this she

went into the cottage to her knitting, leaving Marion outside the hedge **alone.** When **supper was** ready, the little one **came** in with a gilt chain suspended from her neck, attached **to which** was a small locket, containing, under a glass, a bunch of miniature flowers, — a pretty little trifle, such as was to be bought at the booths for a shilling.

"O, look, mammy!" she said, "see **my** present, and I've got sugar plums, too."

"**Poor** Paddy wastes his money to plaze ye, little dear," said Peggy, looking with interest at the bauble.

"O, no, it was **not Paddy gave it me,**" cried the child. "It was a pretty lady that says you're not my mother. But you're a dear mammy, and I love you more than she, if your cheeks arn't red. I love pale cheeks and gray hair best." And the innocent child climbed to Peggy's knee, and covered **her** with kisses as she sat at the table.

"**Her** mother can never surely have found us out, poor thing! I'd **never** a thought she war living," exclaimed Peggy.

"Never," replied John. "It's no mother of hers, but mayhap some evil-disposed body that would be staling her for her beauty or her clothes. How looked she, darlin'? War she a beggar-woman?"

"Oh, no, she was a bit of a lady, or nigh to a lady. She had red cheeks, and roses in her hat, and I kissed her because she gave me this and the sugar plums. She said I must hate Paddy Mannon, poor Paddy."

"No, darling," replied Peggy, "ye must love him. He's kind and good; and if he war not, ye must niver hate him. God bids us love aven our inimies, ye know. If iver ye see this woman more, Marion, do ye run into the cottage at once, lest she run off with ye, and break my heart."

That horrid peal of laughter was recalled to Peggy's mind, and she had little doubt but her old tormentor was in the neighborhood, and had spoken thus to Marion simply to annoy her. She was sure Nan did not want the child, and if she had believed otherwise her faith was too strong that day to be shaken.

Had a host encamped against the cottage, she would have dwelt in peace.

After supper the children led Peggy out to see how they had dressed the cows, deer and lambs with haw-berries. As they came near the cow-house they heard sobs, and looking in, saw Paddy Mannon standing in a corner, with his face pressed close to the wall, weeping bitterly.

"What can ail ye, boy?" asked Peggy in surprise; for Paddy was one of those fortunate mortals who seem exempt from the sorrows of life, — who, having nothing, can lose nothing.

He turned round and replied, "Send the small things into the cottage, and thin if ye'll promise not to turn white and scare me, I'll tell ye what a evil has come to us."

When they were alone he continued, "I had a visit from Nan, and she bid me get the tin pounds I told ye on, or she'd walk into the cottage. I war just quite brave at first, and I told her it war mysilf hired her friend to woo her off, and I threatened her with the magistrate, and the like. And didn't she up and

bate the ears near off my face because I'd not
git her the tin pounds to spend at the fair?
Yerself knows, misthress dear, there's not a
live man as has more respect for woman nor
mysilf; that is whin she kapes in her own
sphare; but when she laves spinnin' and
milkin', and goes aboot chastisin' noble men
as was made to be the head and ruler o' her,
then I'm more afeared o' her, than o' the very
ghosts thimselves! I'll not go out o' doors for
a year, lest the boys taunts me with this blow I
got from a woman. 'Dade, my head tings now
like the church bells with the weight o' her
hand;" and Paddy wept afresh at the thought
of his humiliation.

"Quit yer cryin', poor lad, and never tell a
mortal that ye saw her at all," said Peggy.
"I'm not afeared o' the poor thing; I could
minister to her war she sick, or an hungered,
or athirst, or aven in prison."

"Ah, so could I," cried Paddy, smiling
through his tears, "if I could but once see
her in prison, — that's the place for her!"

"God," said Peggy, "is stronger nor all the

powers o' evil, and we're safe under His wing.
Now mind, poor faithful cretur, ye're not to
breathe you poor thing's name to any mortal,
especial not to yer dear masther, to bring
back the sorrows o' the past. She'll be off
with her friends when the fair and the races
is over, and we'll still 'bide here together in
the pace o' God."

CHAPTER XXV.

A CONSECRATED LIFE.

THE young man, whose visits had been so greatly blessed to John Sheehan, had been abroad about three or four years for study and travel. He had now returned, and taken a place in the counting-room of his father's extensive "works," believing that he was called to honor God in the busy mart of trade. This decision caused great disappointment to his father, who had hoped to see his only and gifted son shine in public life, either in a profession or as a statesman. He now resolved that he should at least become a star in the fashionable world, and saw no reason, except the fanaticism which had taken possession of him in college, why he should not marry a title. He knew that his money would be as highly prized

287

among **the** poor nobility as **a** name would be
be by him, a rich commoner.

With this fine fancy **in his** brain, **the man
of** gold did not choose to see **his** heir seated **on
a** high stool, scratching in a ledger. **So he**
bought him fine horses, **a** startling brougham,
and other vehicles, and gave him means **to keep**
up the style requisite to carry **out his plan**
for him.

But his son's heart was on other things, and
the young daughters of dukes and earls passed
by him, as little regarded as the down of the
thistle. He envied the coronet of an earl no
more than the cockade of a coachman, and all
the efforts of his father and sisters to "rouse
his ambition" were in vain.

One morning **as** he sat in the library alone,
his father entered, with a cloud on his brow.

"Come, my boy," he said, in a tone which
betokened pain rather than anger, "we must
talk over this matter of your future a little. I
need not tell you that I am sorely disappointed
in the son of my pride. I reared you for a

gentleman, but I'm told you have turned out almost a Methodist, forsaking the society which you are fitted to adorn, and choosing your associates among the employes of the house, — even the draymen, — and making yourself 'hale fellow well met' with old Shannon, and Cragin, the cooper. Whence did you inherit such tastes, my boy?"

A deep color rose to the cheek of the young man, as he replied, "I hope, my dear father, I shall never do any thing to disgrace you, or to show myself ungrateful for all your indulgence. But there is One who has a still higher claim on me than you have; and to Him I made vows, as solemn as eternity, in an hour of deep anguish. I was on the brink of ruin, and had almost brought disgrace on you, when God laid His hand on me, stayed me in my mad career, and brought me to my right mind. Those vows I must fulfill, both from honesty and from a love which draws me in the way of His commandments. I implore you not to tempt me from Christ by suggesting that I am cold and ungrateful to you. I enjoy the comforts of

19

wealth as much as any young man can do, but were the choice forced upon me, I would rather be a beggar following Christ, than a prince with my back turned upon Him."

"Your sisters can never induce you to accompany them to rout or play; but you have plenty of time to bestow on people who have no claim on you," said the father, severely.

"Every body has a claim on me, father," replied the young man, "and when those I love at home will not listen to me, I must seek out those who will. Our family friends would scorn me and perhaps refuse my visits were I to remind them that they were mortal and needed an Immortal Friend. But our draymen and coopers listen respectfully when I speak to them of their souls, and they read what I give them, and go where I request them, to hear the Word of God preached."

"You never caught this spirit of fanaticism from my friend Murray; for although he was a church-member when we were young together, he always remembered that he was a gentleman," said the old man.

"I hope I shall remember that too, father," replied the son.

"You did not see Murray waylaying workmen, and running to night services when you were with him, I'm very sure?" asked the father.

"He did what he could in that way, but the lower classes about him are all Papists, and they shun him as if he were a foe."

The father remained silent a moment, and then, as if a bright thought had just struck him, he said, "Well, if this course appears in the light of a duty to you, why not take orders? A clergyman stands in the foremost rank of society, even though he be as poor as the mouse in his church, and with your wealth you would doubtless get speedy preferment. Your sisters accuse you of "preaching" now; why not make that your profession and take some prominent living?"

"Father, should I do this, it would not be in the church of your choice, nor yet among people who have rich livings to bestow. But aside from this, I feel that my duty calls me to a business life. I have never had a call to the ministry."

"A call to the ministry!" re-echoed the old man, who had probably never heard the expression before, "what have you 'had a call to,' pray tell me?"

"To make money, and with it, as well as with all my powers, to glorify God while I live," replied the young man, solemnly. "Do not tempt me to play traitor to the King I have chosen to rule over me."

"I will do nothing to vex you, my son," replied the old man, "even if my heart and my hopes are all crushed. You are a man, and must choose your own road in life. God bless you, my boy, whatever way you go." And taking out a large gold watch with much jingling of chain and seals, he wiped tears from his eyes before he could see the hour on the fair dial plate. Then he took his hat and went out to make his usual morning round among the works; not to see what was doing, as there were men paid for that purpose, but to inspire the workmen with an awe of his dig-

nity ; and also to encourage each of them by
his bland smile and his cheerful " Good-morn-
ing, my man ! "

When the letters by the morning's mail
were laid by a clerk on the desk before the
young man, his eye brightened at sight of one
in Mr. Murray's well-known hand. The very
address gave comfort to his tried spirit by an
assurance that one still lived who could enter
into and sympathize in his trials. He tore it
open as if he knew it held the balm he needed
at that moment, and read therein good news:

" MY VERY DEAR YOUNG FRIEND, — When I
saw your name among the passengers in the
' Iris ' I first thanked God for your safety,
and then took my pen to welcome you home,
and to tell you the ' good news from a far
country,' which I fear missed you in your
wanderings. You remember I told you I
should call Killyrooke your parish, and that
I would be your assistant there. I blush when
I ·remember that I strove to discourage you
in your efforts for poor, fallen Sheehan. God
blessed your work. He was saved, and the

desolate are brought together into a happy and godly family.

"Your success in gaining the ears of these poor people has convinced me of the utility of lay preaching. You, with your blue coat and white hat, were welcomed where I would have been stoned. You were listened to as a young gentleman, while God's more public servant was looked on as a wily heretic seeking to delude their souls. You did more for poor blind Killyrooke the two weeks you were with us than I have been able to do in all the years I have labored at Cloynmally. I have already reaped the first fruits of your labors there. I have received into my church, and administered the Sacrament of the Lord's Supper to, old Monica Burke, long a roadside beggar of little fame for honesty; to the former bar-maid of the poor little inn; and to the wife of Sullivan the poacher, — the woman whose heart and arms ached from emptiness after the dead baby. There was great joy in the church over these poor souls.

"When John Sheehan, 'your joy and your

crown,' brought back his wife to the cottage,
it was as if he had introduced an angel into
the poor hamlet. She had gained much information, and had also overcome, to a surprising degree, her natural shyness by her
intercourse with Miss Grey and her poor Christian pensioners. She at once set out to read
the Gospel to her neighbors. But they were
soon forbidden to hear the Bible read. She
then, with strange wisdom, selected such
hymns and psalms as form a body of divinity
in themselves; and by coaxing, and sometimes
hiring, she fills her little room every evening
with poor lost sinners, and to them she *sings
the Gospel.* They learn the tunes and the
words, and carry them home and sing them at
their toil; and thus your work is going on
here.

"The ungodly see little cause for our rejoicing over these few poor wanderers gathered
into the fold, thinking them small gain to any
church. But you and I, who know the esti-
mate Jesus puts on one immortal soul, know
there is joy in heaven over them. The poor

heart-broken lady at the Hall is in sore need
of the sympathy of Jesus, and is, I hear, fully
convinced of the vanity of her penances and
of the mass. But alas! she could never stoop
so low as to hear the Gospel sung in a
thatched cottage, and she dare **not** hear it
preached in a Protestant **church.** ' Position '
keeps her in darkness, while these poor wo- '
men walk in the light. That little hamlet
will be depopulated ere long. The gentleman
at the Hall, sorely embarrassed by high living,
has let the cottages of the tenantry, as well as
his own grounds, run to ruin; so the poor
people are emigrating to America **as** fast as
they **can** get money for the passage. The seed
which Peggy is casting forth in love and faith
will thus be scattered, and bring in a harvest
in the New World.

" I have often been perplexed to know how
to regulate the matter of amusements **for**
young Christians, so that it might not clash
with **the** injunction, ' Whatsoever ye do, do
all to the glory of **God.'** Your course has
settled the **question.** It is ' for the glory of

God' that you keep the delicate frame He has given you in health and vigor by manly exercise. As your calling has not led you to find this in labor, you have sought it in athletic games. Now that all your powers are consecrated to God, your skill at those games is turned to account for His glory. Through quoits and ball you gained the ears and the hearts of those poor fellows at the lough. Hereafter, when any one asks me, 'How far may a Christian enter into worldly pleasures?' I will say, 'Just as far as he is sure he is thus promoting the glory of God. When conscience tells him that he can honor Christ by going to the play or the dance, let him go there. Otherwise he will by going get harm to his own soul and stumble the souls of others?' Your skill at games gave you an influence over those people, and enabled you to talk to them of heavenly things. That influence has extended to me, so that I can now drop a word when I meet them, without fear of abuse. I believe those 'boys' with whom you met would read any book you should send

them — if fortunate enough to read at all.
Come back at your first leisure, and visit your
humble little parish before it melts away, and
I will show you a wonderful change in the
home of poor humble Sheehan. That foolish
fellow, Paddy, says he is a Protestant now,
and he attends service regularly with his
master. The account he himself gives of the
change is, that when he was homesick after
his mistress, he vowed that if ever she came
back to him he would toss up a penny to
decide the matter of his religion. ·He did
so just before she came. The result turned
him from the faith of his fathers! Do you
not think that many wiser men than poor
Paddy stake their religious principles on
ground as small as that ?

If, in your labors in the city, you meet with
those who dare not read or hear the Bible,
sing the Gospel to them. Would it not be
well for us to avail ourselves of poor Peggy's
invention, and through music to draw the poor
and the needy where they can hear the sweet
sound of the Gospel ? ''

Ten days after this letter was received by the young man, the family at the cottage were surprised by the arrival of a box full of books and colored cards from Mr. Murray's friend. These were to be scattered by Peggy among — so he wrote — " my friends in Killyrooke." Many of the young men, proud of the honor, wished to know what the books contained, but not being able to read, were forced to go to Peggy and John, who held themselves ready for the work. Both Bessie and Marion were brought into the service, and there was more reading in Killyrooke in the next ten days than there had ever been before since the first poor cottage was built there.

CHAPTER **XXVI.**

ONE pleasant afternoon in the **early** autumn, as Peggy sat at her wheel by the open door of her cottage, she **was** surprised by the arrival of guests in **a** smart jaunting-car. They were no other than Barney and his wife, who for the first time in their married life had set out on an excursion of pleasure. There were no cold rules of etiquette to bind down the warm-hearted hostess; and, forgetting that she had never seen the **wife of the " dear** wagoner," she rushed out to the gate **to wel-** come them.

" Ah, good woman," cried the wagoner, " ye see it's true that 'birds of a feather **flock to-** gether.' For the last while I've jist been long- ing to have a word with ye, and to thank ye for the throuble ye took about my soul, and to

tell ye that I'm jist one o' yersilves now!
And here's my poor Molly, a thankful cretur
as lives, and as lovin' a one too. She's never
asked high things o' the Lord in this world,
but what she has asked He's bestowed on her
and on me; and we're come to bid ye rejoice with us that we, poor lost sheep, is
brought into the dear fold."

Peggy folded the wagoner's wife in her
arms and imprinted a motherly kiss on her
pale cheek, but, without speaking to her, continued her conversation with Barney as he
hitched his horse to the donkey-post. "And
how do ye feel towards the Papists now?" she
asked, as if trying the genuineness of his repentance.

"I loves ivery one o' them, from the Pope
hisself down to the manest o' my inimies at
home! I'd travel from here to Limerick on
my knees, if by so doin' I could open one
pair o' blind eyes to see the marcy I've seen
in the sinners' Friend," he replied.

As they entered the cottage, Paddy, who
had been drawn from the garden by their joy-

ful voices, joined them, and taking off his hat
made a low bow, and said, " I'm at yer sarvice, and yer harse's sarvice, too, good wagoner. But afore ye enter, will ye let me have
a word o' ye ? " ·   •

The wagoner stepped back and inclined his
head towards Paddy in the attitude of a listener. But Paddy was a man of deeds as well
as of words; and he surprised the stranger by
stooping down and catching up one of his feet
in his hand. Then falling on his knees, he
put his head down so low that he could exam-
ine the sole of his brogue. " I only wanted to
see," he said, with a confidential wink of his
little gray eye, " if ye had hobnails in yer
shoes; because if ye had, I'd be to pound them
down afore I let ye into our cottage. We've
grown very fine since first ye saw us, and we
has a carpet on our floor, and carpets is not
for men as wears hobnails in their soles, ye
know. *Ye're all right;* so walk in, and a
wilcome to ye ! Yis, yis; it's fine indeed that
we are now — atin' with our tables covered
with white cloth, 'stead o' bare. There's not

PADDY AND THE WAGONER.

a one like us but only the minister and the priest in all these parts. But for all this, we kapes quite humble, and treats dacent poor people with due civility; so don't be afeared, but wipe yer feet well and thin just step on the carpet as if it were no better nor a clay floor. Isn't it a fine thing to be kept this humble when we're grown such grand folk?"

And for two days these humble souls, with a few Christian friends who joined them from the little band in Cloynmally, "did eat their meat with gladness and singleness of heart, praising God, and having favor with all the people."

The girls were now so large and so capable, that they relieved Peggy of nearly all the care and work, both in the cottage and in the poultry-yard. What they could not accomplish Paddy did, so he felt great pride in boasting that "his darlin' misthress didn't have to lift her finger only to plaze herself." But with all this freedom from toil, Peggy was not the woman to sit down in idleness. The love in her heart always supplied work for her hands.

Late one summer afternoon, Bessie and Marion were sent off to search for the ducks, which had, of late, fallen into roving habits, often leaving " the fine accommodations " Paddy had provided for them, and seeking company at a large pond half a mile from home.

As the girls turned into a quiet lane leading to this duck-pond, they saw two women sitting on the grass enjoying their supper ; and yet they were too well dressed for beggars. They talked and laughed very loudly, and as the girls approached, one called out, " Arn't ye Sheehan's girls ? "

Bessie modestly replied, and then expressed her opinion to Marion of the way in which the stranger spoke of their father. " She might at least have called him 'John Sheehan,' she said."

" Come back here and tell us about you Miss Grey. Do she sind ye money by the hape, or do the old fellow fade and clothe ye hisself? " cried one of the women.

The children were startled by this rudeness,

and replied, " We're in haste, as we're bid to be back to our supper."

" Och ye are! Well, thin, pass on, fine ladies," cried the woman. " I suppose that great lady, Peggy Sheehan, forbid ye to spake to poor folk."

" Bessie dear," said Marion, " I've talked twice with you woman on the road. One day, you mind, I told ye she said she knew my own mother, and that Miss Grey bid her come to see us."

" She was jesting with you, dear," replied Bessie, "but may be she's the body that mammy's so ill pleased to hear mentioned — for what reason I don't know. Perhaps she's the one that gave you the locket long ago, that mammy bid ye never speak to, but run from. A rough body surely she is, and very unlike our mammy."

And chatting together, they reached the pond, and saw their ducks, with a large party of friends, on the other side. It was a long way round, but they were forced to go on or return without them. The shadows were falling, and they began to feel a little timid, when, to their great joy, they saw Timmy, the son of Elder Peter, coming towards them. He had been a most tender and affectionate playmate of Bessie for years. It seems that Timmy, now turned of seventeen, did not partake of his father's stony nature, but gave the elder great annoyance by spending his pocket money and his time for the girls. The elder had long ago declared that he'd have " no stuff" about him, and that he would chastise Timmy next time he saw him befooling himself. " How can I tell," he said, " but if the lad's left to himself, he may turn out a gallant, or a lover, or such-like wake cretur' ? He must sure have got this wakeness from some far-back body among his ancestors ; for his father never looked at a maiden till he had a cottage to be kept clane and no one in it to cook him a dinner. And here's him makin' a fool o' himself from the cradle up ! Amazin' wakeness for the son o' an elder ! "

After a few rebukes and many threats, Elder Peter at length devised a plan to mortify the

lad in a manner that should teach him a lesson.
So he took him out of the " classical school
of Maurice Dolan," and put him into the girls'
school taught by his own sister, with a charge
to her " to set him in between two little maids
whenever he needed punishment."

Strange to say, Elder Peter's medicine was
too mild for the disease. Timmy was now in
his element, wedged in between his admired
Bessie Sheehan and another pleasant child not
so old. If his father had found it hard to
keep his finger on Timmy out of school hours
before, he found it still harder now. He
walked from Cloynmally almost to Killyrooke,
either " after flowers, or four-leafed shamrocks,
or something else," every night, till the elder
took him out of the girls' school and sent
him back to Maurice Dolan, with orders to
have the rod laid on if necessary. But Maurice
was young himself, and he saw no great crime
in plucking flowers and hunting four-leaved
shamrocks with schoolmates or friends. So
Timmy escaped punishment altogether.

Hard as Elder Peter's nature was, he had a

very tender spot in his heart for Timmy — his one, only child. Knowing how hard his own trade was, he had resolved that Timmy should have an easier one — perhaps be a tailor. Against this decision Timmy rebelled most vigorously, declaring that he would either be a stone-cutter or a farmer *in America,* and he dutifully suggested that if his plans were interfered with he would run off and go to sea. And that boy's threat from time immemorial, had as great an effect in restraining Elder Peter from carrying out his plans as if it had never been uttered before.

Marion, who preferred the ducks' company to Timmy's, walked on ahead scolding them soundly for the evil ways into which they had fallen. Thus the two lingerers had a rare opportunity to make complaints and to reveal plans, without a third person to listen.

Bessie remembered her sad early life among the baby boarders, where she was forbidden to laugh or to play, and perhaps it was this which had given a tinge of sadness to her disposition. It certainly was not that she felt depressed by her connection with the Sheehans; for so closely had Peggy guarded the children, that they had never heard a breath against John's fair fame. Seeing his pure daily life and sharing his affectionate care, they looked upon him as the model Christian, and the most respectable man in the hamlet.

"Well," sighed Bessie, "I'm just wild about America. Timmy, and I'll not rest till I see it. Bell Shannon and Maggie McRea are going, and they're the last o' the young folk I'm suffered to consort with, and I'll be just miserable behind them. Why can't your father and mine go, as well as other fathers?"

"I suppose," answered Timmy, "that my father thinks folk don't die fast enough for his trade in a country where's no potatoe rot and no starvation. But the few that do die there lave enough behind them to pay for headstones, and that's what few does here."

"Mammy turns pale now," said Bessie, "at the word 'America;' but I know they'd all go if I set my will on goin,' for they'll never separate from me — the lovin' hearts?"

"If ye go, I'll follow, though I **should have
to run off**," replied Timmy.

Bessie **smiled. "That's an** old threat **o'
yours,** Timmy, and will frighten no one but
your father. But here's the turn of the road
for you. Now go your way home, and I'll go
mine. I'll not let you walk to the cottage, **as**
mammy is grieved with you, saying it's you
put America in my head. Good-night."

"Good-night, Bessie. Keep **up good heart,**
and who can say but we'll hear Elder Peter
and **John** Sheehan singing the Psalms **o' David**
to 'Yankee Doodle' yet? They have only the
one tune in that country. Good-night."

When Bessie parted from Timmy, she came
to the spot where **she and** her sister had seen
the women sitting on the grass, and, **remem-**
bering that, **she** hastened on to **overtake**
Marion.

She has gone but a few steps, however, when
she came upon one **of the** strangers **sitting**
alone on the roadside.

"What's yer haste, maid?" she called out.
"**I'm waitin' here** to tell ye **what will plaze**

ye. Ye are too fine a girl to waste yer life drudging over cows, and flax and butter, shut up in a dull old cottage where's no dances nor songs. There's great want o' girls in the linen mills, and great wages given. Will ye go if yer way be paid?"

"My mammy would never suffer me," replied Bessie, as she passed by her without looking up.

"Well, what is that to ye? She's no mother to ye, but only a hard mistress that works ye sore and gives ye no pay."

Bessie was too much afraid to linger and reply in defense of Peggy, and so hurried on. But the stranger followed her, saying, "I know who yer mother is, and there's where ye'll find love. I've read yer fortun' in the clouds that blow over the cottage. There's hapes o' gold, and fine clothes, and gay friends lying' just afore ye. But there's a journey betwane them an ye — ather by sea or land, as ye plaze, and I'll lade ye, if ye like, to the illigant luck that's ahead."

"I'll never leave my mammy for gold or

fine clothes," cried Bessie, and then she ran on with the speed of an antelope.

When she reached the cow-yard, Marion was there housing her rebellious ducks. She passed her, and entered the cottage, resolved not to worry her mother just then by speaking of either America, or Timmy, or the strange woman.

CHAPTER XXVII.

GOING TO AMERICA.

"DARLIN'," cried Peggy, as Bessie entered the door, " there's ill tidings come from dear Miss Grey in a letter to Mr. Murray. She's very ill, and will have us three come to her by the morrow morning's post-chaise — she said partic'lar ' not by the wagon, as ye war not children, now.' If she die, yer best friend is gone, my jewel."

" No, mammy, you are my best friend, and all the world is small loss to me while God spares you and Marion," replied the affectionate girl.

" And yet," said Peggy, reproachfully, " ye would lave me and go to a strange land with the widow McRea."

" O, mammy, dear, Ireland is such a poor, worn-out country for the young," said Bessie.

"I'm longin' to do something more than just breathe, and what can I do in Killyrooke?"

Peggy made no reply to this just question. After seating the family at table, she said, "I can niver ate again till I know how's dear Miss Grey. Oh, the tinder, lovin' friend she's been to me! Ate ye, but let me go and prepare for the setting off."

Twice since they left her had Miss Grey seen "the children," as she still called them, but she could scarcely believe that the tall girls whom Peggy brought to her bedside were the same.

She had loving words of advice, and a little legacy which she was anxious to settle on them while she had strength.

"Are they good girls?" she asked. "Peggy, tell me if they have ever grieved you? Speak the truth to me,—you can speak nothing but truth."

"They have been iver true, and faithful, and lovin', and willin', but," and she turned a mournful look on Bessie, "but, she is weary o' me, and o' poor, dear Ireland, and is restless to follow the crowd to America, and my heart would die without her smile."

The poor girl hung her head, expecting a rebuke, but, to her surprise, Miss Grey said faintly, " I'm glad she has ambition to better her lot. Ireland is ground to the dust by a double oppression, and is no longer the place for the young. If all go who can pay their way, there will still be more left than can earn their bread, and many of them must starve. If you and John should follow me to the grave soon, what would these poor children do in that desolate hamlet? I should be well pleased if part of Bessie's portion be spent in getting her to America. Place her with some trusty friend who is going, and at the end of a year you can go to her, or she can return to you if not happy there. But Marion was never so staid as Bessie; keep her close to your own side. Do not let her cross the water unless you do."

Peggy turned very pale at these words, but Bessie, overcome with joy, burst into tears.

"Might I make bold to ask," said Peggy; "have ye iver got any account of their mother or father ?"

"Never, and I feel very sure both parents are dead," replied the lady. "Why do you worry yourself about them ? I told the woman you sent to ask, that you must never think of them, but enjoy the children that God sent so mercifully into your kind hand."

"I sent no woman, dear heart, nor man, nather," replied Peggy, in surprise.

"One came with questions, she said, from you. I sent replies by the nurse, but did not see her myself," answered Miss Grey.

"Well, it's quite mysterious entirely !" exclaimed Peggy; "but ye are now faint, dear, with the talkin'. I'll send all away and sit this night by yer side, and as many more nights as ye'll suffer me, but niver, niver can I repay ye for all the love and marcy ye showered on me thim days."

Miss Grey rallied after this, and there being no need of Peggy's services, she insisted on her returning to Killyrooke.

Some bird of the air — if not Paddy Mannon — soon dropped a hint in the hamlet that "Miss Grey had left a great fortun' to the girls, and had ordered that Bessie with the gold open out in her hand should set sail as soon as she pleased for America."

Peggy no longer tried to dissuade Bessie from her purpose, but suggested the subject of a family emigration.

"Ye see, John, darlin', how the people is thinnin' off, and how few is left here. What would ye say to us all goin'?"

Paddy sprang to his feet, and catching his hat off one peg and his staff from another, exclaimed, "I'd say ' yis,' and be off by the sun risin'."

"Whist, Paddy," said his master, "and don't be spakin' when yer not spoke to." And turning to Peggy, he exclaimed, "Where would be our gratitude to God as has watched over our crops and herds, and given us plenty while others is starvin?' Could ye lave the dear grave and all the poor souls here without a one to care for them?"

" Shu ! shu ! " cried Paddy, " the grave will take care o' itself, and as for the few **souls** here, there's none left that's worth lookin' afther.   See, dears, I heered at the blacksmith's that all Ireland's goin' soon, and thin we'll be left quite alone entirely, and, —— "

" **Paddy,**" cried John, as sharply as he could say any thing, " if ye don't be quiet when yer masther and misthress **wish to be** talkin', I'll send ye out to the cow-house with yer ' stirabout.' "   .

" **And,**" continued Paddy, nothing daunted, " they said that in England the quane **was** payin' the passage o' whole ship-loads **o' her** paupers to get them to that fine country. And the 'Miricans is that **glad** to get them — bein' all rich thimselves, and not a one to give their charity to — that **they** be standin' on the shores, waitin' the ships to come **in, and thin** they fight to see who'll git the paupers **to fill** their fine empty workhouses."

Peggy and the girls **laughed, but John** cried, sternly, " Will ye be **quiet, Paddy ? "**

" **And,**" continued Paddy, deaf to all reproof, " I shall soon be ashamed to hold up my head in Ireland if the very paupers can go and not we — such a fine, respectable family, — there's not the like of us in that country, though some of thim's richer nor we. Whin will we start off, dears ? " he cried, imploringly, " I'm afeared folk'll think we can't raise the passage-money."

After a free discussion of the matter, it was decided that Bessie should go with the Widow McRea; who, after residing in America several years, and doing well in a little store, had returned to Ireland for her children, Bell, and Rose, whom she had left with a sister in Cloynmally. If, after a year's trial, Bessie was happy, John promised to sell the lease of the farm and join her with the family.

Few poor girls ever set off from that poverty-stricken land with such preparations for comfort on sea and on land as were made by the loving Sheehans for Bessie, who was the light of their eyes and the pride of their hearts. After all was done which the tenderest love could prompt, Mr. Murray, Elder

Peter, and others of the little church were sent for, the evening before Bessie's departure, to commend her to the care of Heaven, and to ask God's mercy on the lonely hearts she was to leave behind. And in that hour this beloved child was committed fully to the care of a covenant-keeping God, for life or for death.

When the tears were all shed, and the farewells all spoken, Peggy and Bessie and Marion set off to wait the post-chaise at Cloynmally. The loving Peggy had determined not to part with her child till the water should separate them. John dared not trust himself to go from the cottage with them. Several of the little church were waiting them at " the turn o' the road," and there was Paddy, from whom they had just parted at the cottage! He had run across the wet bog and got there before them. And panting and sobbing, he cried out:

" O, Erin ! (that's the grand name for *Ireland*) swate Isle o'
    the sea !
Hinchfor'ard no flowers shall blosshom on thee ;
Thy herds shall be dead, and thy birds niver sing,
Thy fowls shall be hatched without feather or wing.
                O-ho-ne !

" Thy trees shall grow down'ards, with roots in the air,
No rain shall fall down, but be drought ivery where.
And why this distrissful confusion ? 'Kase why ?
'Kase swate Bessie Sheehan's detarmined to fly.

O-ho-ne !

" Mad waves, now I bid ye quite paceful to lie,
Wild winds, don't ye whistle once more in the sky,
Old ocean, rock gintle, yer roarin' giv o'er,
Till the gim o' our cot reach Amirican shore.

O-ho-ne !

" And Bessie, my jewel, whin the Yankees ask ye,
Why fine Paddy Mannon arn't crossin' the sea,
Just till thim he's settlin' the farm, and that soon
With masther, and misthress, and Mar'on he'll come.

O-ho-ne !

" Then will we 'bide with thim, and wander no more,
But call yon Ameriky our native shore ; —''

And while Paddy was still howling out his
lament, the post-chaise came up, and Peggy
and Bessie drove off amid the tears and the
God-bless-ye's of the loving little group.

21

CHAPTER XXVIII

A PAINFUL PARTING.

TO Peggy's amazement, as she and Bessie stepped on the ship's deck, the first person they encountered was Master Timmy in his Sunday clothes, looking very sober. He had, for the first time, been as good as his word in the matter of " running off." As he could get neither permission nor money to cross the sea, he was determined to have at least the last look of his old playmate before she left her native land for ever.

Peggy was at first much displeased at sight of him, and said, half tenderly, and half reproachfully, " See, Timmy, what ye've done by stirrin' up my darlin' about a strange land. How could ye be so cruel, boy ? "

" We'll all follow her soon, Misthress Shee-han," he answered, with a frank smile, " for

322

ye'll not 'bide long after her, and my father'll
not 'bide long behind me, for goin' I am, and
that afore long too! So cheer up, since ye belave that all things work for good to thim as
be good, — and who's better nor Bessie and
yersilf, dear? What's tears about?"

This was said very bravely, but the color
deepened on Timmy's cheek, and his voice
trembled a little, and Peggy was forced to forget her own sorrows and turn comforter.
Casting a glance full of pity on the boy, she replied, "I forgive ye, dear child, from my
heart's core; now let's away, for, as poor
Paddy says, ' Our sun is set for ever in the sky
o' Ireland ' — poor, dear Ireland!"

After folding Bessie again and again in her
arms, and calling down, in fervent tones,
Heaven's "swatest blissings" on her head, she
left her sitting in tears by the Widow McRea;
and taking Timmy's hand, as if helpless without aid, she turned to go.

Then Bessie's high heart gave way, and running after her, she threw her arms round her
neck, and cried, "Mammy, go home and tell

father to sell the farm at once and come to me, for I can **never** breathe the breath o' life away **from you.** And be sure to bring poor Paddy, for he'd die if left behind, and **I'm sure** we be just no family at all without him — **the dear, foolish man!** Will you come soon?"

Peggy did not look **at the child of her love.** She dared not trust herself, but answered, "If God will, darlin', **ye'll see us** in a twel'month. Farewell, farewell, my jewel!"

As she and Timmy stepped off the **vessel,** they met a woman in black leading by the hand a young girl who was weeping bitterly, and who had only a shawl over her head. "There's more folks nor **us** in sorrow, Timmy; yon poor lambie's to bid farewell to one she loves, and may be she **has** little **love to** go back to, as ye and I have, lad," said Peggy, looking back pitifully at the weeping girl.

As she uttered **these** words, the **woman in** black **called out in a loud tone to her** lingering companion, **to** hasten **her steps.** Peggy uttered a cry which startled **Timmy.** Then she strove to compose herself, **and** said to the wondering boy, "The voice sounded nat'ral and frightened me for a moment. That's because my heart's weak now; let us haste away, dear." And yet she looked back; but the woman was lost in the crowd, and she heard only the sailors ordering all on shore who desired to go. Pressing the boy's hand, as if thus she could still the anguish in her heart, she led the way to the inn where they were to take the post-chaise.

While waiting the hour for setting off, Timmy strove to divert Peggy's mind from the sea by talking of himself and his plans.

"Father will niver bind me to Ireland," he cried. "A boy has but one life, and should pass that where he wills. What can an old man with a dried up heart know o' the ambition o' a boy?"

"Timmy," said Peggy, reprovingly, "ye have one great fault, I may say, a sin, and —"

"What me, mysilf?" cried Timmy, in surprise; "you surely can't mean that?"

"Yes, Timmy, I do mean just that," answered Peggy.

"A great fault! And pray what can it be?" cried the boy, his fine eyes wide open, and his cheeks aglow with wonder.

"Why, Timmy, it's the onrespectful way ye spake o' yer dear father. Ye remember God bids ye to honor yer father and yer mother, and to obey them in all things."

"It would be sore hard to obey the elder 'in all things,'" replied Timmy, quite relieved to find he was not to be accused of lying or theft. "Now, as yer old Paddy says, 'he's a stone man, made by himself out o' his own matarial,' and has no human wakeness about him. Ye mind, Misthress Sheehan, when I was a small bit o' a boy, and would gather all the girlies in the place about me and sew dolls,' rags with them, he called me 'a sheep,' and bid me be off playing rough with the lads. And now that I'm seekin' to work hard like a man, he turns about and bids me go to a tailor and learn to sew. I'll not do it if I die. I feels the great strength in my bones, and I'll let it out, ather on the stone or yet on the land,—and I'll do it in America, too!

That I will. If the elder likes to go with me he's wilcome, for land's plinty there, and if not, he'll just have to 'bide where he is."

"Ah, Timmy, my lad, yon's no way to spake o' thim that's done so much for ye, and that's so proud o' ye," said Peggy.

"Who's proud o' me, Misthress Sheehan?" asked the boy. "Not my father, sure; he's sore ashamed o' me, and always askin' me why I arn't like Ned McGee and the Carney lads; and they goes about nights howlin' like bears, and stonin' old women's cats, and the like. And all the triflin' *I* does is to whittle thread-winders, and gather flowers, and buy sugar plums, for the girls; and for that he calls me 'a sheep.' No, none is proud of me, but one loves me, — that's my mother."

"Dear lad, Elder Peter is too proud o' ye for a Christian man. He's never done tellin' o' yer fine lessons and yer honest behavior; and both himself and Mr. Murray is just quite proud o' yer Latin larnin', hopin' yerself will be a schoolmasther yet," said Peggy, trium-phantly.

Timmy laughed outright. "Latin is *stuff*
for the like o' me! I'm not the makin' o' a
scholar, and if I should even drag on at the
book till I'd get a school, woe to the urchins
benath me! This great power o' strength
that's within my bones must come out and
strike somewhere; if not the stone or the land,
then on the boys' backs. Spake ye, that has
such power over the elder, and strive to get
the harness off my showlders, that I may be a
man as well as look like one. Here am I,
more nor seventeen years old, and yet askin'
my father may I do this or that to arn my
bread; and so doin' just nothing at all. I'll
sure be ' a sheep' at this rate."

Peggy promised him her influence; and
wliile they were talking thus the post-chaise
drove up. They took their places on the top,
and were off for the home for which Peggy's
heart was yearning. She was hoping the love
yet left her there might fill the blank just
made by Bessie's departure.

CHAPTER XXIX.

STOLEN BY THE FOE.

PEGGY had left Marion in care of the cottage, with many charges to "be tinder o' her poor, lovin' father, and civil to Paddy, and to have all things shinin' on her return."

Childlike, Marion had dried her tears, and begun to picture to herself the beautiful things which Bessie would send her from America, and to anticipate her own voyage thither. She was a great "tease," and was already laying plans to worry the indulgent, easy John into speedy preparations for the change.

By dinner time she was singing about the cottage as merrily as if no empty seat were there, and as if the pillow beside her own were still to be pressed by the bright head which had used to lie there.

John and Paddy had at length dried their tears, and gone to work in a field at some little distance from the house. Towards nightfall they heard loud voices in the direction of the cottage, and then shouts and cries.

"Whist, Paddy," cried John. "What can yon noises be?"

"Och," replied Paddy, coolly, "it's on'y some o' our neighbors bating the life out o' a few o' their spare childer. When my milkin' time comes, I'll go up and quiet the distarbance."

John smiled, and as the voices ceased he thought no more of the circumstances till he returned home and found the stool and pail beside a half-milked cow, but no supper ready, and no bright little Marion waiting at the door to welcome him. He called her loudly, and went from room to room through the cottage, but in vain; all was silent there. His alarm was increased by Paddy coming in from the yard, whither he had gone to milk, holding up the little red, shawl Marion always wore at milking, and crying out, in a tone of agony, " Where's our child? The gypsies or the evil sperits has stole her away, and left midnight in my soul. Ohone! who'll give me my child afore I dies o' fear?"

John grasped the little kerchief, and holding it up towards the light, gazed at it as if he hoped there to read the mystery of her absence. Jacob did not look more anxiously at the coat of many colors.

The two ran from house to house in great alarm, hoping to learn the child's fate. The neighbors had heard a noise, but " thought Paddy was batin' the boys who had stolen his ducks, and that the cries came from them." They almost ridiculed the fears of these two strong men, but they joined in their search through bog and wood, and finally wandered toward the lough. One person had see a strange man and a woman, in black talking with Marion at the cow-yard, and another had seen a strange horse and jaunting car standing at the end of the lane ; but that was all.

There was little sleep that night in Killy-rooke. John and Paddy, weeping like children and accompanied by a band of pitying neighbors, went from house to house, blew the horn and dragged the lough.

While the men were abroad, the women, each with her rush taper in hand, went to the cottage to gossip over the mystery. In their womanly tenderness they forgot all differences, and all forgave Peggy for her neat dairy, her glass windows, her table-cloth and her carpet.

Two boys who had been dispatched for Mr. Murray now returned with him and Elder Peter; the latter, though somewhat anxious about the fate of his own heir, took good care not to allude to it, lest he might expose the weakness of his family government.

Searching proved all in vain; so the neighbors dropped off, one by one, till only Mr. Murray and Elder Peter remained.

"Have you no suspicion, John, where she can be?" asked the minister.

" Niver a one," replied John, shaking his head mournfully. " And how'll iver I meet Peggy after betrayin' her trust thus?"

" You, perhaps, have some thought about it, Paddy?" asked Mr. Murray again.

" 'Dade, thin, I have a fine thought jist come to me," replied Paddy. " But it might be oncivil to spake o't here, as I'd be to name one I'm forbid to spake about."

" Speak out, Paddy," cried John, " and let's have none o' yer long talks or yer nonsense in a time like this."

" Well, Mr. Murray, sir," exclaimed Paddy, " it is jist this: Three nights agone I war in at the horse-shoer's; and more men war there; and in comes the inimy o' this house and this name, and she in black wades, to be sure! And the men all asked her where did she live, and what did she work. And och, sorra me! didn't I, as war forbidden o' my misthress to look on her or to breathe her name, like the fool I bees, go talkin' to her?

" She asked me about the fortun' Miss Grey gave the childern, and where was the gold kept; and I **told her** in a belt about the darlin' childers' waists. And she asked by what vessel would Bessie go, and who would go **with** her, and all that like.

" **She** said *herself* was goin' to America as soon as the passage money was arned; and that now, in the mane time, she was about the country sarvin' a society **o'** holy ladies in the great city, by layin' tax on the people and **collictin'** money and orphints for a new 'shylum they war buildin'. Och! och! if that same sarpint with **a** human face has stole off our jewel! What an illigant orphint she'd be to ornamint a 'shylum with! I belave you one's got her by my folly. Och, ye miserable **man,** Paddy Mannon, will ye niver larn wisdom by **the** sorrow **ye** bring on yersilf and others!"

" Paddy, **did you** tell any one that the children carried Miss Grey's gold **about them?"** asked Mr. Murray.

" Dade I did. I heerd **my** misthress say she was sewin' Bessie's up in a belt for her to wear about her waist. And she always trated the twos quite aqual, so I thought Mar'on's gold would be there, too; and that if yon one thought to steal it, she'd find it unpossible!"

There was now a loud knock at the door, and Paddy leaped half way across the floor to open it. There was Father Clakey's honest old face, flushed with excitement and terror. At sight of him, Paddy darted back more quickly than he had gone forward, and hid himself behind the rough settle on which John was seated, for this was the first time since he had left his flock that he had met the priest face to face. Whenever he had seen him coming down the road, he had always found it convenient to run into the cow-house and draw the wooden bolt behind him, or to hide under the hedge. His allegiance was broken, but his fear remained.

"Any news yet, friends, o' the pleasant child?" asked the old man. "I've a sore fear on my heart that evil's come to her through the mad boasting o' this fool, Mannon. Come out o' that, ye miserable cretur," cried the priest, striking a heavy blow on the back o' the settle. Paddy shrieked as if it had fallen on his head, but did not appear. " Come out and tell what ye revaled to you woman in black, after ye left the smith's shop where ye were boasting about the gold. I'm told, sir," he said, addressing Mr. Murray, " by the man o' the shop, that *this woman* followed him out, talkin' with him, till he got afraid o' her and ran home over the fields."

They could hear Paddy's loud breathing and almost the beating of his heart; but they could not get him out of his hiding-place till Mr. Murray took a seat on the settle and bade him come and sit beside him, promising that no man should lay a hand on him. Then the poor fellow crept out, pale as one of his own ghosts, and whispered, " I knows no more ; I's told ye all."

" What did you woman say to ye, Mannou ? " cried Father Clakey, stamping his foot on the floor.

" She— she — och ! she said she war akin to our chil — childer ! that hersilf was ather their mother or their cusin, — she'd forget which ! But that bein' their kin, she'd get enough o' the gold to carry her across the sea. — whativer! och! my heart!"

"And why, then, didn't ye tell this at once to yer misthress, ye miserable loon?" cried the priest.

"Bekase, yer, — yer riverence, she said if I'd tell a word she spake, she'd bate me afore all the boys! So, so, out o' silf-rispect I hild my tongue; and see ye all what's come o't. Is there no world on this arth that we can 'migrate to where she'll not be? What's iver the use o' goin' to America now, and her there?"

"If this family lave their native land, I'll advise thim to lave ye in it, Mannon. The House o' Corriction is the place for ye, with wit enough to do evil, and not enough to do good," said the priest.

"Please, sir," said John, "he's a paceable cretur' and would lay down his life for the childer."

"More's the pity he hadn't done it then, 'stead o' betraying one o' them into the hand o' an emeny. Yon evil one is no doubt by this time off with yer child, unless she larns there's

22

no money about her ; if she find that out too late, she'll set her adrift in a strange place. Though if she had the two in America, she'd make capital out o' them ; — Heaven help them, the fine rispectful things they war to ivery body. I've had men out sarching for the child till I got this word, and then I thought it vain. But I'm at yer service, and will turn the whole town out o' their beds if ye need; good-night, neighbors." And, to Paddy's relief and joy, he closed the door behind him.

CHAPTER XXX.

PATIENT IN TRIBULATION.

IT was part of Timmy's plan not to appear to have been far away, and, at his leisure, to drop in at his home as if he had only been at his cousins', where he often passed a night. So when he and Peggy were set down at "the turn o' the road," he insisted on walking to Killyrooke with her, carrying her baskets.

It was just at nightfall they entered the cottage. Mr. Murray, Elder Peter and some half dozen other friends were there again, consoling John and Paddy, who had spent the day in unavailing tears.

· When Peggy saw these grave men sitting in her little parlor in solemn conclave, she was surprised. As no smile lighted any face in the group, she took alarm, and turning very pale, cried, " **where's my** darlin' child, that she's not at the gate to greet me ? "

Still no one spoke, **and she cried out,** " **John,** where's my child ? "

Poor John burst into tears, **and could not reply.** Mr. Murray then said, calmly, " Mistress Sheehan, you are not of those who expect **to** receive good at the hand of the Lord and not evil. You have seen too much of His mercy to doubt **Him** now, even though clouds **and** darkness surround Him."

" Is she **dead,** then ? **tell me,** dear hearts, and not kape me in this great fear. **I, that** ha' given all to God, did not withhold her. And if He has taken her to Himself, He's took no **more** nor His own."

Encouraged by her calmness, John began a recital of the painful story. As soon as " the wo**man** dressed in black " was mentioned, Peggy cried **out,** " I saw her, darlin', **with my** own **two eyes, and I heard her voice. It** was *my lambie* she **war draggin'** in tears, on shipboard — och, **it war yon fearful** woman; **and I** might have saved the child — Timmy and I. She war at our very hand, wern't she, dear boy ? "

Timmy nodded, and Elder Peter looked surprised at his knowing what was seen on shipboard ; but he was too shrewd to ask questions.

" If ye had told me the darlin' were hid safe in the grave, I'd ha' done like David when his child war dead ; but to be in *her* hands," exclaimed Peggy.

" She's not in her hands nor yet in her power, Mistress Sheehan," replied Mr. Murray. " She's as safe now, surely, as if she were in the grave, and the same love watches over her. Bessie is on the ship, and will report the woman to the captain and ask protection. Keep you quiet, and soon you'll hear of the two being safe on the other shore. I beg you not to cast away your confidence, which hath great recompense of reward. God has brought you through great and sore trials already, and be assured He will not now give your peace over into the hand of your enemy."

" He will not, dear Mr. Murray," cried Peggy, smiling through her tears. " That's an inimy that's vanquished and that has lost her power. She may plot evil, but can never carry it out agin us, for we're hid under the shadow o' the Almighty. Once, friends, in the midnight, I had a sore struggle about you one; and I thought she'd yet triumph, but the great peace come and rolled like a billow o' love o'er my soul, and the fear was gone, and has never come back since then. Her voice makes me start for a moment, but then I remembers that she's under my feet, and no weapon formed agin me or mine can prosper. Ye may think this bold talk, friends, for a poor weak sinner, but I've had the word o' the Lord for't, and His word standeth sure. I'll yet clasp my two children in the land o' the living."

" O, woman, great is thy faith!" cried the pastor, " and according to thy faith be it unto thee."

When John and Peggy opened the door to let their guests out, they saw several of their humble neighbors waiting at the gate for their departure, that they might go in and sympathize with Peggy. Once within the cottage, they commenced, in true Irish style, to weep and howl; while some few, having got a hint about Nan, began to curse her, hoping thus to manifest in the strongest manner their sorrow for Peggy. But she, pale and calm to a degree which astonished them, said, " Take seats, kind neighbors, and cease this noise. It breaks my heart, and it will not bring back my child. Nather let me hear any that would befriend me curse a soul that God has made. Hundreds o' prayers has gone up to Heaven from these lips for that evil woman, that she might yet be pardoned; and do ye think that after that I could stand by and hear her cursed? Maybe my children will be let to bless her soul. There's many a one, friends, as evil as her, that's been washed and made clean, and at last been let in among the holy."

" And thin ain't ye sorry after the child?" asked an old woman, who was disappointed in not being allowed to curse Nan — cursing being being one of her professions, for the practice of which she always expected to be paid.

" Yes, Betty, I'm heart-sick for my child, but I'm not goin' to rave like an onrasonin' woman. I belave she's in the Lord's hand, and whoever's there is safe. Ye all know, dear women, how I loves the child ; so look at me now and see what strength God can give to a poor weak mortal. This is the comfort and joy my religion gives in distress. Ye mind it helped one long ago to trust Him and be quite asy when a flood covered all but himself and his family. It enabled others to walk calm in a fiery furnace, and others again in a den full up o' lions ; and couldn't it bear me through this? There's only one ocean between me and my children, and I've not got to bridge it afore I can get to them. God prepared a way over the mighty sea long before I was born, and all I have to do now is just to go over it. And that I'll soon do, and gather my family all about me."

This last sentence set the poor neighbors to

howling and weeping again, for they realized the sad loss this family would be to poor Killyrooke, whence the younger people, and indeed all who were able to work, were going as fast as they could get money to pay their passage to America.

"Cease yer howlin' there, ould bodies," cried Paddy, who had slipped off his chair at the departure of "the fine company" and seated himself on the clay floor in a dark corner, where he now sat hugging his knees. "Cease yer noise, will ye, and not put my misthress off the idee o' the voyage? Think what a fine thing this is to be for us as a family, and mysilf in pertic'lar! Why, whin I raches yon illigant country, I'll be no more 'Paddy Mannon,' but 'Mr. Mannon.' Old Tim Marphy got word in a letter from Judy and Dave that the schoolmaster here must direct all their letters to 'Mish Judy Marphy,' and 'Misther David Marphy;' for they was all 'Misther' and 'Mish' in that counthry. There we'll have 'Mish Bessie Sheehan,' and 'Mish Mar'on Sheehan,' and 'Misther Mannon,' as well as the grand lady and gintleman — John and Peggy — above us all ! "

" Paddy, cease yer nonsinse now, like a good man, while I have a few words with the pityin' neighbors," cried Peggy imploringly. " Here's poor Molly waitin' to get in a word to me."

" Well thin," cried the poor woman, wiping away her tears, " will ye suffer us to take the work o' the cottage off ye till ye gits a bit over the freshness o' the throuble ? Norra Burke will do the milkin' with her strong young hands, and Sullivan's wife will make the butter as nate as an angel could do it ; and mysilf, — well, I'll just do the manest thing ye bid me, in mimory o' what ye did for my Mickey when he was laid up o' the shivers."

" Ten thousand thanks to ye all, good neighbors," said Peggy, " but at a time like this I could niver spare my work out o' my own hands. When the hands is busy, the heart's far easier nor other times. Half the sin and sorrow in the world comes o' idleness. I'll put through all the work that the three of us used to do ; and beside that, if any o' ye are o'erburdened, I'll lend a hand with the needle. I'd wish, dear neighbors, to be that lovin' and helpful to ye while I 'bide here, that ye'll miss me sore when I've gone. I'd desire ye to remember myself, and also the words o' my Master that I've so often read to ye. Ye mind that he said, ' I will send ye another Comforter,' and ye see he has fulfilled his word to me. I'd be wild now only for that. He's as ready to comfort ye, as me, if ye'll but go to Him.''

CHAPTER XXXI.

NEW HOMES IN THE NEW WORLD.

NAN O'Gorman had been for some time plotting against the gold which she fancied Miss Grey was to leave in vast sums to the Sheehan girls. Having heard that a mystery hung about the fate of their mother, she had walked all that distance to learn what she could from Miss Grey, saying that Peggy had sent her. Although she got little information for the trouble, she saw enough to satisfy her that there was wealth in the house ; and concluded that, as there were no children, there would be no legal heirs to it. When, therefore, she heard, first by rumor and then from Paddy Mannon, that the girls were now rich, and carried their gold about their waists, she thought her hour had come to reach America — that land of golden dreams. She had therefore laid her plans for sailing in the same ship with Bessie, regarding the meek widow McRea as no obstacle whatever in the way she had marked out. It then occurred to her that she " might as well have both fortunes as one ; " so, after Peggy had gone in the day's post-chaise with Bessie, she, with an accomplice, had watched about the cottage till she was sure Marion was alone, and then leaving their horse and jaunting-car in a by-lane, accosted the child as she came out to milk.

Marion, of course, was fearless of danger, and chatted freely of the family plans. Nan induced her to leave the yard, and go to the lane to see the jaunting-car in which she was to be driven to the sea-port that night. Once there, she was pressed in, and, seated on a trunk, was driven off in a state of dreadful terror, having by this time recognized in the woman in black the one who had shouted so roughly to herself and her sister on the road-side, some little time before.

Nan was very tender in her manner towards her, and told her that she was her mother. She said that **long ago, being in** great trouble, she had " taken lave **of her sinses and** wandered off," **and** that when afterwards **she** " came back **to** her wits," Miss Grey and **Peggy had her** children, and refused to give them up; **but** that now, finding Bessie was going across **the** sea, she had resolved to follow her, and to **have** both her children to herself.

" Why, then, couldn't you tell this to our dear mammy," asked **the** child, **"and not** break her heart by stealing me?"

" A body can niver stale what's already her own, darlin'," replied the woman. " Kape ye quite asy, and ye'll see **ye** niver had sich a friend as mysilf afore."

The man, too, who drove, was kind and jovial, and described America, where **he had been, as** a glorious country, in which it **was** holiday all the week, **and** gold was to be had **for taking.**

Nan wrapped **a large, warm shawl about the** child, who soon sobbed herself to sleep, **from** which she did **not wake for hours;** and then to weep anew at her strange **situation.**

As the sun rose high, the party neared the wharf, and the man, setting down Nan's small trunk, drove off to witness the sailing of the vessel from a hight beyond. Leading Marion by one hand, and dragging her trunk with the other, Nan pushed and elbowed her way. through the crowd, with an independence that would have satisfied the most ardent advocate of woman's right to any work and any post.

Bessie was astounded by the sight of her sister and the tale of the coarse woman, but with her natural delicacy she strove to hide her, anguish from the rude company on the deck. The Widow McRea, holding fast to her own children, lest Nan might claim them too, accused her of kidnapping Marion, but her voice was soon drowned in a torrent of words; and then the deck was cleared of all but passengers, and the ship got under way.

As soon as they were fairly off, Nan walked about on a tour of discovery, to see if there might not be some of her acquaintances on board. Bessie calmed Marion's fears by saying that they would find some Christian hearts in America to pity them.

"Do you think she's our mother, Bessie?" asked Marion.

"No," replied Bessie. "I think she's the body our dear mammy dreaded so greatly. But, dear child, God will 'bide with us on sea as well as on land if we but trust Him; and we will trust Him, come life or death."

It took but a few hours to consign the Widow McRea and the four girls to their berths, where they spent most of their time. But when the Atlantic Ocean assailed the equanimity of Nan O'Gorman, he found more than his match, and came off beaten. It would have taken two oceans tossed by the wildest storms to lay her low, or to "unman" her to such a degree that she could not walk and talk.

At length the voyage was over, and the ship beat up the Narrows towards the harbor of New York. The girls clung frantically to the poor widow, lest they might be separated from her; but on the vessel's touching at Castle Garden, Nan seized a hand of each, and dragged them to the nearest hack. She ordered the driver to secure her box, and then drive them to some house kept by one of her own country people. Bessie told the man she would not go with this woman, and Marion reached out her arms from the carriage window, calling pitifully after the Widow McRea. But before the bewildered creature could reply, the hackman mounted his box, touched his horses with the whip, and drove off through the densely crowded streets.

Nan was very angry when she found that Marion was penniless, and vowed revenge on Paddy Mannon for deceiving her, and thus burdening her with this child. But she made free use of the money she had taken from Bessie, both to rest after her voyage, and to buy fresh widow's weeds.

Bessie and Marion made quite a little stir

23

in the Intelligence-office, whither Nan escorted
them on the third day after their arrival, in
search of nurse places. Such neat, pretty and
modest little maidens were not met with every
day in that place.

Here they attracted at once the attention of a
fine-looking lady who was looking for two girls
to act as child's maids for herself and sister,
living door by door.

" What church do you attend ? " was one of
the questions she put to them.

" We're Protestants, ma'am," replied Bessie.
" It was to the Presbyterian church we went at
home."

" But it's Catholics they'll be in this country, ma'am," exclaimed Nan, looking resolutely, almost defiantly, at the lady.

Bessie turned pale, but collecting herself in
a moment, she looked imploringly into the kind
face before her, and said, in tremulous tones,
" I fear God, dear lady, and I'd never deny my
faith. We are Protestants, like the dear ones
who taught us to love and trust Him only. If
you'll look no farther, but take us two with

you, you'll never repent it, for we'll be faithful, and the Lord will bless you for having pity on us."

This was strange talk in a place where servants were questioning ladies, and making terms for them to accept. The lady was charmed with their pleasant manners, and with their artless expressions of trust in God, and she announced to the person who kept the office that her choice was made.·

"But, ma'am," cried Nan, following her to the desk, "ye can't have ather of them unliss their wages be paid to mysilf. I'll suffer them to have half o't then, and the other half will go to support their poor widdy mother."

"But, my good woman," said the lady, "you look stronger than either of them. Why not take a place and support yourself?"

"Och, dear lady, I'm a lone widdy, don't ye see? The Widdy Sheehan."

"I know no reason why widows should not labor as well as other women, if they have strength to do it," said the lady, who was as resolute as herself.

"Will, will, I must git a bit over the sea-feelin', and hunt two or three cousins first," replied Nan; "and now if ye'll only take them off my hands at once, I'll sind their box after them, and visit them once a week — small consolation — " and shaking all three cordially by the hand, she saw them walk off together, and then seated herself to make new acquaintances.

Mrs. Maxwell and her sister were charmed with their neat little nurses who were capable and patient at their work, and who never lost an opportunity to teach or sing some useful lesson to their little charges, of whom they soon became very fond.

On her second motherly visit, Bessie being in the park with the children, Nan was admitted into Mrs. Maxwell's sitting-room, where she at once began relating her life's trials to the lady.

"Och, lady dear, it's a fearful thing for a woman to come down from great prosperity, as mysilf have done. If ye could know my fate, ye'd cry the full o' yer two hands o' tears. I had a lovely cottage with a farm to't, and cows, and pigs, and a donkey, and ducks, and geese, and hins, and a shilf full o' red and green delf ware, and feather bids, and a row o' milkpans as would reach from here to where our ship landed," — a distance of about four miles. "And och, my heart! the husband I had! He was the ilegintest man in all thim parts. He was high and stout, and had the finest leg for a long stocking in all the country. Och, but he was the man for a beauty!"

"And how long has he been dead?" asked Mrs. Maxwell.

"Dead? Indade, ma'am, it's not dead at all that he is," cried Nan, intent only on making out a good story.

"But you *told* me you were a widow," said the lady.

Nan's memory had failed her for a moment, but she was not one to give up her point. "So he is *dead to me*, dear," she sobbed out, "but he's live enough to the rest o' the world. And if a woman wears wades for a man that's gone peaceable into his grave, much more me

that's lost mine a worse way." And moving
her chair close to Mrs. Maxwell, she whispered, confidentially, " He turned me out o'
doors, dear, and my lovely childer, and there's
an evil woman now enjoyin' all my good
things, — my farm, and my iligant cups and
saucers, and nine skeins o' grey yarn I spun,
and — and — and my husband."

" But your daughters speak very tenderly
of their father, and tell me how he used to
pray for them," said the lady.

" Och, dear heart," cried Nan, " they like
l im because there's much of his evil natur in
thimselves. Didn't ye see how mane they
were, not wantin' me to have all their
wages ? "

" They ought not to give you even half,"
said the lady. " I shall insist on their keeping
most of their wages, and you must go to work
yourself."

" Och," cried Nan, " and what do you think
I came here for ? I could live by work at
home. I had a father's house full of plinty,
and would niver ha' left it only that these two

evil-minded girls ran off and hid in the ship, and I had to follow to save thim from destruction intirely;" and the virtuous creature drew a heavy sigh.

"Well, I advise you to go to work, and come once in a month or so to visit them," said Mrs. Maxwell.

"Once a month, is it?" cried Nan, rising; "indade they'll not 'bide where I can't come in and out when I plazes, and call for money, too!" And dashing out of the room, she slammed the door behind her in a way that told poorly for her gentle blood.

That evening, after the little ones were asleep, Mrs. Maxwell, as was her custom, went into the nursery to see that all was right, and there she found her little nurse in tears.

"Why, Bessie, what's the matter, child?" she asked.

"O, ma'am," cried the girl, "there's a heavy trouble lying on my heart, and I'm afraid I'll die in this strange land, and leave my darlin' sister alone."

"Bessie, I'm sure there's something wrong between you and your mother, and I insist on knowing what it is; I will protect you, if you are doing right," said the lady, kindly.

"O, ma'am, when we were in the park, she followed us and bid us both leave our places, and when I refused, she struck me before all the nurses and the children. Oh please give her all the wages if she but let us 'bide with you till our father find us, — the darlin' man! This is just the hour he'll be prayin' for us. And our mammy too will be singin' — oh no, she'll never sing more till she finds us — I'm sure o' that."

"Bessie, is this woman your mother?" asked Mrs. Maxwell. "She neither speaks nor acts as if she had brought you up."

"Oh, ma'am, she said if I'd tell one word about it, she'd put us both in a nunnery where our father would never find us! She never brought us up — you see, ma'am, we do not speak Irish, like that."

"You are in safe hands, my child," said

Mrs. Maxwell, with tears in her eyes. " Tell me the whole story, and Mr. Maxwell will protect you as if you were his own."

Thus encouraged, Bessie told all she knew of herself and the Sheehans, and the little she knew of the woman who professed to be their mother.

Mr. Maxwell at once wrote to Mr. Murray, assuring him that God had sent these good children to friends who would guard them well till their father came or sent for them.

When Nan called again, Mrs. Maxwell refused to see her, telling her that her husband was now the protector of the girls, and would take care of them till their father's arrival.

While waiting for a reply to the letter, Mrs. Maxwell and her sister did all they could to encourage and comfort the little exiles, who found it possible to be happy even under such painful circumstances.

CHAPTER XXXII.

PADDY'S WISDOM.

PEGGY'S love for the children whom God had placed in her care, was truly a mother's love; and none but a mother can imagine the anguish which at times filled her soul while John was busy settling his affairs to follow them. But scarcely did that anguish come, before the "great peace" would roll over her spirit, and she would see her darlings, not with her enemy, but in the hand and under the wing of the orphan's God. She applied herself to her work and to her religious duties with a calm and cheerful spirit, which those only know whose hearts are fixed on God, and who have entered into an everlasting covenant with Him.

The knitting and the singing went on as usual at the sunset hour; but her guests were

leaving one by one, as their families deserted
their miserable homes for better ones over the
sea. Her work was going before her, and
therefore she felt less reluctance at leaving
Ireland than if her field were growing about
her.

As the preparations were going on, John
said, "And now, my jewel, I must spake to
ye o' the Maid o' Longford. I suppose ye
couldn't sell her?"

"No more than I could sell one 'o my
children," cried Peggy. "She's more than
just a good cow to me; she was the kind
gift o' the darlin' mother, and has always
seemed one o' ourselves. When I was in sorrow, her eyes always looked sad as if she had
the power o' pityin' me; and she loved me,
too. She's not young, the poor dear, more
than ourselves, but she'll be useful several
years yet. So I've resolved to give her to Mr.
Murray; and should his family die, or follow
us over the sea, to have her left for the next
minister that takes his place, and always to
'bide on that land."

"That's wise indade!" cried John. "Elder Peter will buy Silverhorn, and will be as tinder o' her as I have been."

"I hope thin he'll not fade her on granite or marble!" exclaimed Paddy, who had just entered the cottage. "I believe that's what he ates himsilf and that gives him yon stony look."

"And now that we're on the priparations, Paddy," said his mistress, "I beg ye not to take thim clothes o' the old masther's to America. The people that know ye laugh at ye and no more; but in America, where none wears short clothes, they'll think ye're an idiot. Go to the workhouse and give thim to old Dinnis. They'll fit him, and kape him warm many a winter if he nades them."

"Och! but what fine thoughts are always comin' into yer head and out o' yer mouth, darlin'!" exclaimed Paddy. "And won't the old man dance, spite o' his rheumatics, whin he sees himsilf in thim fine clothes!" and springing up the ladder that led to his loft, Paddy tied the clothes up in a bundle and de-

parted, much to the relief of Peggy, who had
feared strong resistance on his part. We are
sorry to say, however, that he went no farther
than the cow-house, where he stowed the bundle away among his treasures in a "deal
chest;" and then sat down long enough to go
to the workhouse and back again, that his mistress might think he had been off on the benevolent errand. Then he went into the cottage
for a good supper.

On the evening before their departure, the cottage was filled with weeping neighbors, nearly
all of whom were either too poor or too old to
emigrate. While Peggy, in gentle tones, was
giving them her parting advice and blessing,
Master Timmy walked in, radiant with excitement.

"The battle's won without blood, Misther
Sheehan!" he cried. I' got twenty pounds o'
money, and the free consint o' the Elder to accompany ye. When he saw I would go, he
gave consint to save me from the sin o' disobe-
dience, the dear man; and he'll soon follow;
for nather he nor the lovin' mother will brathe

long out o' sight o' me. I'll show them what
a strong arm can do when it has a chance to
work. I'll just put myself to the granite, —
that's the fine material to lay out a lad's mus-
cle on. It would ha' been fine, indeed, if I,
after I'd stirred up half the lads between here
and Limerick to go to America, had been forced
to 'bide in the chimney-corner **myself.**"

Paddy was leaning on his elbow, looking out
of the casement, in rather a pensive mood for
him. He thought these remarks of Timmy's
rather personal ; so, turning round abruptly he
said, " Pho, yer nonsinse, lad ! Ye talk like
the small child ye are ! The arth, and the arth
alone, are the fine material for a man to spind
his stringth on."

" I disagree with you, old fellow," said Timmy. " Granite is harder, and so is a nobler
work than the arth. Sure ony maid can hoe
potatoes, if she but have good health and common sinse ; but put the best o' thim on a huge
block o' granite, and bid her hew out a monu-
ment or an ornamental gate-post, and see what
work she'll make on't ! Setting the maids

aside, ye can put an idiot on his knees, and he can pull weeds as well as a giant or a college-larned man ; but set him to hewing the crowned falcon — the coat-o'-arms on the new door for the Harpley tomb, — and see what a fine work he'll make on't ! "

" And so would Elder Peter made as fine work on't as the poor fool, afore he'd larned," replied Paddy. " Ah Timmy, lad, *the arth is the material for an honest man to delve in !* "

"The arth's filthy," said Timmy, to draw Paddy out ; " a man can never work in it without defiling himself ; but the stone is as pure as the sky above us, Paddy."

"List to me, lad. The good God knows which is the finest thing for man, surely ; and the dear, dead Misthress used to read to us that when He made his first man, and had ivery thing afore him to select from, didn't he pass by the stones, the jewels, and the gold and the silver and the tin, and make him a fine garden, and put him into it to till it and to dress it ? That same showed, as Mammy Honey said, what Him as made the world thought

—that farmin's the noblest work at all ; and while I'm doin' what the grand jintleman Adam did with his own hands — him that owned the whole world for his farm — I'll feel quite honored. And yer Protestant Bible tells too, aboot a man that wint out to sow, and about a husbandman that had a vineyard ; but will ye show me the place where's mintioned a man that stood hackin' away at a gravestone or a gate-post ? Ye'll not find it at all."

Timmy was a little crest-fallen by Paddy's reasoning, but laughed it off by saying, " Paddy, the church was chated when ye were put on a farm to work. Ye should be aither a priest or a parson, with all the fine thoughts ye have. What war ye thinkin' so grave about when I came in, with yer head out o' the casement, and yer eyes lookin' up at the clouds ? "

" Well, Timmy, lad, it war fine thoughts I had ontirely yon time ! I war lookin' at the moon, and thinkin' how neglected-like she war, and how light sot by o' most people. Hapes thinks a dale o' the sun, bekase he stares so fierce down on us, and makes such a

show o' himsilf. And bekase the moon only
throws a kind smile on us, they think little o'
her. But I'll till ye what I think, — it's a comparison like; the sun is like frinds that's
very lovin' and helpful whin we don't nade
them. He shines in the daylight whin we
could jest get along quite fine without him.
But the dear little moon, she's like a friend
in nade; she shines when all's dark, whin but
for her we'd wander astray, or fall down into a
ditch and break our head. So away with yer
sun, that only gives light whin we've enough
without him; and up with the moon that's
saved many a fine life!"

"But Paddy, man," cried Timmy, "there'd
be no light at all in the moon, but only for the
sun. The astronomers say the moon gits her
light from the sun."

"Then they lies," cried Paddy. "Don't ye
think I've as many eyes as these 'stronomies
has? And can't I see that the sun's no where
about to be givin' her light? He's gone ontirely out o' the way afore the moon rises at
all! It's a great trick wise men has got

24

o' these days, tellin' such stuff and thinkin'
they'll make onlarned folks belave 'em agin
their wits; but I'm not one o' the fools that'll
do it. I'll belave me own eyes and me own
sinses afore I'll belave Mr. Murray himself,—
'dade I will. One o' his boys was foolin' me
as we walked home together from the post-
office, one night, by tellin' me that some o' the
stars he pointed out was made o' dippers;—
as if he thought I was fool enough to belave
him! Dippers, indade!"

CHAPTER XXXIII.

A JOYFUL MEETING.

IT was a bright day in the early autumn, and the trees, in hues of gorgeous beauty, made the park a scene of gladness to the eye weary of the tame sights of every-day life. Nature and the little children were out on a holiday together.

As the young Sheehan girls drew their baby charges slowly along under a row of bright elms, they noticed, in a corner, a group of poor-looking people, who seemed to be trying to hide, one behind the other, from the observation they were attracting.

"Look at yon poor things, Marion," said Bessie. "I'm sure they're new off the ship, and are suffering from the sport the lads are making of their old-fashioned Irish clothes. Let's cross this path, and give them a hand and

371

a kind word. Maybe some o' them are homeless and friendless. And it may be a long day
before they find such friends as God raised up
for us at the very first. Perhaps there's no
pure hearts at home prayin' for them, either."

And the little nurses drew their baby-car-
riages towards the forlorn-looking group.

"You've just come over, poor thing," said
Bessie, kindly, to the one woman of the party.
"What part o' poor Ireland are you from?"

"Coonty Kirry, me and *these*," she replied,
pointing to three rough-looking fellows on the
bench beside her. "Thim two is from Clare,
and yon man with his back to us, — him in
the breeches and the huge coat, tyin' up his
brogues, he's from Limerick or some other
place."

The girls naturally looked at "yon man,"
who was "tyin' his brogues," when in an
instant Marion dropped the tongue of her wagon, and rushing towards him, screamed out,
"O, Paddy Mannon, this can never be you,
you darlin' old man!" And forgetting that
there was any one else in the park, the child

threw her arms round the neck of the rough old emigrant, and wept aloud for joy. Bessie, too, put her arms about him and kissed him, and called him " a darlin', kind old creatur'," and clapped her hands and laughed for joy, all unconscious, for the moment, of the crowd of idlers they were attracting.

"And where are mammy, and father, and all who came with ye? And will ye take us to them now? And how long were ye on the sea?" These and many other questions chased each other from their lips before the overjoyed Paddy could get an opportunity to tell them that Peggy was "watching the boxes" while he and John were off searching for them.

"Ye see, my darlin's, yer father had the paper with Misther Mixwill's place wrote on it, so I had to trust my mimory. That failed me, and I've been hours sarchin' could I find ye. If I rung at one door, I rung at tin-thousand, kapin' these poor people on the shide-walk, o' course,—not to be lettin' thim walk up jintlemen's steps,—and yet not a body in all Ameriky seemed ever to ha' heerd o' yer comin' at all."

"And who are these with you, Paddy?" asked Bessie.

"Och, dear, they're poor innocent things that come over in the ship with us; and as they were quite ignorant o' the ways of a strange country, I was civil enough to take thim round with me to show thim the fine sights, poor things!"

"But O, Paddy, why did mammy ever let you bring those fearful lookin' clothes with ye?" asked Bessie.

"She don't know I have them on at all, dear, but thinks old Dinnis is jist now orna-minted with them at the work-house! How could I iver come to a strange place, jist like any common laborin' man? I resolved they should see for once that I had fine clothes, and that a respictable man bewilled thim to me, if I niver wore thim again; and I think I niver will, ather, for the lads is hootin' and howlin' after me at ivery turn o' the road."

"Haste back, Paddy," said Marion, "and tell father and mammy that America's the loveliest land on the whole arth ; and that the people, all that we've seen yet, are just angels. Don't stop to walk, dear man, but go on to yonder broad street, and there take a car to your left, and pay sixpence each, and it will land ye safe at the place you're stopping in."

So Paddy stirred up his weary party, and dragging his wooden-soled brogues along, lumbered up the gravel walk, followed by his uncouth shipmates, who evidently regarded him as a man " born for a leader."

But the girls were not done with him yet; and Marion, after feasting her homesick eyes on his awkward figure for a moment, called out, " Paddy, I'm so thankful you're all safe in this dear country ; you won't have to work so hard here for stirabout and herring."

Paddy walked back towards them, wiping away his tears with the sleeve of his coat. " Dears," he said mournfully, " I used to think Ameriky all the hiven I'd iver ask for, but now I'm here, tho heart is as heavy and

cold as a stone in my brist. I've left the
bones o' Meg and little Pat — him as war
Johnny Sheehan — behind me alone. When I
was there I use to go and sit down by their
cold bed and mend my clothes and talk to
thim; but I can niver do that in this fine
place."

"Paddy," said Bessie, "I haven't asked you
how ye left all the friends in Killyrooke and
Cloynmally, — Mr. Murray's family, and — and
— and Elder Peter, too; I hope *he* was well?"

"All's well, dear, and partic'lar the Elder.
He's thrivin' fine on the stones he ates,
and growin' every day harder and grayer,"
answered Paddy, smiling through his tears.

"And Timmy, I hope he's obedient, and
will 'bide his father's will about leaving
home?"

Paddy dropped his head mournfully, and
made no reply.

"There was nothing wrong there, surely?
Timmy was *living* when you left?" she asked,
in surprise at Paddy's manner.

"Well, dear child," cried Paddy, "he *was*

living when we sailed; but Timmy will never cross the sea to America."

" Was *just living* and that was all ? " asked Bessie. " What ailed my poor old playmate, Paddy ? "

Paddy put his handkerchief to his eyes, and turned his back on her, saying, " Now don't break my heart with quistions, darlin'; whin ye come to us your mammy will revale it all to ye."

Bessie wanted to hear no more ; so she said, " Go, now, for yer friends are weary waiting, and we'll find you before many hours."

Paddy's grief suddenly gave way to gladness, and he exclaimed, " Och, but I forgot to tell ye that I found a kin o' mine on the ship — one Teddy Flask."

" Who is he ?   I never heard of him," said Bessie.

" Well, he's ather a cousin to me, or I'm a cousin to him, I don't jist mind which," replied Paddy.   " But tell me where's Nan ? My heart's full o' what I'll do to her," he added.

"Paddy, go on now, and we'll tell you all at night," said Bessie. "Our time has come to be at home."

When the little nurses reached Mr. Maxwell's they found their father waiting them. The joyful meeting was almost as grateful to Mrs. Maxwell as to themselves, for she had now heard all their story from John, and was prepared to welcome the whole family to her heart.

The girls went with John to meet their beloved mammy, and to be surprised by the pleasant and merry face of Master Timmy, who had accompanied them!

"Why, Timmy, lad," cried Bessie, "Paddy made me believe that you were dead. I was afeared to ask my father, lest he'd say you were."

"No Bessie," said Timmy laughing. "I'm quite alive I assure ye! The Elder — dear man that he is — finally gave consint rather than suffer me to come without. And the darlin' mother pladed that he'd give me all the clothes and tools and money I'd nade, and send me off with his blessin'. And it'll be a short day afore ye'll see them all here, that's if the Elder can lave Mr. Murray behind."

"But why, then, didn't *you* come to seek us, Timmy, and not let Paddy give me yon fearful scare?" asked Bessie.

"I stayed here to watch the boxes," said Timmy. "Paddy was that taken up with the new people and the strange dresses, that he couldn't 'bide in at all. He was bid to take off his workin' clothes that he'd wore on the sea, and put on his Sunday ones; and what did we see in a short space, but him in ' the ould masther's shute ' that we thought safe in the workhouse, goin' off the steps in company with half a dozen wild Irishmen he took under his wing on the ship, and at his heels a troop o' boys. The people about the inn door all shouted with laughter, and one man cried, 'There goes old Ireland and young America, hand in hand!' Ye'd ha' thought he'd known the lads all his life by the tarms they was on; he givin' them Irish pennies, and singin' Irish songs to them afore he'd been two

hours off the ship.   He called the stupid loons
he was ladin' about, ' these poor sthrangers in
a sthrange land,' and said he must put himself
about getting work and homes for them on the
morrow !   Ye'd a thought he'd lived in America all his life, and had hapes of influence in
it.   There's one thing we've done for America,
already ; we've brought her a man, the like o'
whom, for wisdom and folly, she never saw
before."

CHAPTER XXXIV.

THE OLD FOE AGAIN.

MR. MAXWELL was so charmed with this new development of Irish character, that he made places for John and Paddy in his warehouse, as porter and teamster. The girls cheerfully kept their situations till, as he promised to do, their father should be able to send them to school again.

With aid of the girls, Peggy found rooms in a neatly-kept tenement house of the better class, and soon made her humble city home shine as brightly as the cottage in Killyrooke had done; and her grateful heart was gladdened every Sunday evening by seeing the pleasant faces of her children again at her table.

But these " Gems of the Bog " did not sit selfishly and quietly down to rejoice in their deliv-

381

erance from enemies, and their safe conduct to
a land flowing with milk and honey. They
looked about at once for work, each one asking, " What shall I render unto the Lord for
all His benefits toward me ? "

Peggy soon found neighbors who needed
help and comfort, and without breathing a
word against their faith, she talked to them of
that which was the joy and the rejoicing of
her own heart. John, also, by his kind and
obliging ways, made friends among the men,
both in the store, and in the neighborhood
where he lived. Relieved from the pressure
of his old conviction at home — that all had
known his sin and therefore regarded him as a
hypocrite, — he began to talk and to labor
more openly. Peggy, through Mrs. Maxwell's
aid and encouragement, opened again her knitting and singing meetings in the evenings when
toil was over. The husbands and brothers of
the women dropped in now and then for a chat,
and they too would listen, and sometimes sing.
Mr. Maxwell, who was himself an earnest
worker in the same good cause, supplied John

with books of interest to read and to lend to his neighbors; and occasionally visited him to cheer him on. He was amazed at the power of Peggy over the women and girls, and charmed by John's humble zeal and his earnest desire for the souls of his countrymen, whom he regarded as bound in chains of error. He was also greatly pleased with John and Paddy as faithful laborers in the store, and he felt sure that God had work for the humble family in their new home.

One day, a few weeks after their arrival, as the redoubtable Paddy was passing through one of the great thoroughfares, he saw a fair-faced blind woman who was relating to passers-by, — not one of whom stopped to listen, — the story of her woes. "For the love o' mercy," she said, "give a shilling to a poor blind lady, whose husband is just after having his arm imputated, and nothing at all in the house to ate."

Such poverty in America was surprising to Paddy, and he stepped up to lay his offering in her extended palm. The face of the blind woman was too familiar to deceive him, even under the green shade; and he exclaimed, "And whin did ye lose yer eyes, Nan?"

"I'm not Nan O'Gorman," she cried, "and I niver heard o' Killyrooke in all my life."

"And who said that was yer name, or yer home, I'd ask?" cried Paddy, his temper rising at her audacity. "I'd inform ye that my masther's nare by, and he'll have ye 'rested for stalin' his childer, and ye'll then have a chance to see what's a Yankee prison like."

"Powers o' evil!" cried Nan, "why did ye iver sind Paddy Mannon all the way over the sea to tormint me? Whist, Paddy, and I'll till ye a sacret. I've jist turned to this business to gather a little money to take me to Cal'forny, where they gets high wages for sittin' still. Don't till on me, for I'm sore afraid o' yon starn Misther Mixwill, who thritened to 'rist me; and I'll promise niver more to go nare the Sheehans while I live. Will ye plidge yer honor?"

"No," said Paddy, "I'll call the first polishman I see, and get ye put into prison for life."

And Paddy, in his zeal to expose the impostor, began to tell her story to some listeners, when she darted down the street, turned into a narrow alley, and was off for " Cal'forny " or some other distant region.

Paddy had little idea of the vastness of the city, and thought he could find her at any time by going to the street in which she had disappeared. So he gathered quite a crowd of idlers about him, and discoursed at considerable length on Nan's genealogy, and on the fate which had " well nigh swipt the blood o' the race off the face o' the arth ontirely."

His audience became quite interested in Nan's history, and Paddy, seeing this, grew eloquent, and throwing back his head, gave vent to a torrent of " varses."

> " Och, lads o' Ameriky ! Sons o' the free !
>   I'd like to be makin' a bargain with ye,
>   That ye'll jine me in sarchin this wide city o'er,
>   Till we bring Nan O'Gorman a Justice afore.
>
> " Nather silver nor gold has poor Paddy to give,
>   But he'll love ye and bliss ye as long as ye live,
>   If ye'll help him to clare her quite off on the sea ,
>   For he'll niver rest asy in the land where she be ! ' "

Of course this and much more of the same

style charmed the boys, and many of them followed Paddy when he moved on, asking him
where he lived, and if he made poetry for a
living.

Paddy was so flattered that he was tempted
to tell a lie, and own himself "a varse-maker
by trade whereby he arned a fine livin', howlin' at funerals and singin' at fairs in the ould
counthry;" but he said he had changed his
business in this city, "and was now tamester
to Mr. Mixwill, ontirely."

At dinner-time Paddy went home, his face
radiant with good news.

"Look, dear," he said to Peggy, "I've fine
news to tell ye. I've found Nan, and I have
consorted with a score o' boys to delude her off
to the sea, and if good luck be with us, drown
her, maybe!"

"Paddy, ye shall niver touch a hair o' her
head. We're raised up beyond her power to
harm us, and I hope the Lord will pity and
save her," said Peggy.

"I'd be very sorry for that, for it would be
quite discouragin' ontirely if she was trated

as fine as yersilf in the matter o' religion.
She's no right to it after all the ill she has
done us. I'd feel myself quite wronged if she
got as good tratement as oursilves," exclaimed
Paddy.

"Oh, poor man, it's little we deserves from
the hand o' the Lord ourselves." said Peggy.

"Humph! I'll niver give in but I desarves
a finer heaven nor she!"

"Ye *desarve* no heaven at all, Paddy. If
any o' us be so happy as to enter in at last, **it**
will be o' free grace."

CHAPTER XXXV.

WHEN the Sheehan family had been about six months in their new home, and all was going on well with them, Paddy came in to dinner one day, evidently much cast down. He pulled his hat over his eyes, — his custom when in grief, — and said mournfully, "No dinner for me this day, misthress dear."

"What's gone wrong, Paddy?" asked Peggy. "I hope you've not angered the jintlemen at the store?"

"No, but they has angered me sore," replied the poor fellow. "I'm disgraced and ruined for iver, and can niver hould up my head more in public. They've turned my masther into a coal-haver."

"A coal-haver?" cried Peggy.

"Jist that. All was goin' on will, Misther

389

Mixwill seemin' to think there was jist only one man in the place ! It war ' Sheehan ' here and ' Sheehan ' there, and more nor once I've heerd him tellin' jintlemen what a fine religious family we war — 'specially himself and ye.

"Will, to-day, when the door was full up with bales, our minister come steppin' over them with a high man with hair like a hay-mow on the top o' his head, and a white nick-cloth, as big as a sheet, about his nick. Misther Mixwill shuk hands with them very glad-like, and bid them into the coontin'-room, and in five minutes more he opened the door and called in my masther, who was listin' bales.

"I made an errand by the place, and put my ear to the window, — not at all with a view o' listenin', for I'm too unnerable a man for that like maneness, — and heerd them ask my masther many questions, and thin say, ' by the will, thin, o' Misther Mixwill ye'll be no more in this store, but be our coal-haver.'

"My masther niver lifted his tongue agin it; but he was very solemn whin he came out from the grand folk. I doubt but the old story has

followed us to Ameriky, and will hunt us till
we hides in the grave. Och, och, why iver did
I lave my own peaceful grave in Ireland, and
come here to be buried in a strange man's
grave ? "

When John came in, and " the lad " was
gone, Peggy said, with a smile, " Paddy says
ye are tarned out o' yer place, and made a
coal haver, dear."

" A coal haver ! " cried John. " The simple fellow has been listening to the talk o' two
gentlemen with Mr. Maxwell about me.   It
seems, darlin', that the hearts of some o' the
Lord's people here is stirred up to make known
the Gospel to them that will nather go to His
house nor read His Word. And they have
bound thimselves into a society like for that
end, and pay men (not ministers) to go from
house to house among the poor and the sinful,
readin' and talkin' to all that will listen.
They had heard through Mr. Maxwell o' our
poor efforts among our neighbors, and came to
see would he let me off to be a worker for
them -- a ' colporter,' as they calls it.   And

that's sure the very word Paddy got hold on; he thought a colporter was a coal-haver, poor lad."

"And what did ye say to them, dear?" asked Peggy, with real pleasure in her eye.

"I said I'd consult ye, and if ye'd think me worthy, I'd begin at once. I really belave, darlin', that I've been doin' a sort o' pinance by keepin' my sin always afore my mind, when that sin was forgiven and to be remembered no more agin me for ever. Och, Peggy, if our own righteousness is nothing to live on, what can our sins be? I'm going to strive hinceforth to think only on the love and the marcy that has washed them all away."

Paddy's only remark, when he heard of this change of work, was, "And sure, thin, he'll be a sort o' a minister, and wear a fine white nickcloth like Mr. Murray. Why couldn't Mammy Honey ha' lived to see this day?"

Timmy secured work at once in a granite-yard, where he had need of all his strength; and "being fine at the pen and the figures," he made himself very useful among the lads whom John gathered into his kitchen in the evening to listen to reading and to be kept out of mischief. Paddy aided greatly in the work by forming acquaintances among the young men and boys, whom he decoyed into the "tachin's" by promises of "fine stories about Ireland," if they would stay till the clock struck nine. He would redeem his word by tales of witches and ghosts, of ball-playing and quoit-pitching, till John was ready for his reading and Peggy for the singing. They would remain, and frequently return without a repetition of Paddy's pious fraud, which was known only to himself and them.

On Sunday evenings, when the girls were always at home, the room was generally full of listeners to the sweet singing; and scores thus heard of the love and pity of the Saviour, who would not have dared to listen to a sermon or a prayer outside their own church.

One day Paddy came in after one of his missionary efforts, and pulling his hat over his eyes, said, "Misthress darlin, there come a very troubling thought into my head when I was strivin' to drag in these wild lads to hear the singin' and the readin'."

"What was that, Paddy?" asked Peggy kindly.

"Will, thin, I thought, here's me takin' all this pains to get other ones to plaze God, and thinkin' very little about doin' it mysilf, or gittin' my own soul saved. Times gone I was asy, becase I thought, bein' a Catholic, I'd push into heaven among the crowd, few o' whom war as good as mysilf. And since I've turned Protestant I've trusted that I'd git in for bein' in such fine company. And jist now I'm thinkin' I'll not be let in at all, at all. If I'll not be saved for yer goodness, nor yet for the dear misthress, sure I'll not be let in for my own,—becase why? Becase I hasn't any."

"I'm glad, my dear man, that ye've found it out," cried Peggy, "for I've regarded ye as the self-righteousest cretur' that ever lived on the arth. And none will ever receive Christ till he's emptied o' silf."

"Will, thin," cried Paddy, "I'm surprised that I've been let live all this time, hatin' ivery body that didn't jist admire us, and scornin' all that warn't equally grand. And now I look worse to mysilf nor even Nan. She did as she war tached, and I didn't. And what'll I do now?"

"Ye'll just have to do what every other sinner does, Paddy, before he finds pace; believe what Jesus says, and give yersilf to Him."

"I'll do that, thin," cried Paddy, with tears in his eyes, "but it's a mane thing ontirely to bring only my grey hair and my failin' strength to the Lord, when I might ha' given Him my bist years, and I'm jist ashamed to do it."

"And yet, Paddy, all the labor of those 'bist years' could not have purchased salvation for ye. That is ever a free gift.

> "'Jesus, Thy blood and righteousness
> My beauty are, my glorious dress;
> 'Mid flaming worlds in these arrayed,
> With joy shall I lift up my head.'"

"Aye, and will ye may lift up yer head with joy, ye that have lived like an angel, with niver a hatred in yer heart nor a lie on yer

tongue! Look at the marcy I've had o' the Lord.
Such religious larnin', — catechisms and commandments and psalms and hums bate into me
from the time I left the workhouse, till this
hour! And I've laughed at the catechism, and
broke the commandments, and twisted the holy
varses into nonsinse. Mysilf it was, who
scared the poor fool who disgraced our fine
funerel, by chasing him near the church yard
till he fell and was tuk up for dead, none
knowin' what ailed him! And I it was that
set fire to our inimy's cottage. And oh, the
lies I've told! It would take seven year to
confiss them to ye. Only tin days agone I
lured two rough lads into the night-tachins by
tellin' that ye closed up by givin' the boys a
fine supper. Ye mind how yon ones sat long
after all else war gone? Will, thin, I beck-
oned them out, and told them the butcher disappointed ye in not sending the young pig ye
war to roast for us! And didn't I tell the
clarks in Mr. Mixwell's store that ye were
niver common farmer people at home, but that
my masther war brother to Harply Hall, and

that we only tuk a freak and came off to
Ameriky in disguish for a little sport,—the
way Victoory of England do at times! I told
them we laughed at the pittance Mr. Mixwill
gives us in wages, and often threw it away
among the boys on our road home, and that I
war yer butler in Ireland as my father war before me! Sure I can niver be forgive for all
that and a thousand evils more."

"O' course they didn't belave a word on't,
and laughed at ye for thinkin' they did; but ye
must confiss yer sin, and humble yersilf before
them, and tell them ye've repinted and are
seeking the Lord," said Peggy.

Paddy shook his head mournfully, and said,
" I used to think if iver I could grow rich and
have tin pounds in the Bank, I ask no greater
happiness. But now, if I could but be forgive
and get pace, I niver care if I didn't look on
another farthin' while I lives! "

" Paddy," said his mistress, " there's one only
can give ye pace, poor man, and ye know
where to find Him. Go to Him and confess
yor sin, and ask Him to pity and pardon ye

for the sake o' His dear Son, who came to save the simple as well as the wise."

"I used to think, dear, that I was wiser nor any other one, but now every word I spakes sounds like an idiot's," replied Paddy.

"In the multitude o' words there wanteth not sin, dear man," said Peggy; "so the less ye talk the less danger ye'll be in o' sinnin'. Even the wise King David had to set a double watch on his lips lest he might sin with his tongue."

"Mammy Honey once told me my tongue gave her great sorrow, and bid me count tin every time before I'd spake, so as to have space to think what I'd be to say. I'll obey her orders aven at this late day, and so strive to plase the Lord. If iver ye hear me boastin', rebuke me, dear, for I have a sore longin' to be rid o' evil and to sarve the Lord the small space that's lift me here; for I jist feel I love Him so, that I'd lay my life down rather nor grieve Him."

There was a marked change in poor Paddy after this time. Although he kept his merry old heart, and still " consorted with boys in place o' men"; his calm and modest demeanor, and his zeal in every work of mercy gave great joy to those who had spent so much labor on him.

At the end of three years, the Sheehans were joined in their new home by Elder Peter and his wife. The hard nature of the stone-cutter had undergone a great change during his painful separation from his beloved Timmy; and the work of softening was carried on still farther by the genial influences which now surrounded him in the church to which he had been at once introduced.

Timmy had grown into a strong and noble man, proud of his trade and of his skill at it. He rejoiced that " miracles o' money could be wrought out o' the hard stone by a strong arm and a powerful will; and the money he thus earned was as free as the air to all who needed help. He had now become a real helper to his friends in every good work. Timmy had not, however, overcome " his old wakeness " which he had inherited from some far-off ancestor. When the Elder saw that he devoted all his leisure time to Bessie, he remarked, "It's just as I always prophesied; he has turned out a gallant, or a lover or some such thing." But the old man was not annoyed by the fulfilment of his words, but, on the contrary, he entered into all his son's plans for the happy future. He established himself at once in a stone yard, and took Timmy into partnership with him. He is now aiding the Sheehans in their good work, and laying up a little store wherewith Timmy and Bessie may ere long set up another new home in the New World.

And here we take leave of these "Gems of the Bog," asking, for their sakes, the sympathy of the reader, in that class for whom especially they labored and prayed.

THE END.